ISLINGTON

Please return this item on or before the last date stamped below or you may be liable to overdue charges. To renew an item call the number below, or access the online catalogue at www.islington.gov.uk/libraries. You will need your library membership number and PIN number.

D0496766

Islington Libraries

020 7527 6900   www.islington.gov.uk/libraries

BLOODLINES

Also by Marcello Fois in English translation

The Advocate (2003)
Memory of the Abyss (2012)

MARCELLO FOIS

BLOODLINES

Translated from the Italian by
Silvester Mazzarella

MACLEHOSE PRESS
QUERCUS · LONDON

First published in Italian as *Stirpe*
by Giulio Einaudi editore, Turin, in 2009
First published in Great Britain in 2014 by MacLehose Press
This paperback edition published in 2015 by

MacLehose Press
an imprint of Quercus Publishing Ltd
Carmelite House
50 Victoria Embankment
London EC4Y 0DZ

An Hachette UK company

A CIP catalogue record for this book is available
from the British Library

ISBN (MMP) 978 1 84866 794 5
ISBN (Ebook) 978 1 84866 409 8

10 9 8 7 6 5 4 3 2 1

Designed and typeset in Cycles by Libanus Press
Printed and bound in Great Britain by Clays Ltd, St Ives plc

to Paola, who gives meaning . . .

CONTENTS

CONTENTS

PROLOGUE

Luigi Ippolito is lying on his carefully made bed. He is in formal dress, the buttons on his soutane shining, his shoes like polished mirrors. As he always has, and always will, he refers to himself by surname first: "Chironi Luigi Ippolito" and, without moving, he stands up to look back at himself, perfectly serene, dead, so ready he could weep. There, on the bed, lies the One, tidy and precise, while the Other stares at him, anxious and turned to stone, yet at the same time turbulent, as straight and blunt as an insult hurled in your face, standing between the bed and the window. Because the immovability of the One is like a shadow and the immovability of the Other is control. At a glance, one would say Luigi Ippolito and Luigi Ippolito are identical in every respect, except that the first, the one lying on the bed, has the imperturbable appearance of a body peaceful in death while the second, standing and observing himself, has the frowning rigidity of someone who is unsure of himself. So that while the first is immersed in the indescribable peace of total surrender, the second is struggling against an overwhelming sense of feebleness. This is why, at a certain point, to end this stagnation, Luigi Ippolito almost holds his breath, like a loving but anxious father who needs reassurance that his newborn child is still breathing. But it is not out of love that Luigi Ippolito is bending over Luigi Ippolito, oh no: the Other is bending over the One in order to read his life. And to insult him too, because this is no moment for dying, still less for playing at death; nor is it a time for surrender.

The One listens without moving, stubborn in his farce of playing dead. He does not move even though he would like to pull himself together.

Giving in to his own obvious obstinacy, the Other sits down on the edge of the rush-seat chair by the bedside table like a young widow who has not yet understood the disgrace she has suffered. He continues to watch the One, who is barely breathing. What can it be like to explore that land of silence? he asks himself. What is that accursed journey like?

Then the light seems to leave the room suddenly, so that the thick eyebrows shading the closed eyelids of the One add force to his pallor. In response, the Other lowers his voice and the intensity of his thoughts to declare himself disposed to playing the mourning game. Can he remember the solitude of exhausted fields during the sweltering heat of the summer? Can he remember the long wait in front of the snare? And life bursting from his lungs after a race? Can he remember? Those battles among the olive trees, the tremendous chirping of the cicadas, the treacherous whistling of the north-west wind. Do you remember? I wanted to live in the void, in the light of a constant present. I was obstinate. But you wanted to be silhouetted against the light. You wanted shadows. I wanted space, remember? Do you remember? It was all a constant repeating. Do you remember? And books in baskets like bread, because there was a body within that had to be fed and the urgency of being prepared for the daily march of time. And the rough surface of our shared life, like a crude rustic table on which the incantations of the past could find order. Luigi Ippolito Chironi, descended from people originally called De Quiròn, then Kirone, who, before their captivity in the Barbagia region, had bred horses that bore the holy backsides of two popes and the very secular back-side of a viceroy . . . Do you remember? The marbles, the narrow-necked bottle, the old magazine. Oh . . . Our whole life balancing in the predestined chaos of memory. Like the secret order of a tidy plan. Do you remember? Do you remember the transparent hope of the glass windows?

But the One doesn't respond to these questions; he knows what it means to be self-confident and abruptly believe himself to be both the One and the Other at the same time. Silence. This is the point they always return to.

By now the light in the little room has faded to that of a mortuary chapel since a black stain has crossed the sun's face. The One and the Other exchange glances. The One, lying down, seems far away, but is watching the Other through half-closed eyelids. The Other, his brow furrowed, responds to this absent stare with a persistent expression of expectation. As it has always been, and always will be.

Then comes silence, set against the constant roar of reasoning. Now there seems to be nothing; nothing to think, nothing left to remember. It has all been a dream, yet no. They are exactly back at the point where being able to change anything has become impossible.

The writing-desk stands by itself in the shadowed corner of the room. Fate has allowed him pen and paper. Outside, the sky is the colour of milk. Luigi Ippolito watches himself with a mixture of understanding and pain. His body is drifting, softer than he remembered it, more pliable than ever before, yielding to the current.

But how can this story of silences be told? You know it, everyone knows it: stories only ever get told because they have happened somewhere. It is enough to hit the right tone, to give voice to the internal warmth of the dough waiting to rise, serene on the surface but turbulent inside. It is enough to be able to tell the chaff from the grain, almost thinking without thought. Because conscious thinking reveals its mechanisms and introduces terror into the story. So, as I was about to say, the stubborn brightness of a sheet of white paper leaps from the shadows enveloping the desk. Which is perhaps an invitation . . .

First Canto – Paradise
(1889–1900)

Scire se nesciunt

First the ancestors: Michele Angelo Chironi and Mercede Lai. Before them nothing at all. And it must be said that if this blacksmith and this woman had never met in church, it is probable, in fact certain, that the family would have vanished into the anonymity that shrouds the stories of this land before anyone has had a chance to tell them.

This is how it happened, she is saying a *novena* prayer to the Madonna delle Grazie, and three metres above her, he is adjusting the metal hook from which the large incense burner hangs. She is sixteen, he is nineteen. He is not even a blacksmith yet, merely a blacksmith's apprentice, but she is already cast in iron, chiselled and magnificent, her face perfect. For him, high above her, it is like looking down into distant depths while she, looking up, feels vertigo. Just that. The air seems rarefied like when a runner pauses for breath.

Michele Angelo is solid and stout, plump as a well-fed animal. His clothes are basically light brown but, seen against the light, his substance almost blond, like the living expression of something as transient as fruit growing from honeyed seed, in sharp contrast to the crow-like blackness that surrounds him. Local girl Mercede's hair seems shining blue, bright as an enamel brushstroke. In fact, it is really jet black, full of presence and depth, but the light on her dazzlingly white parting makes her hair look blue.

And so it is that their moment of unconscious awareness scarcely lasts a second.

Days and months pass. The nine days of the *novena* are over, the feast day that follows is over too, and so is the winter.

In April, Mercede, together with other local girls, goes to collect alms for the festival of San Francesco di Lula. The third house they come to is the home of Giuseppe Mundula, master blacksmith, the place where Michele Angelo lives. And she, who has always before been too timid to knock on anyone's door, knocks on this one; and he, who ought not even to be at home, comes to open it himself. These meetings may seem destined by Fate though Fate is far too solemn a word. Mercede and Michele Angelo are fully aware that they are exactly where they had always determined to be, driven by the wordless force of desire.

Even so, now face to face, they avoid each other's eyes. But she sees clearly that he is robust and not too slim. She is still growing and could end up becoming the taller of the two. But what does that matter? Mercede likes the amber glow that surrounds him, and invests it with a practical genetic quality: it is the seed from which her children will grow. Michele Angelo likes the way she breathes with lips slightly parted. Then there are her eyes, and everything else he would be thinking about if not distracted by the conviction that this is the woman of his life.

Something in the house has made him late for work this morning; and something has made her push in front of the three other girls to be the one to knock on the door. From the other side of the closed door he hears the knocking, thinks it familiar and, against all probability, hurries past the blacksmith to open it.

But, of course, Destiny plays no part in this simultaneity; it is simply a matter of stubbornness. Love lasts one single perfect moment; the rest is merely reminiscence of what has already happened, but that single moment can be enough to make sense of more than one life. And that's how it was: he handed over a fitting offering for the saint, almost equivalent to a whole day's work, and she held out her palm for it in such a way that he would lightly touch her hand. A gesture she would never be ashamed of even though, when she thought about it, it seemed more lustful than if she had offered him her virginity. Because her gesture contained an invitation, and an invitation is much worse than the simple if stupefying physiology of desire. There was nothing surprising in what she had done, only a deliberate conscious intention to make it possible for that man to touch her.

Michele Angelo kept his hand in place for a moment, just long enough to experience the softness of her skin and, perhaps, to be ashamed of the roughness of his own; but then a blacksmith, even if only an apprentice, can never, ever have soft hands.

The difference between them is already clear: Mercede knows everything and Michele Angelo knows nothing.

On their wedding night Michele Angelo is so hesitant and uncertain that Mercede, as always one to take the initiative regardless of the consequences, grabs his hand and places it on her breast. The act of a brazen woman perhaps, but apparently needed because he seems unable to bring himself to touch her, as if there were a

17

cushion of air between her flesh and his hands. Mercede would like to feel herself drenched with explicit desire, because she has always wanted this, while Michele Angelo seems able to do nothing but hover tentatively over her, as over a loaf hot from the oven, brushing it with his fingertips before pulling back. So she looks straight into his eyes, which in the flickering candlelight seem flashing with honey, and presses his hand on her breast. Finally Michele Angelo, from that unplanned contact with soft breast and erect nipple, starts breathing heavily through his nose . . . When he tries to close his eyes, she stops him by pressing his hand to herself ever more firmly, leading it in a circling motion. When she senses that he has finally understood she releases her grip and lets him continue on his own.

The house where the young couple live is small, but it is their own.

There are no lights from human activity outside, so they can gaze into the perfect darkness filled by infinite clusters of stars.

A simple, basic home. A floor added above the forge.

By day, ox-drawn carts go by on the cobbles, then horses, sheep and shepherds. The curate and the doctor pass too. And soldiers: the grey uniforms of the royal army and the blue of the carabinieri. Fugitives and their pursuers also, magistrates and informers. Over that strip of land passes a history in miniature that is the fruit, almost the consequence, of some much greater history. All there is to eat in this tiny slice of the world are the crumbs from the banquet, but if you study those crumbs attentively and taste them carefully, they can teach you many things.

Despite the dark, the walls of the little room above the blacksmith's forge are phosphorescent with quicklime.

They are aware of something beyond the window, Michele Angelo and Mercede, something far beyond the languorous fever consuming them; passing vehicles telling what might be very small or very great stories. And though they are not consciously aware of it, they imagine that conversely, from the lane, the forge of life can be detected in feverish activity. For this reason, as a precaution that is perhaps pointless, perhaps not, Michele Angelo buries his face in the pillow to muffle a deep climactic groan. Without looking at Mercede, he responds to her approval, feeling her opening up to him almost like a mother.

Thinking over it many years later, Mercede says the greatest surprise was to find the attributes of a mature man in her child husband. The light curly hair covering his shoulders and chest made his skin seem even whiter. Then his beard, which from the distance of a mere kiss, could be observed and even felt growing. She is not embarrassed to say he was a good husband, caring and never vulgar. And that he loved her caresses and her breasts most of all.

With miraculous, mathematical, precision Mercede fell pregnant that very night.

But the secret of this perfect conception was their unquestioning acceptance of themselves. Time revealed defects: Michele Angelo was taciturn and touchy and Mercede was bossy and paid too much attention to what other people thought.

Nine months later, again like the precise proof of a mathematical theorem, twin boys were born, Pietro and Paolo. Over the course of the next ten years came Giovanni Maria who was stillborn; Franceschina, also stillborn; Gavino, who left for Australia; Luigi Ippolito, who died in the war; and Marianna . . .

Their love has travelled a long way. They have moved like two pilgrims heading for a distant sanctuary, expecting at every step to see at least the top of the bell tower, but they never see anything. So they have to love each other, again and again, in spite of everything: the dust clogging their hair, the temptation to accept a lift from a cart, or simply, drenched with rain, to abandon themselves to despair, plodding along with uncertain steps in muddy shoes, or with palates parched by scorching heat, or fingers blue with cold, and their eyes fixed on a goal that always, always, turned out to be no more than a starting point.

They have walked straight on, never turning to look back, moving as anonymously as it is possible to imagine. The edge of the road which, from high up on a gig, looks comfortable, but at ground level, trudging on shifting gravel, seems terrible and endless. Occasionally, they meet another person but never, never, anyone they recognise, because they are on their own, two and yet one, seeing nothing and knowing nothing. All they have is their love: obstinate, unyielding, banal and blind.

In just a few years Michele Angelo has extended the workshop, building a new forge behind the old one. The work has involved sacrificing part of the courtyard, but it is good to have more room now the twins are growing and the family is expanding as though spring is a season that will never end. And business has prospered because Michele Angelo has become known as the best blacksmith in the village, which has now almost grown into a town.

Because of the destiny allotted to it by the register office, if we can believe in such a thing as Destiny, the district could now be described as a modest built-up area, as if passing through a sort of restless adolescence, as yet neither fish nor fowl. But it does have the presumptuous expectation of certain suburbs that they will soon become one or the other, or both. Seen from the direction of Ugolio, Nuoro is now like the vanguard of a bare border post, with its landmark cathedral making it look like a village in the Andes. An immense circular prison set down like a bass drum on a grassy plain. To tell the truth, Nuoro now combines two different worlds: in the hills, San Pietro and the shepherds, and in the valley Séuna and the farmers. It is from this clear duality that the life of the place depends. And it is a life Michele Angelo encounters just as the hormone of modernity begins to bubble away in the village's infantile and archaic organism, percolating city ideas (or at least those of a small town), creating via Majore, an extremely modern middle-class street, at the exact meeting point of two ancient souls. Turning two-faced Janus into three-headed Cerberus. This central position explains and synthesises everything: the feeling of caste, the gaze directed overseas, towards History. And it describes the ubiquitous persistence of certain ideas: everybody is convinced they have seen something others have not seen, and they delude themselves that they have thought things that others have not thought, but this is just because someone has taken the trouble to tell an ordinary story in an extraordinary way.

So the connecting road, via Majore, has been created to display – in accordance with a theory of what a town should have – a smart hostelry, a pharmacy and even a rustic town hall complete with market and a weighing-machine for livestock. In addition, of course, to small permanent businesses, mostly run by outsiders, and this among people only recently civilised to the point of being able to read and write and who only recently have given up on bartering. So here is this connecting road, a foreign link between two native realities, a stretch of common land running beside a sort of mossy, rocky riverbed surrounded by trees that the people of Nuoro have named the Giardinetti. But to Michele Angelo this street is above all a building project of small plaster-fronted villas . . . fitted with balconies.

However, in this farce of chained creatures, Michele Angelo is the exception that proves the rule . . . Not much is known about him, except that he must have been the product of a union consummated behind the scenes: his father could have been a charcoal-burner from the mainland; and his mother a local nobody, perhaps a servant girl. What is certain is that she did not know she was pregnant until she was actually giving birth, whereas the man never knew he had become a father at all. And it is also a fact that in that corner of the world forsaken by every sort of god, women gave birth to underweight ugly hairy things, while what this mother produced was like something from a gold and white bundle, as beautiful as baby Jesus in the manger. But, clearly, it was the fruit of a seed ill-suited to such a uterus, so that when they pulled him out she was already dead. Hence the name they gave the child, Michael: the angel with the sword . . . The Sisters of Charity at the orphanage liked the idea that the fruit of sin had itself avenged the sin from which it had sprung.

Mercede's case was different. Her father had wanted that name for her even though he knew he would never see her grow up. The girl was the subject of a dispute over a violated marriage contract. It is possible the facts are otherwise, but the popular rumour was that Mercede's parents were the nobleman Severino Cumpostu and the priest's housekeeper at San Carlo, Ignazia Marras. Known parents, whatever the case. But – and there was a "but" – Severino Cumpostu had contracted to marry a woman of the Serusi di Gavoi family, so that all trace was lost of the housekeeper and her child, until the girl appeared in church sixteen years later at the very moment when Michele Angelo was adjusting the large incense burner.

The Chironi family was the fruit of outcasts, of two negatives combining to make a positive, in itself enough to condemn their union as a rash one. When Michele Angelo and Mercede looked at each other for the first time, he saw her raising her head as if to adore a winged statue – in fact the blond youth was leaning away from the ladder towards the pivot from which the incense burner was hanging and looked as if he was flying. And he, looking down on the girl from above, seemed to see a ruby in its natural setting of rock. He had to place her precisely to be quite sure the impression of beauty he had experienced was real, full and absolute.

24

So, when they looked at each other, they had no inheritance to protect and not even a story to tell; they were at the beginning of everything: he an apprentice blacksmith and she already made of iron.

They knew at once that they must rely on each other. They came from no clan with a name that had to be protected and even their surnames were a sham, dished out by bureaucracy. Michele Angelo was given the surname Chironi after the general inspector of the orphanage at Cúglieri where he had grown up, and Mercede was surnamed Lai after the employer who took her into service at the age of seven.

So there it was: the creation of a new world, one might say, because these people had given them Christian names and surnames from which everything could start.

Seven months passed between their first sight of one another and their marriage, which was almost a secret ceremony, with no trappings. It was witnessed by the blacksmith Giuseppe Mundula and the sacristan Nicolino Brotzu, and held at the church in the side chapel of St John Chrysostom.

But we are running ahead and must slow down.

We must go back to the night when this same blacksmith, Giuseppe Mundula, returning to his home above the forge, found the dead body of his wife at the top of the stairs

The woman had died hugging her chest as if trying to stop her heart escaping from under her ribs. On her face was the worried, disgusted and sad expression of a cook who, tasting a tiny quantity of sauce from the tip of a spoon, has just realised she has ruined it.

Giuseppe Mundula either hardly thought at all, or thought too much. He was exhausted, because his work exhausted him. He was as dirty as a demon. There was his wife lying dead in front of him. She had probably cried for help when she felt her heart bursting but, deafened by the ferocious beating of hammer on anvil – even white-hot iron whistles and complains – the smith had thought he was hearing the soul of the metal and didn't understand that it was his wife's death throes.

All this thinking, or not thinking, had paralysed him. And the stairs, under the weight of his body, were beginning to creak as if with the sound of a tongue clicking on a palate. So after a final glance at his wife, Giuseppe Mundula took a large stride over her body and crossed the landing to the kitchen. There he poured a jugful of water into the basin and washed his hands and face just as he always did. Not even the violence of this drama (when death steps onto the stage it is always as a prima donna), nor that corpse stretched on its back at the top of the stairs, could prevent him from sitting down to eat a piece of bread and cheese . . . Or rather, it was perhaps the discourtesy of death in betraying him by snatching away his wife that made his supper so peaceful, more silent than ever before, because it had always been her defect to talk too much. These pluses: the silence and the satisfaction of not having to give a damn about death, made it easier for him to bear the voiceless pain growing in the pit of his stomach. It was only after he had deluded himself that he had evaded this pain with the large stride he had taken to climb over the corpse, that he was unexpectedly struck by the realisation that he was now alone. Widowed and sterile. He gagged on a taste of iron, and was forced to spit out the cheese and moistened bread.

Rising from the chair, he looked through the half-closed door and saw his wife clearly for the first time. She had never been beautiful; full of life, certainly, but never beautiful. Now that he could see her, motionless in the light of the moon, but no paler than she had always been, she seemed to him as intimate as an amputated limb, but at the same time as distant from him as any unknown woman who might have happened to die at the top of his stairs. She was so light it was easy to lift her, and with her in his arms it was easy to understand how very little she had weighed on this earth: only there at all because there was room for her, as she had always said herself.

Yet there had been a time when even she had meant something and when an ample bosom had finally managed to flourish on her dry ribs. He had known then that she was pregnant from the absent-minded precision with which she had begun looking at things. Every sharp corner of her body had softened, as had every sharp edge of her personality. She had even smiled and, occasionally, laughed. And seeing her laugh had in itself been enough to make him reflect on the silent miracle of procreation.

She had become almost beautiful then, the blacksmith's wife. She remembered she had a name, Rosangela, and that she had once had a few dreams before life had become so prosaic as not even to allow her the concept of dreaming. When Giuseppe Mundula claimed he had never dreamed in his life she had explained that dreams were just like a feeling of real life without the weight of real life.

Now, crossing the threshold like a newly married husband with his wife in his arms, the blacksmith pondered that lightness he had never experienced.

Laid out on the bed, her body did not even crease the coarse sheets. She seemed young yet extremely old at the same time. Rosangela Mundula née Líndiri. That name had no sooner been spoken than lost, at the exact moment when that immature foetus was ripped from her womb.

She had been dreaming of a bushel of grain being constantly emptied and refilled. While dreaming of this infinite abundance, repetitive and perpetual, she had been taken with cramps. She had known at once, on the cusp between sleeping and waking, that something terrible was happening. But it would not be right to say she understood, because it was not her but the other woman who had understood, the other Rosangela, the one with beautiful full breasts who could smile and even laugh. Like the wise virgins in the parable, she had kept a lamp burning in the darkness of deep sleep and the uncertainty of dreams. So that when everything happened, when it was the end, the other Rosangela was in a position to inform the first one.

Sitting on the edge of the bed, she had felt the new life flowing out between her thighs in a tiny mucous bundle.

They never found any way to talk about this. Under their home the hammer went on beating the incandescent bar and the anvil continued to mark the rhythm, the bellows to blow, and the water to hiss as the metal was immersed. The heaviness of life returned just when they had imagined they had escaped from it.

The blacksmith's wife returned to the world sterile, unfortunate and nameless, because that was where there was room for her.

So she began to think that if her husband were to look elsewhere for what he might expect to have, in order to make his contribution to the race, he would have good reason to do so.

But, beware, this was no mere demographic calculation on her part, no: it was the reasoning of a woman. Women always keep their front door ajar, while men always keep theirs either bolted shut or wide open.

To the blacksmith's wife, a son was not just a matter of simple vanity but of continuity, like that bushel of grain constantly refilling itself when empty.

As she saw it, she and her husband had all they needed, yet the bushel still continued relentlessly emptying itself . . . And what if she were no longer there, she asked herself, as though dying were the same as going outside for a moment. So she began suggesting to her husband that he should father a child with another woman and even assured him she would bring the child up as her own. But this would make the blacksmith fly into a rage and thump the table.

So she said no more until a local woman told her that some grand lady had gone to choose herself a daughter from the orphanage at Cúglieri. The blacksmith's wife had never been to Cúglieri and had never even thought of going there, but now she talked of nothing else ... Her husband would shake his head and bolt the door, shouting "Leave me in peace!"

Unabashed, she would repeat, day after day: "Giuseppe Mundula, do you want to die leaving no-one to inherit what you have created?"

And he would say, "To hell with it all, what do I care what happens after I'm gone."

"Just think about it."

And he would say again, "I have thought about it. Get out of my way with all this nonsense!"

He only answered out of a sense of marital duty, but to his wife the blacksmith's words sounded like a door being locked with ten bolts.

Now, as he lay waiting for dawn beside this dead wife who was no heavier than a slice of bread, her obsession came back to his mind.

Before the last handful of earth had been thrown on her coffin, he was already on his way to Cúglieri.

He presented himself washed, and in his best suit, to claim an heir, because he had not the slightest wish to marry again.

He began by saying he wanted a boy old enough to be able to look after himself. He had a letter of introduction from the parish priest of the Madonna del Rosario of Nuoro, which stated that he was a God-fearing and well-off widower with a clean record, an independent craftsman who owned his own business.

In the bare corridor of the boys' section of the orphanage, he was shown about twenty possible candidates, each with a number on his chest. He immediately rejected the first two, thought about number 3, then caught sight of number 7. Number 7 was Michele Angelo. They explained to him that there could be no question of adoption since he was a widower but, having seen his references, they would be able to sidestep the problem by a form of temporary guardianship that would eventually become more permanent – as though it were a question of transferring a *figlio d'anima* or "soul-child" from a poor family to a better-off one. "We don't want to make too much of a fuss," as the prioress of the Sisters of Mercy put it. "It's just a matter of trust, a matter of trust."

Once they got home after a journey spent in total silence, the blacksmith asked the boy how old he was, and the boy said he was nine, or at least that was what they had told him at the orphanage. Then he said he could read and write, not very well, but he did know how to read, if he wasn't hurried.

Michele Angelo started at the forge the next morning.

"The only way to learn a trade is to watch," the blacksmith told the boy. "By watching you will learn what you can, and if you don't understand anything, you can ask me."

While he watched, Michele Angelo helped by keeping the forge in order, tidying away the tools and sweeping filings off the floor . . .

One evening, while they were drinking milk soup, the child spoke without bidding for the first time: "But how can you be my babbo?" he asked.

The blacksmith studied him as one might an unfamiliar insect. "I'm not your babbo," he stated firmly so there should be no misunderstanding.

The boy carried on eating.

Nevertheless, it did not take long for Michele Angelo's habit of saying little and observing closely to pay dividends. Within two years he had learned how to control the bellows and understand the level of fusion from the colour of the flame. At eleven, he was remarkably strong and healthy. In the kitchen he had his own bed which he had helped to build himself.

The blacksmith liked to believe that though two solitary people placed in close proximity do not necessarily form a social group, at least they can make solitude seem less bitter. And it may be that this thought was enough to make it clear that he liked the boy, even though he had no idea how to express his affection.

For his part, Michele Angelo had developed complete confidence in this adopted "soul-father". If the blacksmith said strike now, Michele Angelo struck. If he said wait, he waited. And if he said more bellows, he made the bellows blow harder.

"One day you'll have a forge of your own," the blacksmith said while they were washing their hands and faces at the sink. He spoke as if were talking to himself, because this chestnut-haired boy, who was growing day by day at his side, was simply an emanation of his own capacity to give. That was it: detachment can transform a capacity to give into a marvellous deed as from detachment, para-doxically, can come real advantage.

At this stage the advantage lay in understanding without a shadow of doubt that every road must lead to a destination or goal and that staying in the world simply because there was room for him in it could not exactly be defined as having a goal. But to see oneself again as a boy, inquisitive and trusting, that certainly was. Giuseppe Mundula did not realise it, and he never would, but he was in fact doing his best to keep refilling that bushel of grain that was constantly and so desperately trying to empty itself.

Thus, after ten years, Michele Angelo was almost ready to stand in for his supposed father in the forge. And if the blacksmith felt like relaxing at the tavern for an hour or two, his young apprentice was there to get on with the work.

That was how Michele Angelo came to be responsible for attending to the pivot from which the church incense burner hung.

So there he is at the top of the long ladder, which bends and bulges, as he tests the hook which everyone says is unsafe. And it is, indeed, as loose as a tooth about to part company with the gum. So Michele Angelo, having diagnosed the fault, prepares to climb down to fetch what he needs to solve the problem. Looking downwards, to work out how he might begin his descent, he sees her. Mercede is sitting several metres below, but in his mind she is already so high above him as to be out of his reach. He is nineteen years old and has never loved before, but he understands the body the way males of this world know it, with excess and impatience . . . He understands his own body and its substance, but knows nothing about the bodies of others. The ladder sways under him like a cane, and when he finally reaches the ground he glances from the corner of his eye to see whether she is watching him. She is.

We have already told the rest.

———

Mercede comes on her own to six o'clock Mass in an old but still presentable dress, belonging to her employer. It falls loosely over her chest. She has bound her hair up in a white scarf. She cannot afford more than that. Michele Angelo arrives immediately afterwards with Giuseppe Mundula, in a heavy blue and violet jacket in the Nuoro style. The hair under his cap is combed into place with water and olive oil. The priest is the last to arrive; he had almost forgotten and apologises in the silence of the flickering candles. The wedding does not take long, officiated not at the high altar but in the side chapel, as though for a pair of fugitives from justice or for a love that has engendered sinful fruit prior to any sacrament.

Mercede's dowry is herself and Michele Angelo's desire for her. He brings her a small forge with two little rooms above it, rented to him by Giuseppe Mundula so that he can operate independently. Giuseppe Mundula has married him off, prepared him a future and even passed on several commissions to him.

And he has done this at the very moment when the trends of modernity are making many people feel they must have balconies with good views over the link road.

Two years pass.

As happens, even in the most significant stories, time moves on with little happening to catch the attention. What there is to tell is superficially trivial, but in reality a miracle, the compulsive miracle of generation and regeneration. First the twins Pietro and Paolo are born, then Giovanni Maria who is born dead.

This stillborn child was the first proof that you must pay back in proportion to what you receive, for despite the fact that the craze for balconies, iron grilles and graceful railings was bringing in more work every day, and they had not yet been married a year, it was already clear that the forge would have to be extended on the courtyard side and they might even need to take on an apprentice. Despite all this, which was pure happiness and an almost banal process of growth and multiplication, Giovanni Maria was born perfectly formed but as green as if thrust out of a swamp. They said he had been conceived too soon after the first labour, which had been long-drawn-out but not exceptionally difficult. First Paolo had appeared and then – they say it's the elder twin who decides the order – Pietro. "Too soon," the women of the neighbourhood said, a little critical of this newly arrived couple who were exploiting their good fortune like starving stray dogs.

"Just look at those Chironi," they said. "Who do they think they are? Where have they sprung from? Eh?"

Mercede did know it had been unwise to allow it to happen when she was still breast-feeding. But what could she do with Michele Angelo? You have to care for your husband at table and in bed, but beyond that men should concentrate on their work?

Mercede admonished him. "You've made us look like animals . . ."

Michele Angelo frowned, but continued to concentrate on his soup.

"You can't just pretend it doesn't matter, Michele Angelo Chironi . . ." she insisted.

"Why, what harm have I done you?" he mumbled before swallowing.

Mercede shook her head and lowered her voice. "What sort of an answer is that? It's all very fine for you."

This change of tone took the wind out of his sails, because Michele Angelo was incapable of getting the upper hand with this woman. "You could have told me it was a bad time," he said, pouting slightly.

"Of course, naturally," she said sarcastically. "Just enjoy your food . . ." Then, smiling as if to herself, "Closing the stable door when the horse has bolted."

So the twins were fed on goat's milk, because Mercede had lost her own with this premature second pregnancy that had disorientated her body. She had been tormented with flushes like red-hot irons from her throat to the depths of her belly, and had occasionally lost control of her body. The second pregnancy had been exceptionally difficult with giddiness, constant nausea and acidity – the hair of the foetus, they said . . . And on top of that, which was logical enough, she had lost her milk.

Pietro was the sensible one. Paolo was restless. They were as alike as two drops of water apart from the colour of their hair. Pietro's was light brown and Paolo's a deep black. Pietro ate and slept contentedly, while Paolo constantly searched for the breast. When Mercede came near him, and he opened his mouth like a little bird for the nipple, she would murmur but almost without resentment, "Eh, ask that animal your father for it."

It had been an unbelievably luminous May, almost summery, without any unsettled periods to detract from it: there was no rain, and only a few clouds in the sky. The twins were born in January and by May, Mercede was pregnant again.

Winter had lingered on in a constant leaden light. Until Easter the weather had been so bad it had not been possible to refill pillows and mattresses or prepare dried figs and tomatoes. Suddenly, between one evening and the next morning, May flung open the door to the light. And it was then, while Mercede's breasts were still bursting with milk, that Michele Angelo's desire for her became uncontrollable.

So she became a bad housewife, and was accused of being a harlot. Having lost her milk, she was forced to feed her sons on goat's milk from a desiccated intestine, like orphaned lambs in a sheepfold.

Many years later this would lead to grief. In another spring, another May.

But not now.

*

Now, sudden prosperity enabled Michele Angelo to buy a piece of land at Lollove. A mere handkerchief planted with vines, but the main thing was: it belonged to him. The first piece of land he had ever owned. His own property. In truth, it had been Giuseppe Mundula who had seen the opportunity, but he had preferred to offer it to his adopted son. As he grew older, Giuseppe had softened and had even become able to express emotion. Bolstered by this recently acquired plot, the Mundula-Chironi family, father and son in theory rather than in flesh, threw their arms round each other. It was the closest they had ever been able to imagine approaching one another in the twelve years since they first met in the orphanage at Cúglieri.

"Affluence breeds respect," Giuseppe said, his arm still round his son. He now considered him his son in every respect: Giuseppe was getting on in years, full of experience and with much to give, and he felt secure in the knowledge that he had not allowed loneliness to strip him of all the good things he had managed to achieve. "Remember," he said, "those who have achieved nothing, will always remain nothing. If we leave no trace of our time on earth, we die twice over. You never knew my wife Rosangela, she was a woman and a half . . . Someone who really knew how to tell the difference between what needed doing and what didn't need doing. I think I can honestly say that today she would have been happy."

Michele Angelo nodded. In those days you could die without leaving behind a single likeness of yourself. No-one had ever taken a photograph of Rosangela Mundula née Líndiri, still less painted her portrait. She had gone without leaving a trace, except her husband's brief descriptions of her: she hadn't been beautiful, you couldn't say that, vivacious more like. She would have made you sit up and take notice. She knew what was what, there could be no doubt of that. She would be up at five every day. There were no Sundays or holidays in her life. She was always saying she had too much to do, but one could never be sure what this was.

Neither of them asked how suitable this old man's talk might be in front of that motionless stretch of stunted vines twisting round their overly long poles. The vines were a warning that people dear to one can be absent in good times. And in bad times, whenever these might occur, one hoped they would be looking the other way. All this was life, defying any possible form of death. A life of buds leading to leaves, then bunches of grapes. Perhaps this was why it was worth calling back the souls of the dead to be present at one's own moment of happiness.

But no such soul could have come back to bless that tiny moment of well-being for Michele Angelo, as Giuseppe realised, knowing how things go and and how they have always gone. Of course, there had been Giovanni Maria, Michele Angelo's recently stillborn son, but he had been an incomplete soul, a spirit who could never become a guardian angel. Which was why it occurred to Giuseppe to offer his own immensely powerful personal protection.

So they named the vineyard Rosanzela.

By the time the twins were able to walk the forge had been enlarged, and the house too. The ground floor had been converted into a large kitchen and two bedrooms. The upper floor stayed as it was, but the old kitchen became the principal bedroom, with two other rooms off it: a small one which remained a larder and a second, where

Pietro and Paolo slept. The forge, larger and better equipped, now extended to part of the old courtyard, together with a section of courtyard purchased from neighbours.

Rosanzela yielded a sour, rough wine, but this was their own house wine, and as such a manifestation of the divine. While bread swelled and rose, and was baked and baked again to make it crisp, the wine fermented and quivered and took on colour. But the result was too dark, and had to be mixed with water because it was so strong that a single glass would have gone to your head. Some people dilute wine with honey, and some with sugar and water, but they say such stuff can only be used as communion wine as priests are only half human after all and have no palate for real wine. To be good, wine must leave a stain on the glass, be heavy and syrupy, pressed from withered grapes, crudely planted and cultivated. You did not need a scholar to understand that in that part of the world they knew how to make bread and cheese, but wine, definitely not. Nor olive oil either, to tell the truth.

Anyway, at harvest time, if one can call it that, Mercede was eight months pregnant. It was October, the harvest delayed because September had been cold and the grapes slow to ripen. Michele Angelo seemed transformed into a lord and master because he had called in several local youngsters to work for him by the day and pressed a few small coins into their hands. Everyone was involved, Mercede who had brought something to keep her occupied, the twins running about among the rows of vines, and even Giuseppe Mundula was sitting to one side looking straight ahead. Then there were the three young helpers, two girls and a boy. And Michele Angelo was playing the proprietor with an awkwardness that was revelatory of the shifting social classifications of the period.

Michele Angelo though recalls something he cannot possibly remember. It is a cold night, and he can hear a long moan like a sustained mooing. He is not quite sure what he is remembering and cannot identify it with anything physical. But he is certain it happened at night and that there was this terrible moaning. Whenever he draws a deep breath, as he looks about himself on the Corso and points out the balconies of the Deffenu or Campanelli family homes, and allows himself to say with some pride: I made those; or when he finds himself considering some personal aim and the responsibility of producing a stock of descendants so nothing will be lost; it is at such moments that he is aware of that impossible memory, that coldness and that moaning.

Even now, in front of this land that is his own, in front of his children who already exist and those yet to come, in front of the only woman he will ever love; even now, he is conscious of that moaning, and the night and the cold. It is like a reminder, a sign. That we all see ourselves as predators, but that we are really prey. That we all see ourselves as masters, but are instead servants in perpetuity. Naturally, it takes generations to get used to affluence, all the more so when it has been achieved by the sweat of the brow.

Michele Angelo is telling himself: Here I can be myself and watch my children grow, and I have been able to make sure that they will have what they need to live well in this vale of tears, but above all they must never suffer what I have suffered: the night, the cold, and the moaning.

*

When they get home from the harvest, Mercede feels unwell. The women who immediately run to her aid say she has overstrained herself in her condition. And they look for explanations: she has been jolted in the cart from the vineyard to the village, she has been on her feet all day in the sun, she has drunk too much cold water, or eaten too many grapes with her moistened bread . . .

But Mercede knows there is only one reason. The child inside her is dead. Again. She knows because she has felt the pain of farewell before the pain of childbirth. First an emptiness, then a laceration. Like when what you most fear in the world happens, and happens inexorably, and is made doubly cruel by the fact that you have been fearing it for so long.

So it was. The first female Chironi, Franceschina, was born dead. Pink and white as if asleep, with no sign of what might have caused her death. Mercede knew how gently her little girl had left this world, because she heard her voice just before she was born. Mercede had always seen herself as a solid pitcher, a jar for times of famine, full of candied olives, long-lasting and nourishing. Ready to carry any seed. A woman of flesh and iron. But now she feels as fragile as crystal.

She can see it all clearly, as if observing the world with a fixed stare like a model facing a portrait painter. In this precarious pose she can feel a light taking shape, one that murmurs gold and carmine.

It is clear to her that, beyond this light, is the outspokenness of things unsaid that, like a dark curtain, conceals the substance, contrasting with the invisible. A tenacity of dark shadows thrown on the slippery surface of what has not come into being. A reality that has the delicacy of blown glass, born of breath and fire. A reality that is a constant delaying, a kind of stability created from things attempted but not achieved. A smooth surface serving as a background for uncertain things that had nevertheless seemed to be certainties.

Definite in form, if deceptive in appearance.

This farewell broke Mercede. And the women round her understood that none of the explanations they suggested for what happened made any sense: the ride in the cart, the indigestion, or the heat. Because whatever the real reason, nothing could account for the terrible pain they read in the mother's face.

That evening, while the women busied themselves round the exhausted mother, Michele Angelo left home. He had never done this before. He and Mercede had never let each other suffer alone. Yet in that terrible epilogue to a perfect day, he understood that there was absolutely nothing he could have said or done but run away. And leave in the middle of the night, for the cold of the countryside to howl.

He walked blindly for a long time, and it was not until he reached the bank of a stream that he noticed he was shivering and realised he had put nothing on over his shirt. There were things he could have said, if he had only known how to say them . . .

In the morning when he came home, exhausted by thoughts he could not even grasp, Michele Angelo stopped at the door of the bedroom to spy on Mercede who had fallen asleep, exhausted. The women attending her had nodded off too.

Hearing him, she smiled lightly in her sleep.

He stayed watching her for an indefinable time. The fire was dying out. Pietro was as still as a little corpse while Paolo was muttering and struggling in his sleep. Their suffering, like the silence, was perfect, contained in itself, immobile, unchangeable.

He went into the forge; he had a gate to finish and many other jobs waiting to be done, once there, he did not move, but breathed in the terrible smell of iron that came to him on the night air. There were a few small pieces of work he could have completed at that time of night without disturbing anyone, but he just stood there, in the midst of his creations, some still unfinished and others ready for delivery: every single tool was his, every single sliver of iron. There was nothing in that place that was not entirely his own: the walls, the roof, everything, every stone in the surface of the court-yard. Under that sky Michele Angelo Chironi had made his nest, built his lair, constructed his dam. He had a house and some land. There was a fragment of that cursed land of which he could say: I stand on my own ground, which I earned by spitting blood at the furnace from the age of nine; and here, within the boundary that encloses my land, I can breathe my own air and watch my children grow, and here I am the recognised king and emperor.

He felt a bitterness in his body that he could not have sweetened in a thousand years.

He was the only one awake that night; no-one would have seen him standing there in the middle of his forge, yet he resisted any temptation to weep, because no human race since the beginning of time has ever grown strong and invincible on a diet of tears. He was certainly furious with this fate that took from him with both hands and only gave with one, but he refused to bow his head. He was a tenacious man and had learned that certain alloys that seem inflexible may yield when you least expect them to; you must persist and, often, all it needs is one final blow. Metal is a living thing and it understands the hand that forges it. It knows the heart of the man who works it.

So, regaining full control of himself, he felt he understood that everything depended on how they were seen by others. On how these Chironi, whoever they might be, were regarded by their neighbours. And everything derived from the envy distilled in those looks. In that instant it seemed he had settled everything, as if the solution had always been there before his eyes, but he had not been aware of it. Happiness is never popular with those who are not happy. That was the point, unquestionably. Every single thing confirmed it and cried out to him in a loud voice: after just a few years he possessed a house and land, and a business that had got off to a good start . . . And worst of all, all this had started from nothing. From absolutely nothing. That's what it is, he told himself: you must keep things hidden, I understand that now.

A little after this, Giuseppe Mundula, woken in the middle of the night, listened to an over-excited Michele Angelo's conclusions. The old man confirmed and approved everything. Then, with the same imperturbable persistence with which Michele Angelo had insisted he wasn't sleepy, Giuseppe persuaded his "soul-son" to lie down on his old bed and try to sleep . . .

A sky full of violet clouds dripping thick blood on the ground . . . A terrible fusion of Nothing and Everything . . . Like our consciousness that

wanders among things that have been too explicitly stated until it ends
up producing nothing but silence. There is so much we would like to hear
said to us but that no-one ever says.

In the silence of the rooms gods are hampered by their vestments.
There is a tired old man, like a father compelled to punish his children.
His very thin body seems to struggle to support itself, his shoulders
curved under the weight of the triple crown. All round, angels display the
symbols of supreme martyrdom.

It is a subdued pain that cannot be described.

The moment he woke Michele Angelo Chironi knew exactly what he must do.

When he returned to the house the first thing he heard was the subdued murmuring of women chanting the rosary. Mercede's still swollen belly was covered with missals and images of saints.

Michele Angelo entered the room and stood at the foot of the bed. The look on his face was not human. Even his wife, still dazed, looked worried when she saw him. The women stopped mumbling.

Michele Angelo tilted his head back. "Out of my house," he said, without raising his voice.

It was the fact that he did not shout that particularly frightened the women. So much so that they did not even answer, but hurriedly picked up their missals, put on their shawls and swarmed out of the room.

A second later Mercede and Michele Angelo are left alone, face to face. She is too tired to speak, while he struggles to control the blood throbbing in his temples.

Their silence is packed tighter than a bale of hay.

"Don't be like that," she ventures.

He silences her with a wave of the hand as though not wanting to be distracted from some fundamental thought. In fact, there is no thought in his head, he just needs to concentrate on convincing himself that there is no malignant deity fighting against the most basic aim of his existence: the procreation of children.

It is at this exact moment, immersed in this precise silence, that Michele Angelo understands how the things he had thought insignificant had, instead, definitively marked his life.

And he also understands that he will never be able to pretend otherwise. He is like the survivor of a shipwreck wildly happy to have reached the shore, but not yet ready to face the open sea again. Or like a jockey unseated and hurled to the ground during a race, who thinks he has escaped unscathed because he hasn't broken anything, but who has not foreseen the agony of finding himself once again face to face with a horse in full harness.

He is face to face now with his real fear: not poverty or exhaustion or even sacrifice, but loneliness. As terrible as the old man weighed down with vestments that he dreamed about. Like the silence in the orphanage corridor.

They had only just come back from the refectory when two long rings were heard on the bell. This was the signal for visits and meant that you had to report to the corridor wearing your individual number. He had been allotted the number 17. He was one of the older boys, one of those who were soon to be removed from the orphanage and handed over to life. Decanted from a container into nothing. Like dogs bred in captivity and suddenly released into the forest. And, according to rumour, being decanted was terrible: you left the orphanage to die, that's what everyone said. In the outside world you would be a delinquent, a hired shepherd, an unskilled labourer, a beggar or a cabin-boy, on your own until death. Every visiting time, every time the bell rang, was a chance to escape that fate. It meant fighting the probability of being alone. Of loneliness. For all Michele Angelo Chironi, nine years old, could know, this was what had been missing, that would be missing, outside the terrible prison of his parentless childhood. Because without teeth to bite, claws to scratch, or cunning absorbed hourly from a gang-leader father or from a mother, you're on your own. And if you have no-one to give you, even if only to a limited extent, attention, warmth and interest, you might just as well think of putting an end to your life.

Two things weighed on his mind: the first was, that if he failed to get out of the orphanage that day he never would; the second, that no-one in the world would ever choose a child with a number like 17. So he bartered the only property he possessed, two pieces of fairly fresh bread taken from the table, to exchange his number 17 for a 7. When Giuseppe Mundula appeared in the corridor, the only thing in Michele Angelo's mind was a silent appeal: Choose me, please, please choose me!

But the visitor's gaze rested for a while on number 17, then shifted to the first three. He seemed not to notice Michele Angelo at all. Choose me! Nothing happened: the man seemed incapable of hearing his prayer, because he was distracted, shattered by recent grief, not so much there to make a meaningful choice but to honour some vow. Choose me! The seconds that passed were as long as years and still the man made no move.

Then something happened. The card with the number 7 slipped from Michele Angelo's grasp and fell with a thud that echoed loudly in the concentrated, monastic silence of the corridor. Giuseppe Mundula's gaze shifted and fell, with surprise, on Michele Angelo, as if the boy had suddenly materialised without warning. "That one," Giuseppe murmured.

We have already told the rest.

Now, standing in front of his wife and pointing to an absent god with a menacing index finger, Michele Angelo spoke: "There can be no going back," he declared, "and we won't be beaten. I shall give you many more children, Mercede Lai." Then, deep inside he thought, My darling, but didn't say it. Even so, she heard him perfectly. "Of course," he went on after a short pause, "we have to be more careful, live discreetly . . . No-one likes to see others happy, and to see us happy least of all."

He seemed to be making sense. Mercede nodded and closed her eyes.

A dawn chorus of noise came from outside.

This deference to modesty bore fruit. Within two years Gavino was born, and after another two years Luigi Ippolito.

Four boys and no girls. And two apprentices. And more land at

Marreri for Michele Angelo Chironi, still wearing the same patched trousers. And he always held his head at a respectful angle when he said Yes, signore, or Yes, signora, to all the people who signed more and more work contracts with him.

Invisible, and protected from critical stares, the family prospered. Even so, Mercede still busied herself like a servant cleaning the church. Or joined in her neighbours' communal baking sessions as though she could not afford to bake bread for herself and her family, or have others bake it for her.

They marked the twins' tenth birthday with a secret donation towards the erection of a statue of the Redeemer on Monte Orthobène.

The whole of the local population had been mobilised, each person in proportion to his or her resources, to make sure that this artistic, cultural and religious project enabled Nuoro to take its place among the cities of the nation, at the centre of celebrations for the Holy Year of 1900.

This superficially private act of donation by Michele Angelo Chironi was in reality extremely public. In the way that every secret is public in small communities, especially when they consider themselves to be important ones. The size of the blacksmith's donation was a theme for discussion on the streets. Five lire, some said; as much as fifty, others said. Also up for discussion was the family's arrogance in living as though they had nothing when in fact they had everything, but of course it was equally debatable to pretend to be well off if in fact you were poor. You had to choose your poison. In any case, when the statue arrived in Cagliari – in pieces and ready for assembly, on board the steamship *Tirso* – everyone in Nuoro was able to state definitely which piece belonged to whom according to how much they had donated. And when it had been assembled at the top of the hill, facing that supremely self-important village community, it was seen for what it was: a Christ of flesh and bone, virile, muscular, heavy-browed, a circus performer. A mythical Laocoon only just free from the serpents. The body of a pagan with powerful pectorals. Half naked, with his loincloth apparently held in place by the fierce wind, even if it was to be expected that it would very soon slide down his powerful thighs as he rose. All the Nuoro fathers saw this and, in one way or another, recognised themselves in it. Because there was something familiar in that mass about to take flight. In that bronze lightness.

Then a popular rumour circulated that the statue had cost the lives of those closest to the sculptor Vincenzo Jerace: his little daughter had died while it was being cast, and his wife immediately after it had been set in place. This was said to be why this Christ had such a sad expression. People even went so far as to say that the face, though sculpted with a smile, had later adjusted its expression out of sympathy with the artist's great grief. Which is why the appearance of joy vanished from its face at the exact moment when Luisa Jerace, Vincenzo's wife, weakened by grief after the recent loss of her child, and seeing clouds crossing the sky behind the magnificent statue, had the impression that it was about to fall on her, and in terror dropped to the ground dead. That was how it must have looked to the local worthies and the women in corsets with veiled hats and traditional headbands, those who were privileged to be the first to see the bronze statue exposed to the winds. Because it must undoubtedly have been a windy day even if well into August, a time when clouds would have been crossing the sky. After *Ferragosto** the summer breaks. It was windy on the little paved space round the pedestal at the top of the hill. Everyone who mattered was there: the mayor, the notary, the doctor, the general, the ladies, Jerace himself, and if what they say is true, his wife Luisa as well. Michele Angelo and Mercede were there, in the back row on this occasion, a sign that, whatever the rumour, their donation must have been more than modest, but so far as is known they never referred to the supposed death of the sculptor's wife. And yet they never forgot that day towards the end of August for two quite different reasons: their invitation to be present at the inauguration of the statue, as we have seen, and the fact that it was the first time Mercede felt her child kick inside her.

When they reached the top of the hill in their cart at the end of the procession of local worthies, it seems no-one even noticed them and they could see very little of the statue . . .

Then they went back home.

* Traditional holiday in Italy on August 15

Second Canto – Hell
(1901–1942)

Scire nefas

Before going to see the statue of the Redeemer, Michele Angelo and Mercede entrusted their youngest children Gavino, now five years old, and Luigi Ippolito, three, to neighbours. The twins Pietro and Paolo had been given their first grown-up job: to take food and money for the day's labour to the workers in the vineyard.

Pietro and Paolo are no longer children and have food and money in their knapsacks. But they never reach the vineyard. The workers will say they never saw them . . . Indeed no-one, not a soul, will admit to having set eyes on them anywhere near that tiny slice of land just before everything blends into the countryside. So at siesta time a small crowd gathers in front of the blacksmith's house, people who know what to do and where to look, where all the rocks and caves are. Mercede sees all these people getting agitated and hears them without listening. What she can hear is a storm at sea.

She did not know what the sea was or even what a storm was. She knew almost nothing of things most people think important to know. Because she had only been seven years old when she was entrusted to the foster-mother who was also her employer. And seven when they told her she had no father and no real mother. They told her she had been called Mercede after the nun-midwife who had been the first to wash her, the one who had crossed herself as she made an agreement with God for Him to decide whether this unfortunate little girl should survive or not. She herself, Sister Mercede, had already stated her preference: "Better dead," she had murmured. But it did not turn out like that. God had other ideas.

So the little girl reached the age of seven, and she was taken to Redenta Lai who gave her a surname and a home. The woman had a husband and two children to look after. On her employer's furniture were doilies and baubles, everything you would expect to find in the homes of well-off people who need to collect useless things ... Near the front door, placed on top of a doily on a little table, was the shell, a thing of mystery. It was the first thing Mercede had seen when she came to the house, but she only found out what it was called some time later. Shell. Shell. It was large and weighty and looked soft, but was, in fact, very hard; it looked like flesh, but was made of stone.

The youngest child in the Lai family, only a year older than Mercede, one day shows her the secret of this object that she mustn't touch: "Inside the shell there's a storm at sea."

Mercede agrees, as if understanding everything she is being told. Like Mary visited by the angel, she hears a whisper and understands and at the same time doesn't understand, though it is clearly not necessary for her to understand what is being asked of her. So it is with Mercede when the little son of the Lai family talks to her about seas and storms.

"What a stupid girl you are," the boy says, grabbing the shell.

"Here, take it," he adds, holding it out to her. But she backs away. "Listen," he urges, putting it close to her ear. But she shakes her head. "You stupid donkey!" he says, grabbing her hair and forcing the shell against her ear.

It looks soft and warm, but is, in fact, very hard and cold. The feel of it seems to reach down to her stomach, and she can hear something the little Lai boy calls the sea. Seeing her relax, he stops pressing the shell against her.

"A storm at sea, listen!" he commands. And she hears it. A turbulent nothingness swirling about inside the cold cavern of the shell, which is perhaps an actual memory of the sea the shell comes from, perhaps only the echo of its heart. Perhaps.

——————

The same as now, when her children are not at home, now when the neighbours are whispering of imminent disaster, anticipating what cannot be escaped. Sending two youngsters out with all that money: so unwise in the times we're living in, with this terrible poverty afflicting us all . . .

"These are very ugly times," the priest, Father Salis, says, dropping his voice when he glances at Mercede.

The same as now, when the unknown sea reminds Mercede that a whole lifetime can go by before the most despicable of feelings are revealed. At the moment what she feels is a mixture of fury and impotence, aware of the existence of something beyond her experience: a storm at sea; of course; yes but what is sea? And what is storm?

"Poor, poor mother . . ." the women murmur.

Poor mother, because Michele Angelo doesn't seem worried at all. "The minute I find them, I'll sort them out!" he mutters, as if to make clear that he has no time to listen to all these prophets of doom. He is sure that the right thing is to wait for his sons in the vineyard. So off he goes to do just that.

In a few hours it is dark. A black night fruitlessly searching for the boys with shouts and torches. At dawn, having combed the area inch by inch, a group of men reach S'Arbore, beyond Marreri, because that is the only road the two boys can have taken. Voices can still be heard calling out, and other groups are going even further. Time to sit down and rest for a bit, and Murazzanu, Basilio Boneddu's dog, starts rummaging near a patch of undergrowth . . . He whines like a spoiled girl and attacks the bushes with his snout. Basilio comes up and bends over the dog. What he sees overwhelms him. The others join him.

Michele Angelo has waited all night in the vineyard. That handkerchief of land has gradually become a fragment of earthly paradise for him, as when Adam first understood that he could not live alone. Good soil, hard work, the sensible grafting of plants, and you'll get bunches of grapes bursting with health on the vines. Sitting between the two rows, Michele Angelo says a prayer and asks a question. Why? he says without articulating the word: why? He is not quite sure who he is asking. His anger has been hidden and modest, as is proper when fate has been too kind. We've been discreet and modest, he repeats, we've never thrust our good fortune in anyone's face, never. We've always been modest, always.

So why? As if afflicted by boils, like Job in the Bible, Michele Angelo determines to tackle his suffering head on: Is it my destiny never to see my children grow up? You've already taken two away from me . . .

It is not that he is expecting anything in particular, but when, at the far end of the vineyard, he makes out the shape of Basilio Boneddu, darker than the very darkness around him, he really does hope that someone has been sent to answer his questions.

The funeral with the two white coffins was agonising. The whole of the San Pietro neighbourhood came down to the Rosario church square. How could it be otherwise? This was the place for court-room battles and funerals. And that funeral in particular, those two children killed in such a dreadful manner, attracted people from as far away as Séuna . . .

Mercede is in such an exalted state that it is all she can do not to burst out laughing every time anyone comes up to offer sympathy. So many people trying to say what cannot be said and to show what cannot be shown. Perhaps these uncertain looks, and this explosive suffering, are the sea, and this terrible feeling of alienation, this being present yet not being present, is the storm. Could it be the storm?

The procession moves slowly as though hoping never to arrive; some say the dead are not really dead until they reach the church, while for others the real moment of death does not come until they begin shovelling earth on top of the coffin. Yet for Mercede that death, that absence, never happens at all. In the grip of her storm she keeps asking herself why all these people have gathered in front of her house. She knows her own sons, and is well aware that Pietro is a bit of a sulker and Paolo a bit of a show-off and a chatterbox, but a good boy. They are two children and, by the grace of God and Our Lady, nothing bad can happen to children, because who could be so vile as to pick a quarrel with two little boys? Who could possibly do such a thing?

However, here are all the people, so many of them.

Except for Michele Angelo.

Basilio Boneddu, surrounded by a few inquisitive people at the end of the procession, cannot find words to describe what he has seen.

They had sat down for a rest, he and Michelino Congia, and Prededdu Murrighile and others. They had been walking for four hours along the Lollove road. Not that there were many other ways they could have gone. When they got to S'Arbore, he said it would be about another hour, more or less, until sunrise. So the men looked at each other and decided to sit down for five minutes to drink something to warm themselves up because they were beginning to feel cold.

"Murazzanu barks and runs off, happy as a sandboy, you only have to let that dog see the open country and he never wants to go home, he doesn't know the meaning of being still. The fact is," Basilio Boneddu continues, "the rest of us sit down, and after a bit we hear the dog howling, but it was no ordinary howling. I pray however many years Our Lord grants me to live on this earth I never hear such a sound again, it was sort of more like a small child wailing. When Murazzanu tries to push his way into the bushes with his snout, we look at each other in terror, we know we're all thinking the same thing. So I get to my feet and go to drag the dog away from the bushes. He fights back, so I grab his collar and give him a sharp jerk to send him behind me. By now Prededdu's with me. When I go up to the bushes it's not like you could see anything. So I tell Prededdu, 'I can't see anything,' and he sets fire to a dry branch and moves closer. I don't know, I'm tough and strong, but when I see what is there, my knees give way . . . Dear Lord. Inside those bushes there are bits of flesh and clothes soaked in blood. The light from the flame makes the red seem even redder. I say, 'God forbid!' Prededdu Murrighile leaps back like he's been shot in the chest. The others run up. Michelino, Bustianeddu . . . Good heavens, please . . ." Basilio shakes his head.

Those listening, a few women among them, lower their eyes: "So it's true that they'd been torn to pieces?" Basilio nods; chopped up and thrown away for wild boars to eat. "But what sort of animal could do a thing like that?" Basilio shrugs: "If you ask me this wasn't the work of any one person, there must have been a gang of them, God knows where from; with all this shortage of food, there are people around you wouldn't give the name of human to." The women shudder and cross themselves. "God forbid," they murmur, meaning: God forbid that what's struck the Chironi family ever happens to us. "None of us is safe nowadays," Basilio goes on. "We must all be vigilant, because the countryside's full of wretches with nothing left to lose . . ."

Meanwhile the procession moves on, ever so slowly.

Michele Angelo is looking at his vineyard. He has sent the workers home. He has not gone to the funeral, because there is something he must do. He has a couple of things to settle with the being who has planned such a terrible course for his life.

It's fine, everything's fine, he tells himself, don't forget that I never asked you for anything more than what was due to me: all I wanted was my fair share, only that. And you? Well done, really well done. What's your problem? Is it this vineyard? Eh? Or what is it? The house? The forge? Eh?

He is yelling at the top of his voice to no obvious listener, perhaps only in an attempt to understand his own thoughts. Poor man, it is unbearable to witness his pain. He is like an ox struggling to fight off tormenting flies.

What a terrible day for a funeral. As terrible as it could possibly be. It draws out the minutest details, everything is obvious: swollen, glassy grapes, lizard-green leaves, branches as dry and dark as salted meat. It is impossible to talk to God and at the same time be forced to see the world so clearly and in such detail. At this moment everything is full of sensations: Michele Angelo Chironi is doing his accounts. As he tries to listen he suddenly starts seeing and feeling things more vividly than ever before: a little red ribbon dancing entangled in a vine, a piece of paper blown about by the wind, the rushing voice of the nearby stream, the wing-beat of a magpie. All serenely perfect. He almost believes this perfection in itself must be a definite reply to his question.

Michele Angelo Chironi knows very well what he must do.

When Giuseppe Mundula arrives on a donkey and sees him standing in the middle of what is left of his vineyard, he murmurs: "My son." He has never addressed him in this way before.

It's many years since Michele Angelo asked over the milk soup: "But now you must be my babbo?"

And just as long since Giuseppe replied: "I'm not your babbo."

But now Giuseppe has called him son. From behind, his son's body seems wrung by a constant trembling like some poor creature being eaten up from the inside.

Michele Angelo has heard Giuseppe come, but he does not even turn. When Giuseppe calls him son, he thinks how much pain that word can generate. And clenches his jaw so hard it hurts, absolutely determined not to weep. Giuseppe gets off the donkey as best he can, he is an old man now and his bones ache, but he dismounts and comes up behind Michele Angelo: "What have you done?" he asks and adds, "Everyone's been looking for you."

Michele Angelo says nothing. The fire has devoured the vineyard in the twinkling of an eye; the grapes bursting in the heat. In no time at all those peaceful rows of vines have grown a surface like black satin that turns bright silver when the wind turns. Where there was once a vineyard is now a fever crackling under the ashes, with an occasional fresh wound of red-hot embers. The currents of air mean that there is very little smoke: it is as if the fire has swallowed the vines in a single mouthful. The flames have spread in a flash, almost cold flames like those of the burning bush that appeared to Moses. It all happened so quickly that Giuseppe, approaching, was scarcely in time to see the fire from the valley. One single massive burst had transformed that piece of paradise into the dark fissures of an active volcano.

Behind Michele Angelo, Giuseppe repeats: "What have you done, my son?"

But Michele Angelo is watching an insect walk lightly over a thistle that has escaped the flames, and is thinking some good must exist, if the absolute peace of that perfect lightness is capable of generating an instant of detachment . . . Giuseppe's voice calls him back to the world: "What have you done, my son? What have you done?"

Michele Angelo shakes his head, but his emotional balance is so precarious that tears begin to flow of their own accord.

When Michele Angelo turns, Giuseppe is forced to take a step back. The weeping frightens him, as if a moment he has always dreaded has finally arrived. He backs away instinctively as Michele Angelo comes to meet him. Then he stops and takes his uncontrollably weeping son in his arms. This first embrace is as pure, as immaculate as anything can be in this world, like the smile of a newborn child perhaps. And Michele Angelo embraces Giuseppe as if he is now finally the child he could never be before. He weeps quietly on the old man's shoulder. They say nothing. There is nothing to say.

Four months later, in sadness, Marianna is born. An easy birth, one night of labour and the little girl comes without pain. When the midwife thumps her she gives a little cough and immediately falls into step with the breathing of the Universe.

Then, as God wills, the years pass.

They pass as years should pass, with almost nothing to tell. When you draw up an account, in old age, you realise how beautiful the silent periods in life were. Because noisy times only appeal to those who feel compelled to narrate them; for everyone else silence is a privilege. So the years pass and the Lollove vineyard turns to brushwood, and Giuseppe Mundula becomes so unsteady on his legs that Michele Angelo and Mercede have to take him into their home. The whiplash of that cursed late August has left indelible marks. Mercede still wears mourning clothes, and Michele Angelo's face is marked with lingering melancholy. He sleeps restlessly and works with hypnotic concentration. The years seem to have made the iron softer, much more malleable. Because in the end even iron responds to the passing of time, and to the skill of the arm that beats it, as well as the accumulated experience of the artisan. Now, in the depths of his concentration, Michele Angelo is clearly aware of the metal beginning to surrender, allowing itself to be forged in exactly the same way as he himself has decided to yield his flesh to the passage of time.

Dressed in black, Mercede is like a child, worn down by constant grief. Yet to hear her you would say that, unlike the long-faced Michele Angelo, she is unchanged; you can even feel her smiling.

She is like a raft sailing on calm waters; there can be no doubt that she has been desperately tossed by the storms that have disturbed her sea, but now she is at peace and things are going well; there is no shortage of bread and the children are growing. Gavino is eight now and Luigi Ippolito six, and Marianna is into her third year.

The only thing that clouds Mercede's face is when people say she should go to the cemetery and care for the resting place of her dead. Only that. The women take her aside and, one by one, they always say the same thing: that she should not leave the graves of her children in such a state, strewn with dead cypress leaves like little brown worms; and that the wind is eroding the marble with dry earth and gravel; and that the vases standing on them have fallen over, spilling out rotting flowers. But Mercede cannot take this in. She cannot really hear it. Let the women talk, but what do they know? For them mourning is almost a trophy, their visits to the cemetery like processions at a country festival. They walk among the graves talking about the life of the dead as though they had no connection with their dying. They watch and criticise and draw conclusions. And seem not to understand. Or perhaps they do not want to know.

From the day the twins were buried Mercede never passed through the cemetery gate again and swore to herself that she never would, unless others had to take her there. To her the tombstones make the dead seem even deader, too dead for her to accept. So she has come to believe that all she can tolerate is this partial death. She knows only too well what it cost her to let them take her children to that place . . . The women shrug and pout: "You're not the first woman to lose her children and you won't be the last,

Mercede Chironi! Don't make such a fuss, or you'll make us think you believe the only reason the rest of us go to the cemetery is to gossip . . ."

She doesn't even know what to answer. Because any answer would be as nothing compared to what she is afraid she could say. Mercede knows herself and keeps her fear to herself, because if they really insist on dragging the words from her mouth they had better look out . . . So she holds out her arms as if to say: Why don't we each do as we think best: you look after the graves, while I let the dead bury the dead. And let's leave it at that.

When Gavino finished fifth class, they had to decide whether it was worth keeping him at school. He was a bright boy, but not much interested in studying. Unlike Luigi Ippolito, who was bound to end up with a doctorate. So they had to come to a decision: either Gavino joined his father in the forge or he stayed on for the sixth form, which would complete his school career and that would be that. Eventually it is decided he should stay on for the sixth form, but begin to spend time in the workshop as well.

Where Gavino is lazy, Luigi Ippolito is diligent. In fact, his education is going to have to be planned with care. Michele Angelo has recently done a job for a doctor from Sassari who told him how to find a good boarding-school run by priests, so the boy can do two years in one, then go to the *ginnasio* followed by the higher classes of secondary school. Reading and studying seem absolutely made for Luigi Ippolito, so much so that his teacher has held him up as a model and even entered him as a candidate for an award. He likes staying at home to read, and even sometimes looks after his sister.

He is remarkably domesticated; when the women of the house are kneading dough for bread he always sits in the corner watching and, above all, listening to them . . . And if little Marianna asks questions, he answers her patiently. Unlike Gavino, who has no interest whatever in staying at home. "Always out and about like a gypsy," his mother is constantly telling him. Gavino is heavily built like his father.

Giuseppe Mundula, from the comfortable place by the fireside he has made his own as grandfather, looks at Gavino with a sort of astonishment, as though seeing Michele Angelo again at the same age standing in the orphanage corridor.

Luigi Ippolito is very good-looking like his mother. Slender and sensitive, but with his father's chestnut colouring. His expression, always serious, bodes a significant future. You only have to look at him to realise he is the one who will take a decisive step forward in the fortunes of the family. Everyone can already see him, adult and sober, in one of those large houses on the Corso where the people who matter live.

———

Luigi Ippolito was the first Chironi to know the history and origins of the family. He had read enough to know we all come from somewhere and he was articulate enough to be able to tell the story. His firm and steady, if not yet fully mature, voice echoed calmly through the short November days as everyone grew sleepy round the log fire.

He liked to tell the story of how Don Juan de Quiròn was sent to

Sardinia as a *fiscal* or official representative of the Royal Treasury, with the specific task of arresting the Inquisitor Don Diego de Gamiz.

Listening to him at home they could not understand how all those people with foreign-sounding names could possibly have anything whatever to do with themselves. But the story of the *fiscal* had gradually become their own personal story: somehow, through the tangled generations, the mutation from De Quiròn via Kirone to Chironi seemed to make sense. Michele Angelo never revealed that his surname had been an accident, nothing more than a concession he had been granted, while Giuseppe listened quietly to this story from the distant past with the confidence of one who knows that running backwards over a path that has already been trodden only changes one's concept of the future because of the awareness it brings. Though illiterate, he knew one fact that can never be taught: that it doesn't matter if a story is true or false; the only thing that is really important is that someone should tell it.

So they all sat and listened. Even that blockhead Gavino quietened down when his brother began with the cry: "Open! In the name of the Viceroy!"

There had once been a Viceroy living beyond the mountains, and people who had come to Sardinia by sea . . . At this point, at the word "sea", Mercede always gave a start and stroked Gavino's curly head. She had never been beyond Silanus, where she had been brought up, and Nuoro. For her these places were the whole habitable Universe, no less . . .

69

Did they know what heraldry was? No, of course not. But Luigi
Ippolito did. So he explained: heraldry helped you know the difference between those who came from families that mattered and
those who didn't. And when he stumbled on the story of the
De Quiròn knight, he realised that the man's surname, though
Spanish, was very much like his own. There was nothing remotely
special about the story of this knight; and the fact that he had been
a *fiscal* sent by the Royal Treasury, in effect a paid soldier of the
King of Spain, did nothing to raise his status. But Luigi Ippolito
was much taken with the idea of creating an ancestor. So what had
this knight done that could be worth remembering? The only
known fact was that he had made an unsuccessful attempt to arrest
the Inquisitor Don Diego de Gamiz. But his real story consisted in
the fact that though he had been sent to Sardinia as a punishment,
when they told him he could go home again he had decided to stay.
This was because he had grown fond of the country, and in any case
the locals had already started calling him Kirone.

In fact, he had probably only avoided imprisonment by agreeing
to go to Sardinia to arrest the Inquisitor in the name of the King.
This had been a confidential assignment and, as usual in such cases,
a middle-man was expected to obey orders, whether good or bad.

In telling the story, Luigi Ippolito would always start with the voice of the captain of the Royal Finance Guard, Don Angelo Jagaracho, in his ruff and half-armour, calling out at the door of the monastery where the Inquisitor lived: "Open! In the name of the Viceroy!"

There is nothing very surprising in the fact that the first Chironi appears without warning at this point, still bearing the name De Quiròn. He is a cautious man, deeply thoughtful in nature, and he tries to calm his captain who nonetheless continues to yell at those inside to open the door.

The terrified friars behind the door cross themselves and mutter, "Most Holy Mother, Merciful Mother of God . . ." They do not dare open, but look up at the window from which Diego de Gamiz is observing the scene.

He was a bad man, this Gamiz: on the other side of the mountains, in History, there were terrible priests and friars . . . Not like their parish priest, Father Salis, who was as honest as bread. Luigi Ippolito understood instinctively that telling stories could be a way of establishing distinctions. Now in this small corner of the Universe, they were repeating this rite of knowledge, passing on information by word of mouth, in the way they say the word of Christ was spread. The little so far told already confirms that their Chironi ancestor was of good stock, a wiser and sounder man than his hot-tempered companion in arms.

In fact, while Jagaracho is already ordering his guards to force the door, De Quiròn has planned a more civilised approach.

Whenever he tells the story, Luigi Ippolito, with a certain historiographical bias, emphasises Quiròn's conciliatory attitude by

71

changing the tone of his voice every time he utters the knight's words.

While the soldiers continue to attack the door, De Quiròn repeats that it is in effect the Viceroy in person who demands entry: it is on the orders of Don Carlos de Borgia de Velasco, Duke of Gandía, that the soldiers are insisting on entry.

Imagine the increasingly frenzied rustle of soutanes inside the courtyard protesting against the irregularity of the situation. "It is not acceptable to fall back on the procedures of the Royal Treasury when addressing Inquisitors," a monk says, opening a spy-hole in the door.

Don Juan de Quirón's face appears a breath away from the monk's own face. "We are not here to have a debate," he snaps, forcing the monk to pull his head back.

From the far end of the courtyard, the youngest of the monks comes forward to stand at his superior's shoulder. "Dear brothers, it can't be done," he volunteers, but without poking his head forward.

"It can't be done!" the older monk repeats, grateful for the prompt.

The monks claim that the immunity of the Inquisition is guaranteed by law, unlikely though that may seem. But whatever the facts, the Viceroy's orders must be obeyed. So far from giving ground, Jagaracho continues to urge his men to break down the door. De Quiròn moves aside to let them get on with it, because as far as he is concerned, he has done all he can to make things easier, even if he has not succeeded.

Anyone hearing Luigi Ippolito tell this story would understand how much of himself he was putting into his supposed ancestor.

Well, the soldiers break down the door and enter into a garden, but now they are faced with the barred gate to the main building.

"A metaphor," Luigi Ippolito would say with a superior air. He knows how to use the weight of his studies when necessary. A metaphor then, that is to say an image to illustrate the fact that when you think you have overcome one obstacle you may find yourself up against another. Do you see? They've got into the garden, but that hasn't changed anything.

"In the name of Don Carlos de Borgia y Velasco, Duke of Gandía and Viceroy of Sardinia, we command you to open the Inquisitor's apartments! We have a message for him," Don Juan de Quiròn insists, a metaphor now for inflexible tenacity.

But, after an umpteenth refusal, he has no alternative but to leave the garden in front of his captain. Their two roles now seem to have been very nearly reversed: now Jagaracho seems calm while De Quiròn is angry. The captain, alone but for an escort of a few guards, remains in that garden reminiscent of the garden of Eden. But where has De Quiròn gone?

For the moment, we do not know.

Don Angelo Jagaracho looks for somewhere to sit. Following the example of the few soldiers still with him, he makes himself comfortable on the steps round the well in the middle of the garden. Suddenly Spain seems close at hand, almost within sight, as if thought were enough to bridge the stretch of sea separating him from his home country.

*

Don Angelo Jagaracho could not have said how long he spent in that silent garden with the friars watching him from behind their windows. The acrid smells of the street could not be detected in that corner of the world, that tiny Eden no bigger than the Royal Hall in the Prado, its walls padded by thick tendrils of ivy like the luxurious velvet lining of a jewel casket. As they waited, everything seemed far away. Even the voices that should have been audible now that Porta Castello, the town's main gateway, had been flung open to admit the country folk and the unintelligible dialects they exchanged in the nearby market. And with this noise also came bleating flocks driven on by the guttural cries of shepherds only distinguishable from their animals by the fact that they walked erect. Then the swish of badly shod feet on roads awash with muddy water left by rain, draining from the beaten earth of minor lanes; and the clattering wheels of carts hauled by skeletal oxen. It is no longer a matter of animals, not even a mere matter of men: the Sardinians were taking over the town.

An hour may have passed, or perhaps a day, but to Don Angelo Jagaracho it seems only the flicker of an eyelid before he sees Don Juan de Quiròn return with ten armed men and two axemen.

They spend a good half an hour trying to break down one of the doors to the living quarters, smashing both the doorway and silence with their blows. Finally, the axemen manage to shift the barrier blocking their entrance from the inside, and come into a large dark room. The porter of the Holy Office steps forward holding his palms before him as if he expects his martyrdom to be the final door to be broken down. Don Juan de Quiròn motions to the armed men to hold back. "We must speak to Don Diego de Gamiz, we have a message for him from the Viceroy," he declares in a slow voice, resuming his speech at the exact point where he was interrupted.

"The Inquisitor is in the Hall of the Secret," the porter says. "He cannot be disturbed . . ."

. . . But it was too late to take the story any further: the fire had gone out and eyelids were drooping . . .

Don Juan de Quiñón closes his eyes. "Alright," he decides, conciliatory yet again. "We can wait."

Luigi Ippolito suddenly goes quiet, but no-one notices. No-one asks him to go on.

Nowadays you can breathe the atmosphere of a small modern country town here, but long ago, when the founder of the family – originally Quiròn, later Kirone and eventually Chironi – was alive . . . this was a quiet outpost consisting of two villages full of ferocious little men. The very place-name, "Nur", was at the start of it all. Time has stood still here for millennia undisturbed by plague or epidemic. We have always been a mixed race, and here on the plateau, where the air was pure and beyond the reach of pestilence, the first inhabitants lived as if in a world apart. It was left to insects, fevers, malaria and infected wounds, and to the sea, lagoons and marshes, to free this small population from their centuries of isolation.

Whatever Mercede's conception of it, it was the sea that brought enemies to their shores, but the sea also carried floating images of the Virgin Mary. The first men must have had some sort of primitive religion, and it was exactly on this point that Mercede perceived a contradiction and got lost in her reasoning. So she decided the sea must be the source of everything, both good and bad, and would always be so.

The story was told of how unhealthy, brackish air had driven those who lived beyond the mountains – where there were evil priests and friars and viceroys with unpronounceable names – to flee to the interior, to the high ground, where the air was perfect, healthy and limpid, and where the earliest people had settled. This involved transferring the archdiocese of Galtellí from the fertile but noxious district of Baronia to the savage but healthy heart of Barbagia. We are quite simply the result of a blend of something already made and something that still needs to be made.

In that coming together some people progressed and others regressed. The Archbishop's palace shrank to a villa, and his cathedral to a parish church. But huts expanded into houses and muddy sheep-tracks grew into paved roads. There can be no doubt that we were all born from this give-and-take, all of us. What makes this particularly clear is the fact that History, having crossed forested mountain passes to reach this area, settled in the middle of the plateau, exactly between the two villages: the village of sheep pens and the village of vegetable gardens. From the south came bread and olive oil, from the north meat and milk. And History, which always identifies the best place, occupied the centre where people first traded and bartered. It was first at Nur that the countryside and the rocks came to terms with human beings who understood the gentle rhythms of the sun and animals, after which roads and markets developed, bringing coins and all those enchantments that test men and distinguish the stupid from the sly.

So History, custom, wall-plastering and new words, together with the cult of the Madonna delle Grazie, helped the shepherds, peasants and farmers who inhabited the high ground of Nur to become aware of themselves for the first time and realise they were not alone.

At the blacksmith's home the story was often told of the

sumptuous procession of the Archbishop of Galtellí when he first arrived at Nur and of the knight Quiròn who was among his followers . . . And of the surprise of the first inhabitants when they saw horses in harness, and saddlecloths and ruffs.

But then, it was said, in the rough and tumble of daily life, Quiròn abandoned the saddlecloth for a sheepskin jacket more suitable for the climate, which in winter was cold and dry; and greased his hair and beard and wore them in locks like the local men and, like them, had his ears pierced with a splinter of bone. Finally, completely transformed, he married a local woman. This was when Quiròn became Kirone.

Now our account of this transformation is merely a synthesis to help explain how History can move backwards and forwards, and sometimes in a spiral fashion, or in a circle or in more than one direction, but it never, ever proceeds in a direct line, whistling straight like an arrow . . . No, History slithers like a water snake, starting at a certain point, then disappearing as if under a mirror, and there is never any knowing where it will reappear. All we can see are coils ruffling the calm surface of the pond. That is how we become aware of History: from signs.

By the following century fusion is complete. The new houses reach the Ponte di Ferro which becomes, in some way, the gate to Séuna. Just as the Archbishop's arrival marked the end of prehistory almost three centuries earlier, so now the final trowel stroke on the wall of casa Virdis – where the corner of the Tuffu farm meets the Ponte di Ferro open land – marks the end of the colonial period and the division between the upper village, now renamed San Pietro, and the lower, which remains Séuna. An imperceptible osmosis occurs between the two worlds as the shepherds go down to the valley to find land and the farmers climb the hill to trade, bringing betrothals and then marriages that shuffle the cards. So we now find in succession as we move from the high ground to the low: San Pietro, piazza San Giovanni, via Majore, Ponte di Ferro and Séuna. In time these are joined by the Fascist Chamber of Commerce, the Prefettura, via Deffenu, and even the Finance Office, before the post-war expansion of the Convent area with its new law courts, and the sudden explosion of the economic boom even in this godforsaken corner of the world transforming Istiritta into a suburb and officially inaugurating a new era of masonry.

Separate from this activity, the most important buildings grow by degrees: the cathedral, the prison and the law courts. The cathedral is built on the foundations of an old parish church, dating from the time when churches were confused with megalithic ruins or *nuraghi*; and the prison, or Rotonda as they call it to make quite clear that the state punishes mercilessly those who do not understand that they form part of the state (since ignorance though desirable is not officially acceptable); and the law courts, built beside the cathedral to fill the prison.

Development to the south becomes imaginable, on the ridge above the farm workers' houses, where for some thirty years there has been an outer extension of the Chilivani railway, and where the road branches off towards the Ogliastra district.

It is a period when the Belle Époque does not spare even this little, neglected, out-of-the-way capital of the Barbagia district, where the people of Nuoro are busy creating their own vision of themselves. Reckless and unshakeable, not conformist but worldly. No pure metals but alloys, stronger or weaker according to the composition of the mixture from which they have been made. A touch artistic and a touch stingy; inclined to fuss over details while remaining completely ignorant of the wider picture.

But this is not the story we have to tell.

In piazza San Giovanni, then, the bourgeoisie and the working people congregate, and among the working people are smallholders as well as shepherds for hire. In this open space, young men on horseback, dressed in their Sunday best, do business over livestock, cheeses and seeds while others, on foot, are looking to be hired for the day for the grape or olive harvests. But piazza San Giovanni is above all the setting for political meetings, where orators try to explain to the shepherds how someone in Germany has written something that has a lot to do with their claims on common land. As if to point out that not only ugly things come from the past, as everyone seems to think. At this point the snake of History sweeps round in a big curve to show that sometimes progress means turning back. In this village, by this time virtually a town, everything can now be found: a well-to-do quarter with trends from the mainland, public lighting, Paris-style bistros and a few fashionable tailors and dressmakers. There is even a cosmopolitan circle of intellectuals, made up of painters, writers and musicians, all younger sons in the great family of the newly born Nation. Excited and awkward, many of them will come to understand how closely one has to look at oneself in order to travel far.

It is an intimate world of courtyards and dry-stone walls, which modernity will transform into public life. Like when a gust of wind lifts a young woman's skirt in the street.

But, yet again, this is not the point . . .

Gavino Chironi, who did not like school, spent hours in piazza San Giovanni. It is where he heard about Karl Marx and Bakunin. And he acquired a precise feeling that his was a species on its way to extinction. Because it is not only lack of energy that can weaken people, but an excess of sensitivity too. Everyone judged the bright one in that home to be Luigi Ippolito and Gavino to be the simpleton, but that was not true, it had never been true. They were simply two alloys mixed in different proportions. One old-fashioned and the other modern, if by old-fashioned you meant relating to Nur rather than Nuoro, but this was not what was old-fashioned about him. You would have been making a mistake if you had not taken into account how much the two boys depended on each other. How incomplete each was without the other.

Now that Gavino and Luigi Ippolito had reached adolescence, it was becoming clear to anyone with eyes to see that the fact they had grown up in a family marked by fear of extinction had made both of them incomplete, partial. Not just different, as one might say of any pair of brothers. They were indeed different, but it was not a difference that could in itself explain their indeterminate character.

Luigi Ippolito's extreme sensitivity was tempered only in the presence of Gavino, who in contrast seemed completely insensitive. The one demanded explicitly what the other would have liked to be able to demand. One would ask questions even if he was certain the answers would not interest him at all, while the other would never ask what he desperately wanted to know. Gavino's ability was deductive and his brother's inductive. Not just different, but complementary, like two horizontally pivoted parts of a single mechanism.

When it was decided Gavino should continue in the local sixth form and Luigi Ippolito should go on to the *liceo ginnasio* in Sassari, it was in fact an unconscious and unanticipated decision to cut a single person in two.

As expected, the departure of his brother for Sassari did not seem to disturb Gavino particularly. Yet he began sleeping badly. It occurred to him that the regular breathing of his brother, in the bed next to his, had been part of his own breathing, and he suddenly started suffering a form of asthma.

The empty bed beside him was like an image of what could have been but had not happened. When he was little, something he could hardly remember, his eldest brothers had been robbed, slaughtered and cut to pieces. It had never occurred to anyone at home that it might have been enough just to say they had died and left it at that, or perhaps that they had been taken ill. No: everyone had always liked to repeat that they had been murdered and their throats sliced open like little goats and that they had been torn in pieces and thrown into a clump of bushes as food for wild boars.

This directness altered things. It was like a baton being handed over in haste without those who received it having any chance to reflect on it in any way whatsoever. That empty bed contained words Gavino did not know how to speak and tears he had never learned to shed. Because even if they were to slaughter him he would never shed a single tear, ever.

So when word reached Mercede that, instead of going to school, Gavino was hanging about piazza San Giovanni with riff-raff bigger than him, she went straight to her husband's forge to say this and that, your son etcetera etcetera. And when Michele Angelo spread his arms as if to say: What do you expect? They're just children, she withered him with a look before he could even finish his train of thought. So Michele Angelo nodded as if to agree that he had to be taught a lesson, then waited for his wife to be satisfied. Mercede studied her husband as if to assess how seriously to take him. She was not a woman to be content with mere words, or even with mere actions, what she needed was for words and actions to result from thought. It was not good enough for Michele Angelo to give in to her for the sake of peace. If he agreed with her, it had to be the result of heartfelt conviction, with no wavering or hesitation.

So when Gavino comes home, at a time corresponding to the end of the school day, he is surprised to find his father waiting for him.

Michele Angelo is standing, Mercede is sitting in the corner by the chimney, Giuseppe is walking about in the courtyard.

Seeing his father when he comes into the kitchen, Gavino looks at his mother and understands immediately. There is a heavy silence.

"Sit down," Michele Angelo says, suddenly and abruptly, believing that if he gets his son to sit down he will have the advantage over this increasingly tall boy.

"No," Gavino says stubbornly. "I'll stand."

"Sit down," Michele Angelo repeats, but with a far more determined calmness than a few seconds earlier. Mercede radiates approval from her corner. Gavino gives in with bad grace, propping himself on a chair rather than sitting properly. "What are we working for?" his father asks.

Gavino lowers his head, but not because he is humiliated. He lowers his head in mock humiliation, as if it were not himself facing his father, but only the part of him they extracted when they sent his brother away. He would never admit it, but at this precise moment he misses Luigi Ippolito, because his brother was always ready with words when things needed to be said, and having the right words is essential if you want to make things happen.

"What are we working for?" Michele Angelo repeats.

Gavino shrugs. His eyes search out his mother. He knows she is at her most dangerous when subdued or withdrawn. In fact, enclosed in her image of *mater dolorosa*, Mercede avoids his eyes. A slow thought matures in Gavino's mind, a muffled perception protecting him from an extremely fragile agony. He presses his lips together so as not to cry. But he would very much like to cry.

"I'm so disappointed, my son, so disappointed . . . Knowing you're doing worse and worse at school and that most of the time you're not even attending . . . I'm so disappointed. I can only agree with your mother, who has been saying for a long time that I must have a word with you. It was I who held her back, it was I . . . but I'm so disappointed." Then silence. In contrast with the expression on his face, and his first question, Michele Angelo's words and tone are full of grief and without resentment. But all the more terrible for it.

"I'm not crying, anyway," Gavino says.

84

The corners of Michele Angelo's mouth hint at a smile without going the whole way. Instead he thumps the table with a deafening blow of his blacksmith's fist as if to shatter the marble top. Gavino leaps backwards and Mercede resists the temptation to react. "School's finished for you. No more wasting time. Now you'll have to work for your bread in this house! I shall expect you in the forge at six tomorrow morning."

Gavino does not reply, nor does anyone else. Silence returns.

That night, next to Luigi Ippolito's empty bed, Gavino dreams these words:

I will accept my History, small or great. Though I will come to believe that I am just passing through this world I shall leave my mark on it all the same. I may see the world as a cruel and sick place of oblivion, but that will merely prove my ignorance.

Some father will remind me of what I do not wish to remember and cannot remember.

The substance of Memory is a dog guiding a flock of sheep, a shadow drawn on walls.

The greater part of my coming and going will depend on how accurately I manage to determine the obstinate course of recurring things.

I shall believe myself born into a place reduced to a prison, a land of punishment, though an artisan father, speaking from the deep reservoir of unforgotten tales, will tell me of furrowed seas, of prosperous civilisations and of lands as fertile as Eden. Beyond the mountains.

I shall prosper, certainly I shall. Yet the beyond will always whisper richer words to me, spells of inaccessible worlds.

But I shall always live in this precise, accursed, state of inferior desire.

In the morning, his face staring into a cup of milk, Gavino announces he is going to be a sailor.

Mercede gives him a long look, then says: "Finish your milk." She shakes her head. "Your father has been waiting half an hour for you already."

Luigi Ippolito wrote assertive letters steeped in nostalgia from his boarding-school in Sassari. These letters had an effect, since his words, though often incomprehensible to the people to whom they were addressed, succeeded in conveying an impression of adult clothing on a child's body. What most struck them was his seriousness.

The childlike purity with which he described the world in those letters in no way corresponded to his precocious use of language, and the contrast was so moving it almost caused tears. So much so that Mercede never had the strength to read his letters, or hear anyone else read them right to the end.

If on top of this Luigi Ippolito began his letter *My Dear Mother*, Mercede immediately felt she was losing all control of herself. There was nothing she could do about it even if, thank God, she had no good reason to weep; far from it, having a son in higher education was a distinction to be proud of. And when they pointed out that she was weeping for a healthy, good-looking and intelligent son as though he were dead, Mercede said yes, that was true, but the feeling was overwhelming. And she tried to explain that though her son's absence was a pain she could not get used to, the reason for his absence filled her with pride.

The task facing Mercede at this stage was to rescue her children from misfortune. After the murder of the twins everything had escaped from her. As if they had asked her to watch over a flock and, one stormy night, it had broken out of the sheepfold and run away in all directions.

> *My Dear Mother,*
>
> *Don't let my brother and sister and our father hold it against me if I turn to you, but this morning, on the path that leads us from the boarding-house to the school building, I ran into something that made me think of you. I don't know what the weather is like in our beautiful mountains, but here on the plain the sun has been blazing unmercifully and forcing the ladies to carry little parasols. Here in the city this is the latest fashion, and seeing the women making such affected exhibitions of themselves made me think of you and how you would be just as beautiful, if not more so, with one of these fashionable accessories and that you would be by no means at a disadvantage compared with the great ladies of the city. Then I thought that what makes you so extraordinarily beautiful, and all the dearer to me, is precisely that sobriety of style that has always been such a distinctive feature in you. Now you're blushing, but is it not the duty of good children to keep harping on about their undying debt to the woman who brought them into the world? This morning, in class, Father Marongiu said the same thing, and that our love for our own mothers symbolises our love for the Mother of God . . .*

Choking on suppressed sobs, Mercede was incapable of reading on to the point where her adored son told her how well he was keeping and how well he was sleeping and eating. But she kept the letters close to her as if she wanted to have them at hand when the right time came for her to read them in their entirety.

Little Marianna was a comfort. At five years of age she spoke little, and badly, and some suspected she might be retarded, but Mercede could hear every imaginable conversation in her silence. She knew very well what she had been feeling in her heart while that seed had been growing inside her, and saw the girl's silence as the logical consequence of so much grief. As for Michele Angelo, he was completely infatuated with his little girl. "Mazinedda" he called her, because for him she corresponded exactly to the little Madonnas on the holy pictures handed out in church to those who made offerings. It was impossible not to love her, poised and serious like a little adult. Even Gavino felt tender towards her.

Now that he had grown bigger, and it had been accepted that he would not go back to school, Gavino was becoming tempered like the metal he was learning to work; he did not welcome attentions from his mother and was furious when his father reminded him he was still only a boy. It was with melancholy that Michele Angelo watched his son working beside him; he could not help thinking that watching a part of himself growing and developing was like an assurance that he himself would never die. But, at the same time, he was certain that he could not survive unless he resigned himself to dying. It was not at all easy to teach Gavino anything; in fact it was a pure waste of time. Gavino had a way of seeing the world that was all his own and he stubbornly defended his autonomy. From being taciturn he had become loquacious, and now never stopped talking, commenting and preaching. He talked animatedly about social justice and class war . . . Eventually Michele Angelo was forced to interrupt his work and say: "What on earth are you talking about? Who's filling your head with all this rubbish? First that stuff about going to sea, now this talk of revolutions, what do you want? The only reason you're saying all this is that you happen to have a tongue in your head . . . You'd do better to keep your eye on what you're doing!"

The difference is the way father and son see each other. Gavino, reduced to silence, assumes an air of concentration as if forcing himself to repress everything he would have liked to say. Michele Angelo, watching him, cannot see this, but is conscious that his son is strong and has good hands . . .

Gavino, for his part, feels his father's gaze on him is almost dressing him in new clothes. A warm, rich look, that perhaps contains something approaching affection, if such a word exists beyond its obvious meaning.

A crystal-clear morning, with everything outside the window apparently just about to shatter into fragments. The dry light of January gives everything a fragile look. Almost as if one's very gaze were frozen.

Giuseppe is in bed and cold. He has not slept all night. Mercede covers him. Since the previous day, when he did not even want to get up to eat, she has been full of foreboding. He looks at her, thinking that if he must choose an image to take with him into the grave, the face of this woman will do very well. He feels very cold, and his lower lip trembles slightly.

"I've done alright," he whispers.

Mercede looks at him; this old man fills her heart with warmth. Long ago, left a widower, he had fetched Michele Angelo from the orphanage and had taken on a responsibility for life. Shouldering it without expecting anything in return.

"You've been a good man," Mercede says. "More than a father."

He smiles the best he can, then points at the drawer of the bedside table. In it Mercede finds a black notebook, and between its pages an old newspaper cutting, as crackly as a piece of hard bread.

"Open it," Giuseppe says, encouraging her.

Mercede sees a report on a group of Sardinian volunteers leaving for the Crimea, with an illustration showing a file of men in new uniforms, the rigour of the black and white drawing making them look like glass statues, knick-knacks on display in a shop selling ornaments.

"There's my father," Giuseppe says, pointing at the picture.

This sudden intimacy is far more disconcerting to Mercede than the attack of coughing that simultaneously racks the old man, a terrible dread that death may have come disguised as a confidence.

Giuseppe's eyes do indeed lose focus while his finger still points at the picture . . .

The transparent crowd on the glacial sea. The wedding procession of the tsar's son and heir. The phalanx of crystal warriors. Sergeants in tight collars. Generals towering over their troops, shining with titanium. The arrogance of an army equipped with dark spears and ancient muskets. The stiffness and icy elegance of guards of honour. The frozen emperor hunts wolves silvered in the moonlight. Packs of dalmatians break the silence of the petrified forest. Silent fairies add substance to the liquidity of the air. Further across, a solemn marching makes the ice-bound earth squeak and disturbs the slumbers of the sacred beast. But it is a vibration, like concentrated silence, shot through with anticipation that grips the countryside in the turbulent stillness of an army steadied before the attack. The thick surface of the frozen lake cracks under the weight of the black boyars.

And here is the copse of birch-trees on the blanched tundra. To the north of thought, with the composure of a posed portrait, the trees offering themselves to her gaze, pulsing with channelled life. They are waiting for the fever of jewels, with the wisdom of settled time. But now they have turned whitened skeletons ready to celebrate the triumphant Dance of Death. Very soon when the hurdy-gurdy starts up they will break ranks. Or are they spirits, their destiny ominously transparent? Victims panting for peace? Victims who relate what cannot be seen, and affirm what cannot be said. Poor souls about to enter a crematorium, suffocated by the silvery soot given off by bodies consumed by madness. Struggling to survive in an equilibrium made precarious by terror.

. . . by the time Mercede's cries bring Michele Angelo running, nothing can be done.

Gavino follows shortly afterwards, and looks at the body only just emptied of its soul like an empty box. Then he looks at Mercede and

Michele Angelo talking together in front of Giuseppe Mundula's warm body, father and witness, journeying soul. She is telling her husband about the newspaper, about the Crimea ... When Michele Angelo becomes aware of Gavino at his shoulder he feels the look they share is reason enough to let himself go. So he weeps as he turns to face his son. Gavino steps back, pursing his lips.

"Well, I'm not going to cry," he says abruptly.

Luigi Ippolito is called back from Sassari for Giuseppe's wake. He has grown so tall people hardly recognise him. An unfamiliar, pale, urbane young gentleman. The hours of travel have exhausted him, but even so he is clearly moved. When the two brothers meet they seem to pretend nothing has happened, that everything is absolutely normal and that a mere half an hour has passed since they last spoke.

They all spend the night chatting to the dead man, because during a wake, those closest to the deceased have to settle any unfinished business. The problem with Giuseppe Mundula, with his calm face and luminous skin, is that there is no unfinished business. He worked all his life, brought up a son who was not his own better than if he had been the boy's own father. And he lived modestly, and thanks be to God, was spared hunger, thirst and serious illness. He went out like a lamp running out of oil. As simple as that.

This generates a calm grief. When we mourn the death of the old we grieve calmly for them. We calculate in our minds how far short we still are of the age they reached and reassure ourselves that there is still plenty of time. When we mourn the death of the young we grieve for ourselves because the fact that their time has run out too soon proves that we cannot depend on any rule or any sense of justice.

So it seems quite normal to everyone when Giuseppe Mundula is raised to a sitting position on the bed. The vigil is for him, but from now on it is he who will be asked to keep watch from above. That is what the contract stipulates. As they lift him it becomes clear how much death has desiccated him: the buttoned collar of his white shirt reveals a neck as thin as a bulrush. Aware he is dead, Giuseppe speaks with encouraging calm: "Everything's fine," he says in a whisper so as not to disturb anyone. "Everything here is just as it should be, nothing to be afraid of."

At these words Luigi Ippolito shakes his head and opens his eyes. Seeing that Gavino and Michele Angelo have also dozed off, he gets silently to his feet and goes to the kitchen where he finds Mercede, who really has kept watch. She is the only person in the house to have truly given a worthy farewell to Giuseppe's soul as it leaves this vale of tears.

"Go and sleep, my child. Go and sleep, you've done enough now," she says.

Luigi Ippolito shakes his head. He is afraid to go back to his room alone.

Mercede stands up, determined to make him something to eat, but Luigi Ippolito says no, he isn't hungry. So she pauses in front of him and looks at him. Now he can see her more clearly, Luigi Ippolito realises time has passed, and that this is why they are studying each other in amazement. When she goes to sit down again Luigi Ippolito follows and crouches beside her to stare at her.

Neither of them speaks, but their gestures, which would have been natural a year or two earlier, have become clumsy with absence and distance. Touching his cheek, Mercede is embarrassed to realise her little boy has begun to shave and feels a sudden sadness. Luigi Ippolito sees his mother is abruptly overwhelmed by this small revelation.

"Have you read my letters?" he asks as if she were a lover.

She answers with a non-committal gesture. Then turns to look behind her. Gavino is standing at the kitchen door. Luigi Ippolito, also turning, jumps to his feet as if caught in a guilty act.

"You still have a couple of hours left to sleep," Mercede says. "Make the most of it, because tomorrow will be a long day."

With his brother lying in the next bed, Gavino feels complete at last. He smiles in the darkness. The sound of Luigi Ippolito's breathing is no different from what it always was. As if nothing has happened at all. As if Gavino is in front of the fire again listening to the story of their first ancestor, Quiròn, who became Kirone and then Chironi.

"How does it go on?" Gavino suddenly asks his brother.

"What?" asks Luigi Ippolito after a very long pause.

"The story of our Spanish relative." And Gavino thinks: My God, it's like yesterday, it seems only an hour ago . . .

Luigi Ippolito clears his throat; his voice is becoming an entirely new one while Gavino's voice, despite his size, is still childish. "How far did we get?" he asks.

"That they wouldn't let them in," Gavino replies at once.

Luigi Ippolito gets up and goes over to the bag he has left next to the bed. He pulls out some pages filled with tight handwriting.

"What's that?" Gavino asks.

"I've written it all down," Luigi Ippolito says.

Then he adjusts the light.

*Foaming with rage, Don Angelo Jagaracho bore down on the secretary-
doorkeeper of the Holy Office, grabbing him by the ruff before he could
back away: "You have time to say a* Pater, *an* Ave *and a* Gloria *but not
a word more; that will allow time for the Inquisitor to learn that the
representatives of the Viceroy are here and that they must speak to
him in person." So saying he advanced on a friar who was standing
to one side, grabbed him by his girdle and pulled him into the middle of
the room. "Kneel down," he commanded. The threatened friar looked
for the doorkeeper's eyes. "Come on, say your prayers!" hissed Don
Angelo Jagaracho. "Pater Noster," he prompted, pressing down on
the friar's shoulder to force him to kneel. Watching the doorkeeper
disappear towards the Hall of the Secret, the friar sank to his knees.
"P...a...t...e...r...N...o...s...t...e...r..." he stammered.*

    Throughout the Ave Maria, *Don Angelo Jagaracho kept his eyes fixed
on the door that had closed behind the Inquisitor's secretary. Halfway
through the* Gloria, *Don Giovanni de Quiròn got to his feet, finishing
the prayer and making the sign of the cross as he entered the Hall of the
Secret followed by the captain of the guard.*

    *They were surprised to find the door unlocked, but came into an ante-
room. There thick smoke from tallow candles enveloped them, and
it came from a table behind which a scribe was sitting. This elderly
friar, half hidden by the smoke, raised his head, allowing himself to be*

distracted for a moment from his work. Adjusting his heavy spectacles, he looked with astonishment at the intruders. Wasting no time on formalities, Don Angelo Jagaracho pushed past the desk and made for the entrance to the Hall of the Secret. The old friar tried to protest, claiming the Inquisitor had personally ordered that no-one, on pain of excommunication, could enter the Hall until the Inquisitor himself had given permission by ringing the bell twice. Hearing voices from the ante-room, the secretary-doorkeeper of the Holy Office came out of the Hall. Addressing Don Giovanni de Quiròn, he asked him in a more civil and conciliatory tone than before if he would be good enough to wait for the short time "till the end of the hour of secret audience". But unfortunately the elderly friar tried to grab Don Angelo Jagaracho by the arm and ended up flat on the floor, apparently unconscious. A blow from the captain's elbow had displaced the right arm of his glasses which were now perched in unsteady equilibrium on his shoulder, though still attached to his left ear, while a splinter from one of the thick lenses had cut his cheek.

The sight of blood was enough to defuse Don Angelo Jagaracho's rage; he bent down to see if the old friar was still alive, as indeed he was, breathing stertorously in rhythmic puffs.

The secretary-doorkeeper joined his hands with the index fingers together. "For the love of Heaven!" he implored, still addressing Don Giovanni de Quiròn. "Allow time for a seal to be affixed to the Legal Action . . ." He tried to bar the way as he spoke, though at the same time determined to placate his interlocutor.

Meanwhile, attracted by the uproar, a number of soldiers of the Royal Guard had burst into the badly lit anteroom. Don Angelo Jagaracho ordered two of them to lift the scribe-friar from the floor. They hoisted the old man onto a high-backed chair beside the writing table.

"Time for a seal to be affixed to the Action," the secretary-doorkeeper repeated, holding the criminal assessor back by his shoulders. He was gaining in courage.

"We've been waiting too long," Don Angelo Jagaracho said, once he was sure the injured scribe was not seriously hurt. He headed for the Hall of the Secret. The old friar, realising the captain of the guard had decided to take action, suddenly leaped off the chair and launched himself at him, pulling him by the belt. Don Angelo Jagaracho took a couple of steps, trying to shake himself free. The soldiers were too slow to react. To separate their captain from the friar they were forced to club the old man's thighs with their rifles. The friar pulled back his left hand with a strangled moan. But with his right he kept a grip on the purse of scudi tied to Don Angelo Jagaracho's belt. The little bag came away in an explosion of coins that bounced and rolled across the floor of the ante-room. With every obstacle to the intruders apparently overcome, the secretary-doorkeeper eventually gave in, letting his arms fall, and he stood aside to leave the entrance to the Hall of the Secret free.

The first to break into the Hall was Don Giovanni de Quiròn. The lighting in the Hall was restricted to the space occupied by the table – round which were sitting the Inquisitor, a guard from the Holy Office, a friar and an apparently dirty and bloodstained man who was probably an offender. The lighting in the Hall was insufficient for Quiròn to become aware in time of a shuffle of footsteps retreating on the far side of a small door a few metres away from him. He sensed a form wrapped in a dark cloak, possibly bloodstained. This impression only lasted an instant, just long enough for Don Angelo Jagaracho to move to his side.

Don Diego de Gamiz, the Inquisitor, did not stand on ceremony, but supporting himself on his hands jumped to his feet, turning on the intruders a look of pity and anger.

"I draw the attention of Your Lordships to the fact that a religious ceremony is in progress in this Hall!" he exclaimed, sticking his hooked nose forward. "Therefore I command you to leave at once!"

Unabashed, Don Giovanni de Quiròn announced, "By command of Don Carlos de Borgia y Velasco, Duke of Gandía, Viceroy of Sardinia, and of the Royal Council, and by decree of his most Catholic Majesty King Philip III of Spain, I command you to come with us!"

The Inquisitor merely signalled to the Holy Office guard to remove the offender from the Hall. The guard was for a moment undecided, but seeing that the Viceroy's envoys made no objection, obeyed the order and dragged the offender through the little door behind which the figure glimpsed for an instant by Don Giovanni de Quiròn had disappeared.

"Are you giving me orders?" Don Diego de Gamiz asked in disbelief, as the Holy Office guard returned to his place.

"Our orders come from the King and the Royal Council and we act in their name!" Don Angelo Jagaracho stated. "You will be escorted by an armed guard to Alguer, whence you will embark for Spain on a vessel of the Royal Court, even now ready and waiting to convey you."

The Inquisitor rubbed his face with both hands as if trying to wake from a bad dream.

Don Giovanni de Quiròn stepped forward to show the seal that identified him as an envoy of the Crown. "Only one thing can render our orders null and void: that here and now, and in the presence of trustworthy witnesses, you withdraw in person the excommunications pronounced by the Holy Office that you represent, on Don Francesco

Scano and Don Matteo Querqui." There was a barely concealed hope of reconciliation in his voice, a desire to bring this dispute to a satisfactory conclusion.

"Impossible!" the Inquisitor shouted angrily. "They have contravened Clause Three of the Concordat of 1613, resulting in the unlawful arrest of Don Sebastiano de Carbine, servant of the Holy Office."

"The Holy Office," Don Angelo Jagaracho interrupted without letting him finish, "should have published the warrant of his status as a servant of the Inquisition within the time prescribed by the same Concordat and demonstrated that it received this information from either the Governor of Sassari or the Viceroy in person! Furthermore, in accordance with the requirements of the First and Twenty-Sixth Clauses of the same Concordat, it would have had to prove that this grant of service had not been made to Don Sebastiano de Carbine at a time when the maximum number of such servants allowable to the Holy Office had not already been surpassed."

This was followed by a moment of heavy silence, which the Holy Office guard tried to break with a decisive gesture of the head to indicate that he was about to speak. But Don Diego de Gamiz stopped him before he had a chance to open his mouth. "If I were a simple citizen, I would bow my head and be obliged to go with you, but as Inquisitor of the town of Sassari and as a senior legate of the Holy Father and Defender of the True Faith I cannot submit to the presumption of such quibbles," he said, looking directly to the Holy Office guard and ignoring the royal ambassadors. Then he turned to them: "Leave this Hall immediately or I shall be forced to invoke excommunication on your heads."

"You are not being asked to commit an act of humility," Don Giovanni de Quiròn insisted, "but an act of justice. The excommunications of Don Francesco Scano and Don Matteo Querqui are an abuse of power unacceptable to the Royal Council!"

"And is not this attempted arrest an abuse of power?" the Inquisitor argued. "Hostility to my person and the Tribunal I represent!" he went on, increasingly angry.

"It would be possible for the order of excommunication to be revoked," Don Giovanni de Quiròn continued. "That would be an act of justice."

"May everyone present be witness to the fact that I have stated my decision not to accompany the envoys of the Viceroy, and that I refuse to leave this Hall unless forced to do so," the Inquisitor shouted to the Holy Office guard, and to the friar who during all this time had not even dared to raise his head. Now both, as if suddenly waking up, made a gesture of agreement. "Si de protegendis!" the Inquisitor continued to shout, once he was certain he had the attention of his witnesses.

Don Giovanni de Quiròn smiled out of sheer nervousness. "So you refuse to come with us, and you refuse to obey your king!" he concluded, keeping his eye firmly on Don Angelo Jagaracho, who was gripping the hilt of his sword.

Don Diego de Gamiz waited a moment before answering. "All things come from God," he declared. "Even my sovereign cannot but bow before Him. And if laws exist that require me to answer to the King rather than to God, those laws need to be changed."

"As you wish!" Don Angelo Jagaracho thundered, moving menacingly towards the Inquisitor's table. The Holy Office guard leaped forward and reached for his sword. The friar raised his head with a pleading expression. The secretary-doorkeeper, who had kept out of the way during the whole of this scene, rushed into the middle of the Hall. Don Giovanni de Quiròn stepped closer to Jagaracho. "No," he said, "let us not allow him this advantage." Don Angelo Jagaracho took his hand off his sword, but continued to advance until he was close to the Inquisitor. "So you refuse to recognise the King's authority!" he hissed in the Inquisitor's face.

Don Diego de Gamiz sighed and shook his head as if trying to rid himself of a troublesome insect. "I refuse to put God second," the Inquisitor stated firmly. He held his ground, chin in air, his gaze fixed on his interlocutor.

The burly Don Angelo Jagaracho responded to the shock of this answer by banging the table with his fist.

Don Giovanni de Quiròn intervened. "This is an argument we are in no position to resolve," he said, rising to his full height. "We are responsible to the Royal Power and live in the present, and it is our duty to ensure that the commands of His Most Catholic Majesty are obeyed. We shall not leave this Hall until, like any other loyal subject, you have made up your mind to follow us. God granted this prerogative to our King, who is your king no less than ours, as you yourself have admitted!"

"No blasphemy, no blasphemy!" the Inquisitor interrupted. "This is not a market-place or a money-changers' table! Our dispute cannot follow the course of any common negotiation. The primacy of God is not open to question, no matter what miserable power may assume authority over us in this world. God's supremacy cannot be contested by anyone, whether priest or layman: this is the simple fact!"

"Render unto Caesar the things which are Caesar's and unto God the things that are God's!" Giovanni de Quiròn quoted. "It is your function that requires you to obey, because if you of all people, a beacon of the True Faith, yield to pride, we shall all become hostages to chaos. Come with us and Caesar's tribute will have been paid."

"That's too much!" the Holy Office guard exploded, drawing his sword.

The Inquisitor intervened before Don Angelo Jagaracho could take up the challenge. "Leave us," he ordered both his guard and the friar who had not moved during this exchange.

"I'm impressed," he continued when the two men had gone. They've picked a theologian to arrest me. I shall not leave this place of my own free will. If necessary, I shall pay Caesar's tribute with my life."

Having stated this he began to take off his clothes. The secretary-porter ran forward to dissuade him. Several moments of confusion followed.

"Is this your last word?" Don Giovanni de Quirón asked, observing the thinness of the man's body and the whiteness of his skin. "You know we cannot carry you away by force, not from the Seat of the Holy Office. And it is too late now for us to reach Alguer before sunset. I must order you not to leave your own rooms until you have agreed to come with us. Your ship will be waiting in the port."

"I'm too old and ill." The Inquisitor seemed about to give in. He propped himself on the shoulder of the secretary-doorkeeper, who had taken the garment from his own shoulders to wrap round the Inquisitor. "I could not come with you even if I wanted to; I should not survive the voyage or the discomfort of the road to Alguer."

"Our orders are to transport you even so; as far as your health is concerned, there will be doctors to pronounce on that." Don Angelo Jagaracho's voice had suddenly become feeble, as if he had used up all his energy.

"I shall not come with you! And the excommunications will stand," Don Diego de Gamiz said in conclusion, dropping his gaze.

The years pass. Five of them.

There are days in May when the pallor of the air fills the country-side with a hazy sadness. And it is possible to persuade oneself that this subtle melancholy is what conveys a sense of something indefinite, like a lump in the throat. And on that very day in May, perhaps for no more than an instant, a subtle fever of change could be felt. An inevitable pathology, a foreseeable event. Old people said if you were in the countryside at that exact moment you could clearly hear the screech of the seed as it divided, slashed by the blade of germination as it was once more called back to the light by irresistible force. And you could hear fear and relief in the song of the bud and the lament of the earth. Letting yourself be carried away by this inevitable force, you could come to understand the prolific language of animals and the mad onward rush of fore-boding.

Now note that on one such day in May a woman no longer young woke from a troubled dream, and was forced from her bed before daylight by an overwhelming thought, driven out of her house into the dawn of the new day by deep disquiet. Note too that, almost unawares, this woman then finds herself just beyond the village, right in the countryside, surrounded by an aroma of thyme and wild fennel, a passionate desolation of blackberry and thistle and a quivering expectation of budding borage and euphorbia seedpods.

Everything round her centres on a nameless feeling. The heart beating inside her ribs is like a caged bird. She has got out of bed and left the house so as not to have to explain her feelings, not to have to admit the burden tormenting her.

In any case, it was an ugly dream, so ugly that waking so suddenly from it has not only made her rush out, but has also saved her. Which is why she has dressed in the dark and fled into the country-side almost as if to the open sea.

In her dream she has just seen intensely ugly things like babies born into a rusty basin, and her own children with their chests ripped apart by dogs with foaming jaws. This is why she has dressed blindly and rushed out in such a hurry at break of dawn . . .

This woman has seen a mountain of corpses and does not even know where, because they were piled up in a closed room and were all young, all the children of some poor mother waiting for them in an unknown place.

Staring at her bedroom ceiling, she has opened her mouth wide as if unable to breathe, still feeling, with her open eyes and apparent wakefulness, unbearable physical agony. She sits down on the bed and finally becomes fully aware that she is awake when she sees her husband snoring, which convinces her it is not yet five o'clock.

So she slides off the bed like a snake, fighting the nightgown which is trying to hold her back, and with a thrust of her thighs rises to her feet. The chill of the floor makes clear a horrible bitter-ness in her mouth and that she is clutching her stomach with her hand.

She knows what she has to do, that if she does not get out of the house and run to save herself, the whole building may fall in on her and on her children and sleeping husband. Because she believes that what she has seen in her dream must be inseparable from her own presence in the house. She is convinced the only way to save her family and her home from destruction is to get out.

In the kitchen, despite the faint light, she can see the white marble table top and the newspaper announcing that Italy has officially entered what everyone is calling a worldwide war.

Worldwide means that the whole world, which is to say that every Sardinian including those living beyond the mountains and even beyond the sea will be called on to fight. A few people can still remember Garibaldi's ex-servicemen or those who lost a hand or an eye in the Crimea, and it is not as if those were worldwide wars, for heaven's sake. To this woman the word "worldwide" seems much worse than the word "war". Because women have always been fighters: fighting themselves, fighting poverty, fighting drunken husbands, fighting children who need sorting out. But the whole world, dear God – worldwide is quite another thing.

When her husband came home the previous afternoon and said that now worldwide war had broken out even Italy would have to join in, she initially heaved a sigh of relief because, after all, she told herself, what have we to do with Italy? But no, on the contrary, her elder son explained, worldwide means everybody. In fact, unable to read or write, some men had already taken to the hills to hide, while the carabinieri were scouring town and country in pairs to serve them with call-up papers.

By God, the woman was thinking, "worldwide" and "call-up papers", what uglier words could there be? And while she is thinking this there is her husband, emphasising his words by waving the front page of the newspaper with WAR printed in heavy black type, as if engraved in stone. She crosses herself and sighs, hoping to keep at bay the ugly thoughts overwhelming her, but it is an unequal struggle. In fact, the moment she lowers her guard a heavy weight begins pressing on her chest. She hardly speaks all day, certainly not because she has nothing to say; but because everything she wants to say terrifies her. Now she understands better what the women in the public wash-house have been saying. About men being recruited by force, about soldiers crammed into ships like animals, and unheard-of places where they are taken to die. Arrested by carabinieri hunting in pairs who claim to have orders that mean sons are no longer sons but soldiers. The women say war means men repeating on earth the anger of the heavens, with thunder and lightning and earthquakes. And that in the end the only winner is the one who survives longest.

And they say that when the call-up papers arrive it's like a thunderbolt striking your home and ripping the life force from your family, like a healthy tooth brutally torn out by forceps.

All night she repeats these things to herself, unable to understand how everything round her could be so silent, and how all the other people in the house were able to rest. Is she the only one terrified of words?

She has buried many children of her own and has seen many other people's children buried. And she knows it is a relentless curse to outlive one's own children. An avalanche crushing homes, a breath of deadly poison, a flood of water that can sweep everything away, a storm whipping the rocks.

She feels each catastrophe in her own flesh. And she knows

the only way to survive total disaster is to run from that room, from that house, from those words "worldwide" and "war". But where can she go? Worldwide means everywhere . . .

She rushes out, running as best she can, her smock held together in her lap to keep it from tripping her up. She lets her headscarf slip off. She must go far, far away. Beyond the lane and then further, because she is still too close to her home. A long way beyond the village, into the open country where the winds of May blow.

Michele Angelo, at table, stares firmly ahead without touching his food.

"No-one here will join up," he states.

Mercede is holding a letter in both hands. As far as she knows, as far as she can understand him, Luigi Ippolito has decided to volunteer. His education means he will be able to go in with a non-commissioned officer's pay.

To Michele Angelo the idea seems mad. Any sensible person runs away the minute they see the carabinieri combing the streets and here is this boy saying straight out he wants to join up as a volunteer. "What? You want to go and join up? This boy thinks it'll be like living next door, but it won't even be like going to Sassari."

"What he means, son," Mercede intervenes, "is don't let it tempt you . . ."

Luigi Ippolito does not even answer, staring into the room with unfocused eyes. He is as sure of himself as he can be for one so young. He sees himself as a warrior, hardened and craggy like the infantryman staring out from the posters.

Michele Angelo shakes his head, because he knows that look on his son's face. He knows it only too well. "But have you seen what neck of the woods you'll have to go and fight in?" Luigi Ippolito nods. "And where's the other one?" he asks, referring to Gavino.

It is not clear who he is addressing this question to, but it is obvious why he is asking it. Because Michele Angelo has learned to sniff out the danger lurking in every ordinary day. His curse is that things change without warning. It is not foresight that tells him this, but experience. He is a craftsman in hand and head, he knows that in time the body can begin to react without any apparent instruction from the brain. Day after day, his arm acts on its own, striking perfectly; the iron yielding to three or four well-aimed blows where earlier ten were needed, or fifteen . . . That is what happens. So this morning he woke like any other morning, but became immediately aware of something preoccupying him: Luigi Ippolito's suitcase was in the kitchen and Mercede was already up heating water.

A morning in May, then, and it is almost as if, with the new century, a breath of modernity has reached even that outlying community. You can identify ladies and gentlemen now because they dress in the continental manner. And it has been made clear to the children that if they want to be accepted as full citizens of the Nation, they must work hard at their studies. There is unrest and war. The debates that reach the square from overseas are like echoes from far away.

Gavino has hurried to the old olive press, where he has an appointment. He has arranged to meet that mad dog Josto Corbu there early in the morning, as it is the place where they are the least likely to attract attention. Gavino has known Corbu since he was a small boy and he used to waste his time in the square instead of going to school. Other people go there to look for work, or to deal in livestock, or to seal transactions or commissions, but Gavino goes to find out what is afoot. And what is afoot is that Italy is entering the War, that much is clear now. And, above all, there are patrols about, looking for recruits whether voluntary or otherwise. It is obvious that the wind must have changed in Rome because what was true the previous year now seems completely contradicted.

"Whatever happened to 'neither join in nor sabotage'?" Gavino asks, a little contentiously.

"What's happened is that things change," Josto Corbu answers calmly. He is the personification of a mad socialist dog. It is said of him that as a baby he refused to enter the church for his christening. That even in swaddling clothes he cried so bitterly when they tried to baptise him that the priest was forced to give up. In fact, Josto Corbu was truly godless, brought up on bread and Socialism. Fruit never falls far from its parent tree and even his father Gedeone, a doctor who cares for mad people and animals, knows a thing or two about atheism. "As things stand at the moment," Corbu goes on, "neutrality is simply a leap in the dark."

"But . . ." Gavino says, ". . . but that must mean that what was important before now means nothing."

Josto Corbu is small and very thin, with a fierce stare, neither sweet nor bitter, the glare of a man who knows what he is talking about. "The secret pact with France has changed our relation to the Triple Entente; that's the fact of the matter."

The result is we now enter the War for the very reasons we

declared ourselves neutral earlier. To Gavino this does not seem like good History. "Surely that's not the right way to decide things," he protests.

Josto Corbu gives him a long hard look before answering. "What do you want to decide, Gaví?" he asks. And Gavino realises that the doubt hanging over this inexplicable idea is nothing but fear. And he realises that the rush of History not only goes as and where it likes, but also, if it comes at all, arrives when it suits itself . . . "We are revolutionaries," Josto Corbu concludes.

"But that's just why we are against war, isn't it? What was it we used to say? That conflict only serves the interests of the middle classes . . ."

Josto Corbu doesn't answer. He pulls an old copy of *L'Avan-guardia* from his back pocket. "Listen, Gavino, read what Deffenu has to say on the subject then tell me . . . I must be off because I have to get on with the milking . . ." Without even waiting for Gavino to say goodbye he slinks off like a ferret, leaving Gavino with the newspaper rolled up in his hand.

There's a very bitter smell of crushed olives in the heavy, sticky air. A vitreous May, ever so fragile, as if it might shatter from one moment to the next. A season so uncertain, in every sense of the word, has never before been known. A gusting wind has swept away the clouds. The windowpane is filled by the turquoise of an utterly clear sky, yet there is no heat from the sun. Gavino looks for a comfortable spot to sit and read.

"So Luigi's home?" Michele Angelo asks his wife as he comes into the kitchen that morning. Mercede tests the hot water with the tip of her finger, then nods. "Has he decided to surprise us?" Michele Angelo continues. "He was telling us he had exams and wouldn't be back from Sassari this month." Mercede spreads her arms. "Or has something happened that you don't want to tell me?"

"He says he must talk to us—"

"Is he in trouble?" Michele Angelo interrupts, worried.

Mercede again opens her arms wide.

"No, there's no trouble." It's Luigi Ippolito himself who answers, coming into the kitchen. Freshly washed and shaved, he looks like a small boy again.

"I was just going to bring you some more water," Mercede tells him.

"Thanks, I've finished. There was plenty," he says with his nonchalant city-dweller air. Then he sits down opposite his father and starts straight in, "I wanted to speak to you. Something I've already said in a letter to Mamma."

As if called to give evidence before a public inquiry, Mercede produces the letter in question.

"I've decided to join up," Luigi Ippolito fires off abruptly, so as to hit his father full in the chest.

Michele Angelo gives the pout that usually means he has decided not to answer without careful reflection. "If you've made up your mind . . . Why is there no food this morning?" he says rudely to his wife. Mercede knows well his anger is not aimed at her, but is caused by the fact that her husband is battling with severe distress. So she rapidly lays the table for his breakfast.

"I'm telling you because I want you to hear it directly from me."

"I'm glad you said it, then... Anything else?"

Luigi Ippolito shakes his head. Mercede places a cup of steaming milk on the table. Michele Angelo looks at his wife as if to apologise for what he's just said.

"Just that my education will be taken into account in deciding my rank..." Luigi Ippolito adds in the silence.

"Those who love portraying those among us who are not only professed but indeed actual revolutionaries, and as such are favourable to the theory of intervention, as people who have become (as a result of some unexpected backsliding of opinion) sensitive to the concept of institutions – they love to portray such people as having lost their way when they confess their errors and set out to make amends for them – but I say such people are merely failing to realise the full significance of the historical fact of War and the probable tendencies of the political and social forces being unleashed in Europe at the present time.

This War, even if it has no other advantages, will at least have one beneficial result: it will be a great instructor that will teach us many things and bring us down from castles in the air and our illusions to the bare facts of the realistic examination set for us by the actual conditions of the world and modern civilisation, and of the forces capable of removing these and revolutionising them. The lightning flash, in fact, that disperses the shadows and shows the road to the traveller previously led astray by dense clouds and fear..."

Gavino folds the paper carefully, then rolls it up and grasps it in his fist. He looks up at the sky: not a single cloud... Nothing at all.

*

In the kitchen, Mercede takes the initiative again because she cannot stand the silence. Father and son are sitting opposite one another without speaking. Michele Angelo is staring at the milk in his cup without drinking it, while Luigi Ippolito is gripping a piece of bread but not eating it.

So Mercede tells the story of Tzia Mena, a woman of a certain age who was recently gathering herbs in the country when she saw two carabinieri approaching her with an envelope. Dropping the herbs, she ran off across the field with the speed of a nanny goat, followed by the two men calling out, "Signora, where are you going? Signora, Signora!" Tzia Mena took no notice, because she had been told you must never accept anything from the carabinieri, because that would make it official and it could be call-up papers for one of her sons. So, despite her age, Tzia Mena ran like a young girl, so fast that the two young carabinieri had the greatest difficulty catching her up . . . Mercede laughs a lot as she tells this story which isn't really a story at all, because all the carabinieri wanted was to find out where she lived so they could leave the papers at her home while she, thinking she was escaping them, simply led them there.

"That's what happens when someone thinks themselves a wily fox or *mariane* but instead just ends up *marianato*," Michele Angelo comments.

"*Marianato*?" Luigi Ippolito repeats. "What do you mean? There's no such word . . ." He tries not to laugh in his father's face.

"So what? I've just made it up, right? It means that sooner or later these clever rogues always end up meeting someone cleverer than they are . . ." Then, after a short pause, Michele Angelo adds: "But have you seen where you'll have to go to fight?" Luigi Ippolito nods. "And where's that other boy?" Michele Angelo suddenly asks his wife, realising Gavino has not been seen.

"He went out early, before Luigi arrived," Mercede answers hastily, before picking up her story at the point where Tzia Mena shut herself in her house, leaving the two carabinieri out in the court-yard, and shouting that the notary had told her not to accept any-thing from them, because if the papers were not officially delivered the call-up would not be valid. But the carabinieri answered that, in any case, she had seen the papers and if she did not open the door she would be in trouble; she could not claim she was not at home. And they said it was one thing not to be there, but quite another to pretend not to be there. This distinction was beyond Tzia Mena.

But this is not quite what Mercede is trying to say. Her real purpose is to use this story about a simple-minded and rather stupid woman trying to fend off a storm with an umbrella to make it clear to her son that when in this earthly life we have so many terrible trials to face we have no need to go out of our way to look for more. Well, the fact is even the very stones know all about this business of forced recruitment and everyone else wants to escape it while this son of hers is so perverse that he is determined to join up as a volunteer.

"That's not how it is," Luigi Ippolito argues. "Lots of men are going out as volunteers and many more will. When they call on us to make a contribution for our country what are we supposed to do? Run away?"

"Make a contribution," Michele Angelo echoes sarcastically. He stands up. "Let me get back to work, I have two bulls to shoe for Molimentu. When that other boy turns up remind him he has those firedogs to finish for Serra the notary." Michele Angelo leaves the room.

Luigi Ippolito and his mother look at each other.

A week later Luigi Ippolito leaves. The only ones to go with him are Mercede and Marianna, who is now almost a young lady, slender and rather tall for her age. It is a melancholy send-off. Most of the troops go by train, but the educated ones, and there are not many of them, are allowed to travel to the recruiting centre in the mail coach, which has been placed at the army's disposal.

Everything is precarious, held together by a shaky breath of air. The light has the brightness of summer, but a dry cold pierces to the bone. The whole situation seems to Mercede like an experience someone else is going through. Marianna, at her side, has the composure of a young religious novice. And the other mothers and the occasional father seem calm too. So Mercede tells herself to ignore the rapid breathing that will not let her think; probably she seems calm too, seen from the outside, dressed suitably for the occasion. But she is far from calm. She has not slept for four nights.

Marianna holds her brother by the hand as if she has decided at the last minute not to let him go. But when the moment comes, she releases him. This reminds Luigi Ippolito of everything he should have said but has not said: Love to Babbo and Gavino; Don't worry about anything; And you, Marià, don't forget . . . And so on.

But Mercede has realised she may never see her son again. Marianna catches this thought in flight and shakes her head as if to dismiss it. Luigi Ippolito smiles and climbs into the mail coach. The air shatters at the first rumble of the coach's motor.

At home, that evening, Mercede sits quietly on her stool by the fire and says nothing. Gavino and Michele Angelo sit stooped over their soup like weakened hunchbacks. Marianna plays the housewife. No-one asks anything and no-one answers.

No-one mentions the front in the Chironi home. They buy no newspapers and they never even say the word "war". They wait for letters. And it is only when he writes that they learn that Luigi Ippolito is no longer in Sassari, but has reached the great pronged fork that forms the front.

Then one morning Michele Angelo has an idea.

But first it must be said that since Luigi Ippolito left, Gavino has seemed restless. He works badly, fidgets constantly and, as his mother puts it, never makes a nest anywhere.

Many of his friends are no longer at home; a few have already died on the front, and little is known of the others. Josto Corbu, together with a couple of "revolutionaries", has decided to jump in at the deep end and volunteer. Gavino, like a diver choosing the best moment to dive, has preferred to wait. Not an inappropriate metaphor, since Gavino has never been able to do anything without thinking it through a dozen times first. At school, he would let minutes pass before answering a question even when he knew the answer; indeed the more certain of the answer he was, the longer he would wait before speaking. You had to know Gavino not to lose patience with him, and even to love him much, or your hands would want to slap him of their own accord.

This occasion was no exception as after the departure of his brother, Gavino was slow to pull himself together. His father, who knew him well, watched him carefully. Then one evening, before supper and in front of his wife, Michele Angelo said, "That boy's planning something." Mercede nodded, because the same thing was very clear to her too. "He's got a little trick up his sleeve for us," the blacksmith added.

Meanwhile Luigi Ippolito's letters from the front were full of a disturbing enthusiasm. For two months no day passed without Gavino drawing attention to the fact that everyone had already gone or would soon go. And no day passed without Michele Angelo remembering the two or three words he and the Eternal Father had exchanged several years earlier in the vineyard, at the time Pietro and Paolo disappeared. To Michele Angelo it was quite clear that Gavino knew perfectly well what he wanted to say, but was simply not yet ready to say it. So, like a gardener who knows his own turnips, his father never relaxed his guard because he knew that when his son finally did speak that would be the end of the matter. But, in the meantime, the fact was that for every son who volunteered, another in the same family would be excused compulsory recruitment. But it was no less clear that two volunteers from one family were entirely acceptable.

When a lawyer, older than herself but not too old, sought Marianna's hand in marriage, Michele Angelo and Mercede decided on a diversionary manoeuvre. Gavino had no idea that his wavering was about to involve him in a war no less tactical, if not as bloody, as the war in which Luigi Ippolito was fighting.

The plan consisted in making good use of the time before Marianna was officially engaged to create an infallible distraction for Gavino. The name of this distraction was Agnese Desogus.

This girl, a childhood friend of Marianna's, was beautiful, healthy and intelligent, and had already for some time been "interested", as the saying went, in Gavino. He was every inch a man's man: serious, hard-working and creative. Closer in appearance to his stout father than his slender mother, and with exotic fair colouring, Gavino was attractive to women, though he showed no particular interest in pursuing them. His preference for the company of his male friends was a continual source of worry to his parents: "This boy shows no interest in getting married and the other one even less . . ." So his parents hit on the idea of arranging two engagements rather than one. Michele Angelo is convinced that all it needs is for Gavino to have "a taste" and everything will fall into place. If the boy's at all like me, he tells himself, all he'll need is a sniff of women to drive all the fantasies out of his head. So, on the pretext of helping get Marianna ready for her engagement, Agnese is encouraged to come to the house as often as possible when Gavino is around. Encouraged by her new status as queen bee, Agnese delights in constantly buzzing round her favourite flower. Gavino, whether conscious of what is happening or not, and perhaps just pretending not to understand, seems more embarrassed than anything else. But there can be no doubt that he escapes whenever he can.

"It's the same old story," the women tell one another, "you have to stick a man's food right under his nose to get him to eat." "Even Michele Angelo was slow at first," Mercede admits, making the women laugh, "but he soon found out what was required."

Then came the afternoon Agnese kissed Gavino and he let himself be kissed. But that's not all . . .

Here is how Agnese tells the story: the two of them are alone in the kitchen, he is sitting and she is standing. She tells Gavino his hands are very beautiful despite the kind of work he does. They are alone and she cannot take her eyes off him, especially the golden halo of afternoon light round the nape of his neck. And it is his neck she brushes as she passes behind him . . . At her touch the silence deepens.

It is a heavy afternoon in late August, smelling of clean sheets perfumed with quince. Agnese says he seemed not to realise she had touched him, but thought he had imagined it, which she could well understand because in the brooding silence of the kitchen she heard him swallow as if from too much saliva in his mouth. But he did not move, seemingly not wanting to encourage or discourage her. So, far from discouraged, she walked behind him again in exactly the same way, except that this time she touched him more firmly and let her hand linger. Gavino, now fully aware, saw Agnese begin to walk round him for a third time and when he thought she was about to touch him yet again he gave a start and grabbed her hand as if it were a buzzing fly. They looked at each other. He is not grasping her tightly, yet she pretends she can't pull her hand away and gives him an almost imperceptible smile. And everything rests there, in a feverish immobility of gestures, looks, smiles and breathing.

Well, according to Agnese, in the next half an hour she loses her dignity and Gavino loses his virginity. They have to act quickly and one of them has to take the initiative. Gavino, seen, chosen and taken, does his duty according to his cautious nature, halfway between real and ideal. Then buttoning his trousers again, he feels as if he has escaped from a fire, after acting without thinking. As for falling in love, if he knew what that meant he would be able to reason about it, but he doesn't know.

What next? Empty, more sad than happy, more embarrassed than proud, all he can think of is getting away quickly. Agnese, apparently not wanting the same thing, with a slight movement adjusts her blouse to cover her breasts. This visible intimacy is more embarrassing than their actual intercourse a little earlier, since enough time has now passed for what has happened to become a recorded fact, an experience achieved and completed; though too little time has passed for it not to be seen as a myth. But it seems that everything that happened in the kitchen, amid the smell of lamb and cinnamon, can only be seen in terms of leaving the room quickly. Outside, in the courtyard, it feels better already, and on the road, the whole thing becomes a story that can be told, and thus a secret that can be kept.

This is how the women see it. Agnese tells them how quickly Gavino gathered himself together afterwards, and how she had found him kind, strong and clean as a well-cared-for child. Good seed, she believes of him. And I'm fertile ground, she believes of herself.

The land where they live has become a realm of women. While the men are falling in clusters at the front trying to face down gunfire with arrogance.

*

But judging from Luigi Ippolito's letters the front is nothing but a womb infested with mice where whole days are spent in waiting. For each day of gunfire, for each massacre, many days of nothingness pass. So there is nothing left to do but write, so far as that is permitted, because sometimes there is a danger of setting down what is not allowed without even being aware of it. To judge from what he says, the offensive provides some hope which is then cancelled out by the hopelessness of the interminable waiting. But he cannot write that. Luigi Ippolito cannot say what he knows, that for every metre gained on the front dozens of soldiers are lost. That is blotted out and replaced by the single prosaic word CENSORED. All that it leaves of Luigi Ippolito is a story-teller, possibly a patriot, a soldier without a war . . . .

In the hours of waiting he has told his fellow soldiers the story of how Quiròn tried to arrest the Inquisitor and was disgraced for his failure to the extent of having to leave civilised Capo di Sopra for the savage interior in the manner of Pizarro and Cortés. And how this also led to him becoming papal chamberlain to the Bishop of Galtellí and finally, to avoid malaria and plague, to settle in the ancient territory of Nur as part of the household of the bishop who had decided to move his diocese there. Luigi Ippolito's voice, echoing round the karst walls of the underground shelter, adjusts itself to accompany the bombardment. "And then," he goes on, "Quiròn became Kirone and finally Chironi, like the man you have before you now."

Meanwhile the diversionary manoeuvre arranged by Gavino's parents seems to have failed. In the forge, Michele Angelo makes discreet enquiries, but his son's attitude shows no sign of any change. So when Mercede sticks her chin in the air and asks him whether he is showing any interest in the possibility of marriage, he can only shake his head to indicate there is nothing to report. What the boy has sniffed has not been enough, or perhaps he has not sniffed it properly.

Two depressing bits of news mark the week before Marianna's official engagement: Luigi Ippolito will not be coming home on leave, and Agnese Desogus has married a businessman from Genoa thirty-two years her senior. This second piece of news, so disappointing to others, seems not to disturb Gavino much. But the first piece of news does. He is again beginning to have difficulty sleeping at night, and hears breathing from the empty bed beside him as though from a soul in torment.

Not only this, but Josto Corbu, minus one leg and with half his face in tatters, but with a bright medal on his chest, has been sent home to be cared for by his family. In pieces but home again. A shattered local hero of no more use than a splinter in the eye. What could be easier than to pay a visit to this brave fool who, in fighting a stupid war, has been literally shot to pieces?

Three days before Marianna's engagement, Josto sends for Gavino.

As soon as he sees his friend, Gavino understands why he has not hurried to see him sooner. What he sees is a fragment of a human being thrown on a bed. Near his bedside table is a grotesque dark wooden leg with a strap, wearing a small tightly laced shoe.

"Do you think I can wear that?" Josto asks, following Gavino's gaze. "They've given me a shoe for the artificial limb, but no shoe for my good foot. Do you think I can go about in two shoes that don't match? Better with only one leg." And, true to his habit of laughing at terrible things, Josto laughs with half his face, because the other side looks like unrisen dough. Every crease has gone from it, every line, every shape. His lower lip has lost its curve, and the shapeless padding with which they have patched his cheek and jaw, reveals the gum and several teeth. One brown eye seems the only thing still living in that texture of scars, but it has lost its light. "Pretty, aren't I?" Josto Corbu says, reading Gavino's thoughts.

"You were never a beauty," Gavino says, with enough sadness in his voice to darken the earth.

That's how peace ends. To Gavino it is like facing a dead man returned from the grave, like a Lazarus bearing news from the depths of darkness. He swallows saliva, and with it, the one question he is desperate to ask.

"I saw your brother," Josto Corbu says, once more a step ahead of him. "Twice. First at the front; then in hospital with a light wound to his foot, a grenade splinter. He was fine, at least he seemed fine," he says, correcting himself.

The correction says everything. Now that he has become a puppet fit only to scare children, Josto's ability to lie seems severely compromised. Nor does it help that he has lost the power to soften his expression. His words become terrible because they are spoken by a shape from hell that cannot articulate anything at all without a huge effort. His mouth seems unaware of the horror that has distorted it into a shapeless cavity.

"He's not well," Gavino prompts him.

"A wounded foot, what do you expect?"

"That's not what I meant . . ."

That night Gavino waits until his parents have gone to bed. Then, knowing where to find them, he goes to get all his brother's letters: two years of correspondence from the front. He knows everything important has been blotted out and marked CENSORED, but he is not thinking of that. He is trying to imagine everything his brother has not been able to write.

Removing the pages from their envelopes, he spreads them out in order on the floor of his room and understands many things that have not been said . . . The handwriting, for instance, was firm and precise in January and February 1916, with very few censored sections. By March, April and May, the censorship had increased. In one letter, dated April 24, there is almost nothing left apart from the heading and final greeting, and the handwriting is sharper.

This ordered succession of letters feels like a cemetery full of identical gravestones, making the war seem like a stubborn chronicling, like a battery of howitzers whose function is to prepare the way for an offensive, a swelling wave that eventually dashes itself on the rocks . . .

Hardly anything remains of a letter dated June 1916:

Do you remember the discussion we had about duty in war not long before I left? That seems a thousand years ago now, but it was less than two years ago. Do you remember you said don't talk about duty, but I argued duty is essential, even sacred? I know you remember that, and also how passionately I tried to

*prove that there is no more warlike race than the Sardinians,
with their particular culture and nature and their preference for
settling matters in a quick, virile way rather than fiddling about
with diplomacy. Well, now that the facts seem to have proved me
right, now that we shepherds and peasants, the newest members
of this fledgling Nation, have been voted champions on the field
of battle . . . Now, as I was saying, I feel that you* CENSORED
   *Many of us needed immediate care, but not me as you know,
don't worry: the pain in my foot caused by a grenade splinter*
CENSORED

At this point what is left of the writing borders on the absurd . . . But
it is his own hand nonetheless. Shakier, but still his own, proving
the writer is still alive. The page has been marked by the barbed
wire used in transporting it:

   CENSORED *I do that now, and with no less love I ask you to
   forgive me and kiss your feet and hug your knees, defenceless,
   unarmed, without body armour, stripped of certainties . . .*

But what on earth can they have been reading up to this point? How
is it possible that in all this time they had not noticed that something had happened? Or who it was that was writing? Two years at
the front without leave, with never so much as a hint of coming
home.

   To Marianna, who had written to him a month earlier announcing her engagement, he answers among other things:

Great news from here too! I've been to the Plesnicar notary office
to perform a duty I'll tell you and everyone about face to face . . .
CENSORED *I'm not tiring myself out, don't worry, I'm being*
looked after better than I could ever wish and I eat regular meals;
I force myself to take at least an hour's exercise every day, which
I need for my foot which was injured by the grenade, as you know.
I hope it's a comfort to you to know that I haven't had to walk with
a stick for two months now. And I hope it's also a comfort to you
to know that it has been my constant care not to disappoint the
hopes you have placed in me. Even if, occasionally, I feel certain I
must have disappointed you and brought you nothing but worry
and pain. As I write now, I am able to believe that everything that
had to be done has been done, in the end . . .

No mention whatever of Marianna's engagement.

It is late at night, now, in the silence of impending autumn. Gavino,
sitting on the floor like a pilgrim at a sanctuary, is beginning to
feel cold; the pages of the letters are breathing round him, like
his brother's empty bed, like everything connected with Luigi
Ippolito.

It takes him some time to put the letters back in their correct
envelopes, and most of all to stack the sacred letters back up neatly,
tying them together with a red ribbon, for Mercede to venerate
and guard like a holy relic.

Exhausted, Gavino goes to lie on Luigi Ippolito's bed, but
finds very little peace. There is a thought at the back of his mind,
something he cannot quite catch. As he lies between waking and

sleeping, invisible threads seem to be trying to weave a cocoon that is slowly suffocating him.

Suddenly wide awake, he leaps into a sitting position on the bed, suddenly understanding what he had been unable to grasp until that moment. Barefoot, he goes back to the table. The letters are still there. Feverishly, he opens them again.

November 1917:
I hope it's a comfort to you to know that it has been my constant care not to disappoint the hopes you have placed in me.

And again:
With no less love I ask you to forgive me, and I kiss your feet and hug your knees, defenceless, unarmed . . .

December 1917:
. . . I hug your knees, defenceless, unarmed . . .

January 1918:
I hope it is a consolation to you to know that it has been my constant care not to disappoint the hopes you have placed in me. Even if, now and then, I feel certain I must have disappointed you . . .
Do you remember you said don't talk about duty, but I argued duty is essential, even holy?

"I've been expecting you." Josto Corbu points to the chair facing him.

"What's been going on?" Gavino says aggressively, tired after his sleepless night. "Why has Luigi Ippolito never come home? You've seen him . . ."

Josto Corbu takes his time. "I'm not sure you really want to know the answer. Sit down, relax."

Gavino remains standing. "What has happened to my brother?"

"He's written to you, hasn't he?" Josto Corbu's voice seems to change, as though coming from a different room. Gavino looks at him and waits. "Sit down," Josto says again.

I'll tell you about one day. Just one single day.

Those of you here don't understand, you can't even imagine what war is like. For months we suffered cold, hunger and exhaustion. Oh, that exhaustion, it was like a permanent burden on our shoulders! We used to call our equipment "exhaustion", thirty heavy kilos on the shoulders of boys who ate little and slept even less. The rats and lice ate better than we did, they really did. The lice drove me mad and stopped me sleeping; they were worse than the rats, worse than the hunger . . . You couldn't even think of sleeping at night. Ever. When we came out of the trenches we were already dead. Stuck on the Isonzo front. Even so I ended up falling asleep despite the constant din, the never-ending boom boom . . .

In August they said we'd taken Gorizia, but it wasn't true; all we'd done was break into an open cemetery infested with snipers, and that was the only advance we made for months and months.

The day started in silence; they had warned us to be ready for an offensive towards five in the morning. During the night we were joined by contingents from the Veneto. Your brother was with them. To begin with I didn't even notice him with his helmet down over his eyes, but when he began shouting orders I recognised something in his voice. Then I heard the capitano say, "Tenente Chironi, make sure everyone has understood what they have to do."

Then your brother repeated the command to fall into line, one detachment after another, and so on. He spoke in Sardinian, because many of the soldiers couldn't even understand Italian. So I went up to him and said, "Excuse me, tenente . . ."

"Yes, caporale," he answered.

"Are you by any chance a Chironi of Nuoro?" I said. "Related to Micheli Anzelu Chirone, the master blacksmith?"

"I am."

"Gavino's brother?"

"*Eja*," he answered in Sardinian, "so you know my brother?"

"We're the same age."

Gavino put his hand over his eyes.

So the day passed, sheer hell, just to gain a metre or two of ground, but it did pass. When we were back in our holes there was a roll-call. Then we lit a fire and slept without sleeping, like animals. I didn't see your brother again for a whole week. You never know where they're going to send you next, and we lived like moles in a labyrinth of tunnels. You can live side by side with people for months without ever seeing them. But I did get a good view of Luigi Ippolito: thin, with a bit of a beard, extremely serious. You know what he's like. Always seems to be telling you one thing while thinking of another.

Gavino nods.

He looks good in uniform because he's tall and fair and to the senior officers he doesn't even look like a Sardinian. The fact is, Gaví, after that time I introduced myself to him he was very good to me and always made sure I got extra rations. Very good to me. I say to me because he didn't have a good reputation with the detachment . . . I have to tell you this, no point in hiding it. They said your brother was a bit too familiar with Capitano Sermonti and was a man who had to be watched . . . And then they said your brother, Tenente Chironi, even had a screw loose, do I make myself clear?

Gavino shakes his head. But he is beginning to find the distorted phrases emerging from Josto Corbu's twisted mouth easier to understand.

Yes, well, they said he was the capitano's guard dog and worse, all nonsense . . . It was quite clear he wasn't relaxed, but who the hell would be relaxed with the Austrians less than a kilometre away?

I kept saying: You're all fools, I know the Chironi family well and they're decent folk, the tenente must have good reasons for behaving the way he does.

But one day Caporale Tinti pops up and says they're not even letting your brother out of the officers' quarters. For whatever the reason, everyone had his own idea about it . . . Some said he was no longer right in the head, for instance. And so we come to the day I wanted to tell you about from the start. And the reason I'm telling you is because it was the famous day everyone started saying Tenente Chironi had lost his mind and that to protect his own back so far as the senior command was concerned the capitano had not allowed Luigi Ippolito to leave his bunk. He was indeed in bed and out of uniform, but feverish, with dirty hair and as thin as Jesus Christ, looking older. Just like all the rest of us, in fact. I'm sure there are evil tongues among the troops that actually kill more men than any weapons . . . But anyway, your brother sent for me for a precise reason: he wanted to know if I was married and had a family. I said, No, sir! Then he wanted to know if I'd written to you and if you had written to me. And I said again, No, sir! He smiled as if I'd given just the answer he expected: Written to Gavino, no, eh? he said. And I said, No, absolutely not. Then he said, How long have you been away from home? And I say, A year and seven months, sir! Then he took a piece of paper off the table and held it out to me. It was a warrant for me to go on leave.

Silence. A tear fell heavily from Josto Corbu's good eye.

*

So that day was memorable for me because, with that piece of paper in my hand, I realised I had not been happy for a very long time, or cheerful, or even merely content. That was the day I finally realised I'd been sucked into hell. I looked around me and recognised myself over and again, trembling underground in the trench, stuck between rocks, hanging from barbed wire. I was everyone and they were all me.

An attack was imminent so we took up our positions, but I had my warrant to shield me against death. So when the earth exploded I felt nothing wrong; my leg flew ahead of me and I just thought, Oh well, people are fragile. What seemed to be a hook ripped off half my face and again I thought: I'm fragile. But I didn't die. I shouted out: I'm strong! I'm alive! The stretcher-bearers ran to me. I felt fine, I swear. Later there were problems, yes, but at that moment, though torn to pieces and with my blood soaking into the ground, I felt no pain. Nothing. Flung to the ground by the explosion, all I could think of was my permit, nothing else.

Who knows how much time passed, but the important thing was the stretcher-bearers took me up. I heard one say, He's more dead than alive, and the other added, Poor sod. He said it as if he were an older man when in fact he was even younger than me.

I realised I'd gone deaf in one ear. As they were carrying me I saw day dawning. I tell you, Gaví, I felt really at peace in that dawn, though the intense cold almost cut me in two. The sky was like a painting. I looked at it and asked myself: How can such beauty exist in this world? Then I realised I had been an animal cursed with always having to stand upright and stare down at the ground. But now I could not take my eyes off that sky just because it was so simple. Perfection is its own justification. I really thought I might be at the point of death. Why, I asked myself, why am I granted this revelation at the very last moment? The revelation is that beauty is simple; that peace and life, and what from either fear or convenience we call God, is pure and limpid. Nothing else exists, my friend, my brother; nothing else.

To cut a long story short, after four months in the military hospital they had me standing again. The medical officer said: Well, Corbu, you must thank the cold for saving you from infection, and then your temperament, you Sardinian devil!

Then he cried out: What is it you people say? *Ajò?* and he laughed. And I, with half my face bound up, repeated as best I could: *Ajò!*

I should have been walking again by then; but after so many months in bed it wasn't so easy. I was better off lying down, looked after hand and foot, like one returned from the dead, not so much a child even as a new-born baby. I liked that, because it made it possible for me to live as an adult, as a conscious being, the way I'd been able to live before when I was unaware. When you come from where I've been, Gaví, healing is almost a punishment, because it's like coming back from the grave only to come to terms with everything you took for granted when you were buried.

They say what happened at Caporetto can never be put right. Have you heard anything about it here?

Gavino shrugs.

Not much, obviously. What can you expect from the newspapers? In time of war, especially . . . However, we've now reached the point

I was aiming for and it's all to do with the day I got my leave warrant.

In fact, I'd had the warrant in my pocket and it was looked after by the nurses during my convalescence. The first thing I remembered the morning they stood me up on my surviving foot was that months before I had been given a warrant by Tenente Chironi to go on leave. The nurse told me not to worry, all my personal effects had been carefully kept, and I no longer really needed the permit, since my dismissal as an invalid was inevitable. Yet that very day, now I think of it, they took me for a walk to "strengthen my remaining leg"; as, of course, the other had run on ahead of me and, by then, must have long been buried somewhere.

So there I was in the hospital grounds, hopping about and sitting down, trying out my crutches, my muscles unable to hold me, out of breath.

At the far end of the path I saw a group of ghosts being shepherded by some massive male nurses. A strange little group of marionettes guarded by four enormous men in white uniforms.

Those are the madmen, said the nurse helping me with my exercises . . . There was also a woman in the uniform of a volunteer with me, doing her best to hold me up, but it was too much for her. So very soon they led me back to the ward. It was at the very moment when they decided we had done enough for one day that I saw your brother pass us by. He was at the back of the group they called the madmen . . . There, you see, I've ended up by telling you. The nurse said that after Caporetto he had been seconded to the firing squads in charge of executing deserters. Did you know that? Did you know that after the enemy routed them those poor boys were further humiliated by being condemned to death for cowardice? It's no surprise people went mad.

But it was impossible to go into the ward where the madmen were held; people said they were being treated with electric shocks and cold baths. They were said to have been normal when they arrived at the front, but then revealed a mental weakness that made them suddenly unstable.

The front was full of boys who had imagined they would count for something, and when they realised they counted for nothing they lost their minds, but we Sardinians have always known from the moment we were born that we count for nothing. So what's new?

There was a lad from Bergamo, in Lombardia, with me in the trenches, who almost went mad at every explosion. I wanted to tell him to relax because after all it was always the same slaughter time and time again, it was just the weapons that changed.

That's modern warfare for you, where each centimetre of earth matters more than the thousands of lives sacrificed to win it . . .

Gaví, I'm talking about Monte San Michele, June 29. We had a whole battalion in waiting and something new and previously unknown began to rain down on us from the Austrian lines, smoke bombs stinking of rotten hay. Strange, but apparently insignificant. Except that next morning some of the boys began to feel bad, seriously bad, coughing till they were blue in the face, then foaming at the mouth before falling to the ground. Those who saw them claimed that those smoke bombs with their stink of the stall wouldn't kill, but they turned out to be weapons without bullets, a poison that our boys breathed in. The Ultimate Evil, people say, striking inside the lungs like the wrath of God against the worshippers of the molten calf in the desert. Worst of all, they took many agonising hours to die, as if drowning on dry land, their lungs dissolving into putrid liquid. No-one survived at Monte San Michele; sixty thousand lads wheezing to death in the trenches, blinded, scalded, distorted by blisters. Until eventually the Austrian high command ordered the lines cleared by a platoon armed with clubs bristling with nails. Did you get that? No point in wasting bullets on those who would die anyway. They've written about that somewhere, Gaví?

Gavino shakes his head. He is paralysed in a strange position, neither sitting, nor standing, as if he had caught Medusa's eye as he got to his feet.

How many are sixty thousand people, Gaví? Eh? How many is that?

Gavino falls into a sitting position, victim of a shattered spell.

How many towns the size of Nuoro would it take to make sixty thousand people, eh? Nine? Eight? Something like that. Well, imagine eight or nine Nuoros destroyed in one day, with every single inhabitant dying; every man, woman and child, every boy and girl, all the old men and old women, the sacristan, the priest's housekeeper, the notary, the maresciallo from the carabinieri, the doctor . . . Imagine that no-one can escape this massacre, blood-thirsty criminals, rapists and thieves dying together with mothers and the victims of rape and theft. Every single one. Sixty thousand. Twenty thousand in a single minute. It was like that at the front in France. Did you know that?

Gavino has something he could say, but realises the time has passed; he should have said it a year earlier.

Josto Corbu can read his face as if his thoughts are etched on it in fire.

And what difference would it make if you went off and enrolled too, Gaví?

Don't you realise they're recruiting underage boys now? Gavino says in a thick voice.

So what? Do you think they specially need you? You fought your war here.

Gavino remembers the time Luigi Ippolito woke him and asked him to come into his bed. Which wasn't really so strange, just a young boy looking for protection from his older brother.

He remembers the evening vividly. He was just five years old and it was a night when the house was full of people and no-one was asleep. Pietro and Paolo had not come home and everyone was asking what could have happened to them, even if the question was a mere formality since no-one had the slightest doubt of their fate.

Yes, that night Luigi Ippolito, moving restlessly on his bed: Let's sleep together. We'll be warmer that way.

It was August, for sure, but it was cold; Gavino can remember that too. And he can remember his brother smelled of iron and solder. And he can remember the extremely nervous feel of his dry little body.

All this comes back to his mind now. When what he particularly does not want to say is that if he had stayed with his brother everything would have been different. Warmer, safer.

But he also believes Josto Corbu's words have solved the mystery, and that he understands why Luigi Ippolito virtually stopped writing . . . Or perhaps he did try to write, but could only write the same things obsessively again and again. And Gavino now understands why Michele Angelo's attempts to find out whether his son was missing or dead had come up against such a wall of silence. Because Luigi Ippolito is not missing, and not dead. Yet in a sense he is both missing and dead.

Josto Corbu breaks in on his thoughts: Don't think your brother has no lucid moments. They tell me that kind of madness is not real insanity. It's just a repressed fear that can suddenly burst out. I've seen it before, with my father's line of work, I know the symptoms: neurasthenic people can gaze dumbfounded without any word or gesture on a highly animated nothing; they see events in a frenetic sequence of disconnected fragments of light and dark because they have no idea how to link them together; they stammer over the words that struggle to come out. Boys who have never dreamed before suddenly have to face their deepest fears: it's as though they've regressed to childhood. Boys who have been forced to run for safety with bloated corpses exploding under their hobnailed boots, and then have to spend days smeared with stinking body liquids and guts because they have no chance to wash.

141

How firm and steady do you need to be, Gaví? Eh?

These are the ones who end up in the madness ward, where if they are lucky they are no longer aware of themselves. The least thing can make them cry. They may froth insanely at the sight of a red uniform or a flower, or at the sound of a whistle. Each has a different obsession.

Silence.

Josto Corbu says no more, but takes a sealed envelope from his bedside table drawer. It is quite thick, and there is only a single handwritten word on it: *Gavino*. With an effort, propping himself up in the bed, Josto holds it out to his friend. And explains that two days after their meeting in the grounds of the hospital, and the day before he was discharged and sent home, one of the massive nurses brought him this envelope, saying it was from tenente Chironi. Josto Corbu adds that when he asked how the tenente was doing the nurse didn't even bother to answer, but just threw the letter on his bed and left.

A very long silence, during which Gavino feels himself revert to being a child. You can see from his face that he is in the grip of a terrible doubt. What shall I do? he is thinking with the envelope in his hand. What can I do? Go home and tell Mamma and Babbo that Luigi Ippolito's not in fact dead or missing, yet at the same time really is dead and missing? What's worse, a mad son or a dead son?

So he goes home and says nothing. But, when someone is as transparent as he is, those who know him well take him to task. Mercede cannot take her eyes off him. "What's the matter?" she presses him. "Where have you been all afternoon? Your father's been looking for you, there was work to do . . ." Gavino says, "Nothing, nothing." To which Mercede says, "I don't believe you, you're strange." And Gavino replies, "I'm tired, I'm off to bed."

Mercede watches him go, well aware that an insurmountable wall has risen between them . . .

When Michele Angelo comes in that evening he finds her standing halfway between the window and the larder, like a jar of olives . . . And nothing is ready, not even the shadow of a supper. He looks around and asks, "Nothing to eat?"

She is not even listening. "You must speak to Gavino," she hisses as if having difficulty getting her voice out. "He's brooding over something."

"I've talked to the lawyer Offeddu about Luigi Ippolito," says Michele Angelo.

"Did you understand what I said?"

"He says it's really strange there's been no news of him for so long . . . but that he has friends in the War Ministry and will be in touch . . ."

Mercede presses her fists into her temples.

Michele Angelo looks at her as if he has only just noted that she has spoken, and asks, "What's happened to Gavino?"

"He's no longer himself," his wife answers promptly like a diligent schoolgirl, but very much on edge.

Michele Angelo, feeling the weight of centuries on his shoulders,

143

collapses into a chair. "What are you talking about?" he says.

"The way things are we'll end up by losing everything, that's what I'm saying. The trouble is, you keep looking where there's nothing to see . . ."

A sudden change has come over her, an unexpected change of tone as if until now she has tried to keep calm but has just realised for the first time that she can't any longer.

"What?" Michele Angelo says, disconcerted.

"Everything . . . Everything," she says, losing control.

"What?" he shouts. He knows the only way to calm her is to shout. And, in fact, she does suddenly seem to calm down. "I know you're worried," he says, moving towards her. She backs away almost imperceptibly, but that millimetre is enough to make clear to her husband that she wants him to keep his distance.

"You don't know," she says. But she is aware that she has confused her husband with her abrupt awareness that there is a problem.

"You don't know," she repeats, as if a door has swung open, letting gusts of air into the room.

"We have to be ready for anything," he concludes after a moment, perfectly in harmony with the chord she has decided to strike. "I know you don't like talking about it, but this business of Luigi Ippolito not coming home and not sending us any news is not good at all."

But she shakes her head as if that is not the point; so much as the thought that Gavino may run away from home and end up as a soldier, which seems about to drive her mad.

All she can think of is that very similar evening seventeen years before. Can it really be seventeen? Yes. The kitchen has not changed and it was even the same time of day all those years ago. Mercede would like to believe that a few things have changed: she has more grey hairs, and possesses a few modern objects she did not have before. And yet, despite this evidence to the contrary, it seems to her that absolutely nothing has changed.

It was seventeen years ago, and husband and wife were discussing whether or not to send Pietro and Paolo to the vineyard to pay the workers. If she is to find any explanation for the bad mood that has overtaken her, she must force herself to go back to that evening many years before. It seems clear to her that the whole of the intervening time has been like a sort of long seething under-current, a kind of gurgling preparation for what she is now at last beginning to understand clearly: that it is up to her to save her sons. And if she cannot save them both, she must save at least one of them.

Mercede has this cynical, blind thought, which is blind and cynical in the way that a wave slaps a rock as it breaks against it. If Luigi Ippolito is lost, she thinks, absolutely everything must be done to save Gavino. It's as simple as that. The thought comes to her in this way and in these exact words. Because running through her is a sense of something she has already experienced and that freezes her blood. Michele Angelo seems totally obsessed by an aim as discon-certing as it is simple: to have news of a son who went off to war as a volunteer and whom he has not seen for two years. While she is terrified by the possibility that Gavino may be swallowed by the same whirlpool that has taken her other son. Of course the letters exist, and there is also Marianna. But why then does she suddenly

145

feel such resentment of the man before her? Michele Angelo, who saved her and whom she has saved. They gave each other meaning. But now, she cannot escape the fact that she hates him. How can you hate a person you love so deeply so much? Without half measures, with no holds barred? This man has devoured his own sons, like a scornful godhead annihilating what she has created. The twins for example; and her mind goes back, obstinately, to seventeen years before, if only she had known she must insist, if only she had had the strength to act on her fear, her worries . . . But to him it was nothing, the boys were old enough to look after themselves. Who could possibly dare to lay a finger on his sons? The seeds of her repressed hatred had been planted that day, but had only now germinated with the wisdom of tender leaves. He had let his sons die. Like a cannibal father who kills for love but nonetheless kills.

"I've got the point that there won't be any supper this evening," Michele Angelo says, breaking the silence.

"There's plenty of food, get your own," Mercede says.

Gavino has been listening to them arguing. As happens more and more often now, he has been lying on his brother's bed. It's not yet eight but he is already half asleep.

He has put the sealed envelope Josto Corbu gave him under his pillow. He must come to a decision. He closes his eyes almost as if he expects in this way to be able to shut out his thoughts as well. But no. Mercede and Michele Angelo have been arguing, but now there's silence. He doesn't know which frightens him more, the noise or the silence. But this is life, he believes: a sleeping beast suddenly waking and shrugging off years of slumber, shaking the earth and leaving tracks like craters with its heavy tread before disappearing again. And what seems like peace is no more than a pause between one setback and the next. Now, for instance, the light is the same, the hour is the same, the bed is the same. And the putrid breath of the wakening beast is the same. It is not easy to define this beast; it is of no particular race and can be found in no zoology textbook. Since childhood, he has imagined it as a cross between a wild boar and a bear, even though he has never seen a bear. It is this indefinite quality that makes it so terrible. It is a beast yet no beast at the same time, indescribable but quantifiable. It has no voice but breathes, no body but only weight. A nothing that leaves tracks. What particularly terrifies Gavino is the idea that it devours like an undertow, chews without teeth and can swallow you alive. Perhaps – and it is only now that this occurs to him – this indefinite beast is merely an image of himself, of his own inconsistency.

Gavino does not know how to weep, he has never been able to. He certainly does not consider weeping an act of weakness. He simply does not know how to go about it. He knows what weeping means and where it springs from, but it is as if he is cut off from his tears by a dyke. Yet it is irrelevant that he does not understand the extreme limits of happiness and unhappiness, which are always touching without ever blurring. He has watched Josto Corbu slaver out his story from his deformed mouth, and has smelled the acrid odour of his martyred flesh. And he has not wept. Now he can reason about Destiny, and he has the power to transform a destiny full of misery into a calm presumption of normality. And he can help wake the beast, even provoke it. All he has to do is get up and go into the kitchen and say: Stop searching. Luigi Ippolito is both alive and dead. All he needs do is show an envelope and say: Here's your lost son, naked before you, lost inside himself.

I don't weep, Gavino tells himself, I do not weep.

It is as though the envelope under the pillow were quivering in anticipation, waiting to release its contents.

Michele Angelo cuts himself a slice of sausage and moistens a piece of *pane carasau*. He places the wine flask in front of him and fills a glass to the brim.

"I've had an idea," he says, his throat refreshed.

"Really?" Mercede seems caught by surprise.

"Really," he says with confidence. "You know your son better than I do. If he gets something into his head no-one can shift it. So I've had an idea: I must maim him." This jerks Mercede back into the land of the living. She opens her eyes wide. "I shall maim him," Michele Angelo repeats, as if to clinch the matter. "Let's see whether they'll recruit a cripple. A convenient accident can easily be arranged in the forge. And that will be the end of the matter."

"But how?" Mercede stammers.

"I'm not sure yet: a weight dropping on his foot, or a hammer hitting him on the leg or the shoulder . . ."

"Better on the leg," his wife interrupts.

"The leg then; he'll get over it, and if he doesn't, better lame than dead, don't you agree?"

Mercede nods.

*

Dear Brother,

What I'm going to write to you needs an introduction. Do you remember the discussion we had about duty in war not long before I left? That seems a thousand years ago now, but it was less than two years ago. Do you remember you said don't talk about duty, but I argued duty is essential, even sacred? I'm sure you remember that and will also remember how passionately I argued that there was no more warlike race than the Sardinians, culturally, by nature and by their preference for solving matters in a quick, virile way rather than fiddling about with diplomacy. Well, now that the facts seem to have proved me right, now that we shepherds and peasants, the newest members of this fledgling Nation, have been voted champions on the field of battle . . . Now, as I was saying, I feel that you were absolutely right. They have abandoned us at the extremity of our strength in a particular town. A magnificent town. Of such quality as to make one think that the Habsburgs did some good after all. Many of us were in need of urgent care – but not I, as you know, since the pain in my foot inflicted by the grenade splinter is now no more than an ugly memory.

Gorizia is a city of ghosts, of poor bodies deprived of everything: of food, of illusions, of History . . . You were right! It has been enough for me to see the frightened faces of old people, children and women prey to uncertainty, ready to cross the border with their few remaining possessions. Women, old people and children: there are no men. The men are either victors or dead! Slovenes and Croats, the coast dwellers press, en masse, towards the borders of the new Yugoslav state; they throw themselves into the wild countryside, the mined fields, the bomb craters . . . An exorbitant price, a burden that weighs on my chest . . . Yet I have been a warrior. Now no longer. I understood this for certain this morning when I was walking in the hospital grounds and a very thin layer of snow settled on me. Gorizia is a city of ghosts and I am one of them. A phantom city. An empire reduced by us to a kingdom, and I'm not referring to political arrangements. A joyless victory, rivers of blood spilled in the name of purely statistical superiority. Here too you were right: better a happiness that is not ours than an unhappiness caused by us. Now I understand those words: now I understand that it is always true, and that it always will be true, but I doubt that many will understand it . . . It doesn't matter . . . You'll ask yourself, or perhaps you won't, what can have caused such a fundamental change in my thinking? I could answer that I don't know, or rather that I can't find the words to explain it, it's mainly a matter of images, terrible and transitory as in an early morning dream: it's the faces, the hands, the cries of women and children coming to blows over a piece of stale bread or leftovers from the barracks. If I lift my head I can see a square of pure white sky like a flag of surrender. A white peacefulness made of fine snow settles on my soul . . . But to you, at least, I must tell everything, if not to you, to whom? I'll entrust you with my secret because when we meet again I won't be in any position to give you reasons. And it may be that someone else will assume the task of not telling you the real facts. The truth is I shall have died mad. It'll be up to you to decide whether or not to reveal this to those dear to us.

Let's go back to the beginning. You know all about what
happens in war from my earlier letters which Mamma has read
to you. You know I was wounded in the foot, and have been three
times decorated for valour in the field. Then came Gorizia. If
only you could see the wonder of it! But let's stick to the point . . .
I'm in Gorizia and here the war seems to me something else.
Terrified faces, whole populations with no ground beneath their
feet, and this is no metaphor. Everything that looked resplendent
and heroic seen from the nearby Carso district, seen from here
appears deadly and diabolical. This is how it all started in
me. Two weeks ago, Tenente Colonello Pugliese sent for me and
made me a speech more or less in these terms: "Tenente Chironi,
the Public Health Committee of the Town of Gorizia has asked
us officially for assistance in stopping thefts from the bakeries;
take a platoon of trustworthy men and prepare to intervene."
So I moved into action. New heights of enthusiasm: the boys of
Sassari are on the march again! We arrived at a bakery, where a
crowd of old women dissolved at the mere sound of our boots on
the pavement. We commanded those inside the building to come
out with their hands in the air. They emerged slowly, and turned
out to be children. Loaded with bread loaves, white with flour,
like little corpses. Surprise paralysed us; for a moment a heavy
silence took over: even the gulls stop squawking above our
heads. Then came a volley of stones, a hail of pieces of porphyry
from the upper windows of the houses overlooking the road. It
only took a second: while an infantryman was trying to protect
himself a shot escaped from his rifle and a little girl fell to
the ground, loaves of bread still clutched in her arms . . . And so

the nightmare begins. Nothing has been the same since. Since then this town has seemed to me veiled in dazzling whiteness. A funereal nothingness. I've yelled at the top of my voice, brother. I've been terrified. I've wept as if I had lost someone very dear to me . . . I have to tell you everything: now I'm locked up in a hospital. They are looking after me and giving me treatment. But I'm no longer myself.

In October things definitely got worse; we were forced to give up all the land it had cost us so much blood and toil to win. Madness has overtaken this sorry Universe. Boys who had been fighting earlier were put up against a wall . . . A few hours ago, during a walk in the hospital grounds, I met a common friend of ours from when we were young who has been very severely wounded. He is about to be discharged, so I thought I'd make the most of it by sending you these lines without incurring censorship or other controls. If you are now reading this letter from me this postal service has obviously been completely successful. The brother writing this to you will always be your brother, but your eternal brother is no more . . . He no longer exists . . . The electric shock treatment calms me, but lasts such a short time, not nearly long enough . . .

I'm really at peace, and when I come home it will be as one you can all – you yourself, Mamma and Babbo – be proud of still . . . I'll find the way . . .

Me, Luigi Ippolito Chironi

The body of Tenente Luigi Ippolito Chironi reaches Nuoro just in
time to find a place in the newly built shrine to the fallen in the
middle of the cemetery. It is a small area of grey granite stones
embellished with iron fittings. The Chironi foundry works full-
time casting names and numbers for these bodies who will find
peace in the glory of this paradise for heroes.

The letter from the ministry that arrives ahead of the body is
simple: *Died while gloriously committed to the service of the Sacred
Soil of his Country.* Nothing more. The zinc coffin arrives sealed at
the barracks two weeks later to be handed over formally to the relatives and is immediately buried together with the other heroes
at the shrine. Beyond that, no explanation. No report. No further
details. After all, in war as the rest of life, one rule applies: one
moment you're there and the next you're gone.

Gavino, newly forgiven and saved from his father's "idea", stares
at his brother's coffin and tells himself that if it occurred to anyone to open it they would be surprised to find a corpse with its
neck furrowed by the scar of the hanged, or its temple perforated
by a bullet fired at close range. But he has decided to keep this
to himself. The personal calvary of Tenente Luigi Ippolito Chironi, driven mad by the war, must not be exposed, because it
would provide food for the beast at present grazing heedless of his

existence and apparently persuaded to return to its lethargy. People shaking his hand disturb these thoughts.

All Mercede and Michele Angelo think about is that they have saved Gavino from disaster. And today, under that sky that seems fine enough to suit the ungodly, this half-victory seems sufficient for them not to let themselves be beaten down by a half-defeat. Now they have understood, and they have understood it together, that nothing can be too terrible if they set this protective device in motion. In any case, consolation must relate to grief.

Marianna is in tears. She too has a secret she cannot confess, but which must come out sooner or later. Now, faced with her brother's coffin, she weeps tears she has resisted for too long.

Josto Corbu arrives at the ceremony supported by a more fortunate former comrade-in-arms. Both are in uniform. The trouser leg intended for Josto's missing limb has been folded back and fastened in place with a large safety pin. Looking at Luigi Ippolito's coffin, he remembers the enchanted look he had several months before, and the hospital grounds and his smile. Propped on his crutches, Josto struggles to make a military salute to honour the tenente who was kind to him despite his deformity.

But we must now turn our attention to Marianna, who has been waiting all this time in the wings. She is not destined to remain a minor character since, in the structure of this bloodline forged by suffering, she represents a secret hope hidden in a bottom drawer.

In fact, promised a good match at the age of seventeen, she is like the tributary of a major river, hidden in a gorge by bushes. Being female, she cannot offer the straightforward navigable course to be expected of a male river, but in full flood during the rainy season, she has always fulfilled her function of contributing fresh water to the main stream. Now that the arrangements for her marriage have been made – arrangements that seem perfectly agreeable to her, according as they do with her own code and common custom – her main task is to prepare a trousseau to justify her dual status as underling and empress. Mercede has firmly directed her to this end, instructing her that the more ready she is to submit, the greater will be her power to command. This has nothing to do with men; it is a matter for women, and this principle governs everything. It is not an attitude that can be exactly defined or explained: it is a matter of having knowledge without revealing what you know, because this will entirely reassure the man to the extent of giving him the illusion that he is in charge.

Meanwhile, quite simply, he will do what is expected of him.

All this is achieved through an arcane process more akin to alchemy than psychology. "Because," Mercede says, "if you want to avoid doing something you have to prove that you know how to do it. There's no point in saying, 'I refuse to do that!' That's being a bad housewife; what you should say is, 'Yes, of course, I could do that, but I prefer not to.'"

This is why the bride-to-be has been spending all her time for several months now embroidering her trousseau in the company of cloistered nuns. It is not clear how much longer it will take her to get the job done. Everything will depend on the quality of the embroidery she manages to add to the sheets, pillowcases, tablecloths, napkins and curtains, and even to the delicate little hand-kerchiefs. Because a trousseau always carries a woman's sense of self, a physical representation of her own specific gravity. The how and the how much. The many thousands of stitches, the hemmed borders and little open-work perforations, that can transform basic linen into a floral wonder.

Mercede sees the perfecting of this rite, the precision of this liturgy, as the achievement of the privilege of the rich in owning objects that have no practical value. And, in fact, it is with genuine surprise that, seeing the result of all this dedication, she exclaims, "Amazing, I could never even have dreamed of sleeping in such sheets!" Though she knows perfectly well that when you are tired enough you would be happy to sleep in sackcloth. It is also important to be able to say, "This curtain is muslin, or this tablecloth is hemp," because it signifies: In our position we can name things; it's not just a matter of covering ourselves and falling asleep; now we can baptise objects as though they are themselves Christian flesh and blood.

Marianna was born in a time of prosperity, but she was not aware of it. No rich trousseau or high-ranking marriage could have been predicted for her. So that when both these possibilities became facts she found it hard to believe that a blacksmith's daughter could enter the homes of the gentry. But the war has changed the order of things and what once seemed impossible now is no longer so . . .

The men born in 1899 have been lopped off like bunches of grapes in the frenzy of extreme sacrifice, their sad victory celebrated with ranks of gravestones. Now servants are becoming masters and the masters, not even realising it, are forced to yield to their eternal enemy, change. Not everything they have seen in these few years can be told, but we can limit ourselves to the highest mountain peaks and the most beautiful women, to the conscience of the world . . .

So when old Serra-Pintus, with more debts than credits to his name, himself suggests his middle son, Biagio, as a possible husband to the blacksmith Michele Angelo Chironi – who has credits and no debts – no-one is particularly surprised. Except Marianna. To her this period of fundamental change seems anything but reassuring. Every time she misses a stitch, or mistakes the colour of a thread, or misjudges a hem or border, she tells herself these are signals of the clearest possible kind. But the mother prioress and the other nuns, all working with her and for her, tell her this is not foresight on her part, but a form of superstition. Because, they say, God doesn't waste time on signals. God takes action, it's as simple as that. Oh yes, God takes action; you only have to look around you to see that, they say.

It occurs to Marianna that there surely must exist some way of seeing things that has escaped her, bearing in mind that none of the holy women around her has ever set foot outside the convent for at least ten years. But, and there's always a but, if their understanding cannot have been sharpened by close familiarity with the world, it may have benefited from close familiarity with themselves. This is, in fact, what the more astute nuns claim, the few who speak at all. The others are said to have devoted themselves to silence to such an extent that they have even lost the ability to form words, with the result that if they ever did want to start speaking again they would not know how to do it.

In this purely female world Marianna feels at peace. Now and then, like a little Penelope, she misses a stitch or stretch of tacking, or pretends she wants to add an extra leaf or flower at a point where none has been planned. And the nuns, the more astute ones at least, exchange looks as if to say: This girl's an artful one.

By the time she gets home each evening everything that should happen has always already happened. During these months of apprenticeship with the nuns Marianna is spared everything, even the deadly uncertainty of men returning from the front, whether on their own feet or not. Thus she is the last to hear that Luigi Ippolito has come home in a zinc-covered box, and she hears of it almost by accident, when a novice from Siniscola, spontaneously embraces her to commiserate with her. And so on that day her embroidery goes wrong. She happens to be working on an extremely delicate vine branch to decorate the corner of a pillowcase; if you saw her you would be struck by the serenity of her expression until you noticed an ill-controlled tremor in her hands making it impossible for her to sew accurately. In fact, the cluster of grapes comes out so awkwardly that it looks like a careless repair pulling the material towards the centre, and the pattern resembles not so much a bunch of grapes as a strange fish. The Mother Superior suggests doing it again, but Marianna decides to leave it as it is. It becomes her way of mourning her brother.

At the ceremony in honour of the fallen soldiers, Biagio Serra-Pintus looks the part: a modest man, both in appearance and attitude . . . Marianna's future husband is like a cabin boy surveying his own retreating horizon from the top of the mainmast. He has blood but no money. He is like a coat made from quality cloth. It has been decided that the prenuptial agreement shall pay tribute to his excellent family name in cash, so that, as always, due attention is paid not only to form but to substance as well. Beside him, Marianna looks like a Chinese vase accompanied by an earthenware pot. Those who see her grieving simply in her well-cut grey coat raise their eyebrows, because they hardly recognise her in her continental clothes. She has been out of the limelight so long that it is the first time anyone has noticed that she is no longer a child.

Mercede did not attend the ceremony. As far as she was concerned the cemetery did not exist and her children were not there. There was no more to be said. The whole of her was now wrapped up, as if in a piece of embroidery, in the complicated weave of organising her only daughter's wedding. Marianna could contribute no more than a cadet branch to the family, but even so she could ask for her surname to be added officially to the two surnames her husband already possessed. If he accepted this, any child born to the couple would have at least one first name and the triple surname: Serra-Pintus-Chironi. Urgency was added to this by the fact that Gavino seemed to have no intention whatever of marrying.

These were times of infantile euphoria when many soldiers returned in pieces from the front and many others did not come back at all, either buried far from home or having started families of their own in the north. The north seemed the other end of the world, but it was precisely what they had all been fighting for.

Grief conjugates like a defective verb: it changes radically, yet at the same time remains obstinately the same. Mercede believed she had forded the river to maturity with an inner strength that empowered her to tackle the many reverses allotted to her. But this was not the case; faced with trials beyond her strength she persisted in believing that in the end there must be something else, and pushed back her breaking point. Thus she persuaded herself that the death of Luigi Ippolito was merely the logical conclusion of his silence and absence. She reminded herself that we all die sooner or later and that her son had simply died sooner. It seems impossible, in these circumstances, to describe grief as bringing a form of incredulous immobility. But this is exactly how Mercede explained the death of yet another one of her children to herself.

When Gavino, Marianna and Michele Angelo came home from the funeral ceremony they found Mercede undressed and in bed, sleeping like a child in the middle of the afternoon. So they took off their shoes and whispered to one another so as not to wake her.

That was the first night Gavino became conscious of the emptiness of the bed next to his own. So he decided the moment had come to try and weep. He was disconcerted to find this was more difficult than he had expected, despite the fact that in the cemetery he had had to struggle to control the trembling of his lower lip, forcing himself to maintain a masculine calm despite the fact that everyone round him was in tears. No, it wasn't easy.

So when he saw Luigi Ippolito sitting on his bed it seemed entirely natural to ask him why he had done it.

The other asked: What?

Gavino replied: You know what, you haven't changed, asking things you already know. And the other: Do you remember when you thought you would soon be dead?

Yes, but what has that to do with it?

And do you remember the time you broke off that lizard tail and stuck it in your mouth while it was still moving and everyone thought you'd swallowed the lizard whole? And when Marianna was a baby in her cradle and you said let's sell her to the nougat-makers in exchange for sweets?

Do you remember? It was all a constant repetition of Do you remember? Pain can reappear as powerfully as a memory, complete with smell and taste.

Do you remember pushing a loaf of bread down your trousers to make your bum look bigger? And the time you pushed a button up my nose and Babbo gave you a hell of a hiding? And when we made holes in the sacks on the cart to steal the grain? The things we got up to! And when Mamma ran after us screaming, saying we were thieves and that thieves ended up in prison. Do you remember?

What I remember is the fragrance of fresh laundry and dried figs; and meat being salted, and a pig's ears and snout smelling like rusty iron; and the acidic boiling down of gelatine. And the stench of sheep's wool soaked with rain and cold smoke from the chimneys . . .

Now that his brother was sitting beside him, Gavino felt everything could be explained. What happened to you? he asked. What happened?

And Luigi Ippolito said: It was all too much.

It was too much, do you understand?

Too much.

Do you remember the transparent hope of the sheets of glass? I remember my time like crystal, I really do. And I remember your time like a dagger of light, inside me and beyond me, like a dark brushstroke forming the foundation of the picture. I couldn't cope, really I couldn't! I went away, but above all I abandoned myself. I struck a pose, leaving you to paint me as a still life in real time. Like an object incapable of resisting the embrace of colour, and fighting against the darkness it exposes itself as tactile substantiality. Do you remember? It was a gash of reflections, it was like knowing one had weight and substance. It was a promise. It was like establishing definite points of view, from which one's eyes could see the object of their gaze. This was the fierceness of the painter. This was the substance of memory. Oh . . . Reduced to one single voice, things came together to flow in the course of a time to which we did not allow time. The roaring silence of the life that fills the convex form of a pitcher or jug. The vigilant eye of a predatory nocturnal

animal, the wakeful eye pierced by the printed page. Do you remember?
Everything I have given you is darkness; everything you have given me
is light.

Hearing that great boy sobbing has a terrible effect. Michele Angelo
drives his fists into his temples, then jumps up in bed. He finds
Marianna standing red-eyed in the kitchen. He asks her some
questions to which she barely answers, while the sound of weeping
still comes from the boys' room. He wants to know how long it has
been going on.

"Have you taken him something hot to drink? There's some
broth."

She shakes her head. "I haven't the courage," she explains, "I
can't do it."

Michele Angelo understands her only too well; his son's
weeping is tearing him apart and terrifies him. It frightens him as
much as Mercede's endless sleeping. She has not woken since the
afternoon.

When Michele Angelo goes into Gavino's room with a steaming
cup in his hands, he finds him lying on Luigi Ippolito's bed, shielding his eyes with his arm.

"Have some of this," he says.

Gavino does not move.

"Do you understand now?" he asks his son.

Gavino finally lifts his arm. He has two deep wells in place of
eyes. "What?" he asks.

"Have you understood that to gain anything you always have
to lose something?" Michele Angelo sits down on the bed where

not long before Luigi Ippolito was sitting. The cup is still in his hands.

Gavino raises himself on his elbows.

"Your mother's asleep," Michele Angelo whispers. "You're a good-looking boy, and there's nothing wrong with you. Why don't you decide to start a family of your own?"

Gavino falls back on the mattress with his arms spread like a figure of Christ.

"No need to cry, my son. Every tear . . . Every tear is a victory. He is the winner."

"He? Who are you talking about?" Gavino asks. His voice seems to emerge from the depths of a cavern.

"He, He," Michele Angelo insists. "You haven't eaten anything. Have some broth."

Gavino refuses. "Some things only happen if they happen."

"No, no," Michele Angelo interrupts. "Things like this must happen, or there's no point in anything."

"What do you all want from me?" Gavino says.

Michele Angelo puts the cup down on the bedside table: "For you to save us."

Gavino seizes on this. "Such things have to happen naturally. And this hasn't happened, Babbo. I know what you want to say . . ." He leaves a very long pause; Michele Angelo waits. They remain locked in silence till one of them gives in.

"For you to save us," Michele Angelo says again. "I was sure you would be the one to go and enlist, and I said to your mother: You'll find out, that boy will play a trick on us. That's what we really believed, especially after all your friends had gone . . ." He stops to look his son in the eye. "We were certain you would be the one to go. But no. We really didn't understand it; we thought we had been saved, then your brother said he wanted to go. And went. Him. We couldn't understand it, because you were the one . . ."

"The right one?" Gavino suggests.

"No, no," Michele Angelo insists, waving an arm to reinforce his words. "Don't even begin to think that. What I mean is, we were thinking . . . Oh, how can I say this, your mother and I were sure that if you had been the one to go, you would have come back. But after Luigi Ippolito went, things changed . . . There, we said, we have to save this boy at all costs, even if we must cripple him to do it . . ."

"Cripple me?"

The hint of a smile escapes Michele Angelo. He nods. "Yes, cripple you, if all else failed . . ."

"What do you mean? What might have failed?"

"If the marriage failed." Marianna answers the question, coming into the room.

"These things happen if they're meant to happen," Gavino says without even looking at her.

Marianna points at the cup on the bedside table. "You've drunk nothing and it's gone cold."

Gavino shrugs. Michele Angelo gets up and moves towards the door. "Let's get some sleep," he says. "We need to sleep."

Left together, Marianna and Gavino look at each other in silence. In the dim light the girl sees her brother's face has got thinner. She strokes it, barely touching him. Gavino half closes his eyes as if to say don't stop. A tear slowly begins to run down to the corner of his mouth. She hugs him.

"What did Agnese Desogus tell you?" he asks.

"Nothing, nothing at all," she says.

Gavino looks at her as if he doesn't believe her.

Now I'll tell you what happened.

It was an August afternoon of starch, yeast, dried figs and sour wine. We have reached the time of day that ends the *controra* or siesta, when the gassy breath of soot exhales from the spent fireplace. Through the window, from the courtyard, a lizard-green blade of light falls, swarming with filaments from the medlar tree. The air is full of roast coffee, honey and mustiness, with wasps buzzing, veering and whirling, avoiding the sticky yellow insecticidal spiral, on their way to treasures of amber-scented grapes.

Everything is still to happen.

Agnese circles round me; I'm aware that she is brushing against my neck as she walks behind me, a strange feeling.

What are you doing? What's going on? I ask.

Nothing, she says. And starts circling again.

Next time she passes behind me I stop her hand before she can touch my neck again. She thinks I'm trying to get her to kiss me so she kisses me without giving me time to understand, all I feel is that her lips are too wet. I want to get away, but don't know how. She starts unbuttoning my trousers and manages to pull them down, and I feel her tongue trying to get into my mouth. I can hardly breathe so I give her a push to get her off me. She suddenly stops, then smiles a little as though thinking, then adjusts her blouse which has come open over her breast and without taking her eyes off me goes to the door.

Doing up my trousers, I feel like a man who has escaped a fire precisely because he acted without thinking. And now? Empty, more sad than cheerful, more embarrassed than proud, all I want is to see her leave quickly. Agnese does not seem to feel the same and with tiny movements she continues to fiddle with her blouse over her breast. Now it seems the only thing that has happened in that kitchen fragrant with lamb and cinnamon can only be seen in light of that hasty escape.

Agnese stops smiling and immediately leaves the kitchen.

And that's how it went.

––––––––––

Marianna shrugs, as if to imply: So what? What she actually says is, "What difference does that make?"

Gavino smiles bitterly. "Oh it does, it does, it makes a huge difference. You see . . ."

He is about to say more, but his sister silences him with a finger on his lips. "Leave it to me," she murmurs. "Leave it to me."

That night lasts for several years.

November brides have a sad smile. If you speak to them they barely answer. They sit apart thinking of what they are about to lose. November brides move with the slow agony of autumn, and they respond to the confusion whirling around them with the inertia of imminent sleep. They are preparing for silence.

The whole house seems filled with the muffled warmth of women arranging sweetmeats on trays and carefully measuring coffee into the little cups from the best service, while the men, clean and freshly shaven, chatter in the courtyard. Their early-morning voices warm from the bathtub go with their smart clean shirts and the festive spirit. They smile over glowing *toscano* cigars and a tiny brimming glass of wedding wine balanced between thumb and index finger. A chorus ready to comment, shielding the red eyes of their cigars inside their left hands, careful not to spill a drop of their dark wine.

Inside the house, Mercede, erect as a queen mother, seems more like her old self. Anxious, but controlled. Each detail must be perfect, everything neat and clean. Marianna is waiting in what has always been her room. The men in the courtyard are relatives of the bridegroom; their function to mime the proposal of marriage. They have all said yes and been offered wine. Also in the yard are the bride's close relatives, who must go and fetch the bridegroom together and bring him back to the same courtyard. A ritual of shared complexity, whose coming and going seems somehow to represent the infinite compromises necessary for any marriage to survive. "Compromise" is a word Marianna knows well, as she sits on the bed she had as an unmarried girl and which has now been completely remade with the lace coverlet. But it is she who must perform, since Gavino has no interest whatever in marrying or starting a family.

The previous evening he promised his sister he would not drink, would change his clothes, shave and do all the things nobody ever now expected of him. Least of all Mercede and Michele Angelo, who have been watching him drift away from them, becoming an unreasonable stranger without being able to do anything about it.

"But you must do this for me," Marianna had told him the evening before. "For me," she insisted, "as my wedding present from you."

He nodded, but almost as if the effort might be beyond him. "Why on earth are you marrying that man?" he asked her.

"That man is to be my husband," she said firmly. "Meanwhile, you must promise me not to play any of your—"

"Don't forget, we no longer live in an age when women can be forced into marriage."

"That is exactly what I meant when I asked you to give me a present . . . A special present for me, Gaví. Haven't I always been on your side?"

Gavino had lowered his head. "Alright," he murmured. "Alright, of course. Even if you didn't need to ask."

"On the contrary, Gaví, no-one recognises how you are nowadays." Marianna's sorrowful attitude to him is perhaps the only thing that keeps his feet on the ground now he feels alien to everything. "What's this beast that has made its den inside you, Gaví? Eh?"

How could he explain that? He couldn't. He claimed he didn't know.

But of course he did.

However, the following morning he gets up early and prepares himself with care, dressing in the clean linen that Mercede has laid out on the chair beside his bed. And when he comes into the kitchen life seems back to how it was when Luigi Ippolito was alive and Gavino knew nothing about anything, especially about himself.

His mother sees him come in, as handsome as the sun and thin. She had not noticed him losing weight, how could she if he was never at home, always busy with all those political activities and heaven knows what else? So Mercede studies him carefully, for a long time. Even Michele Angelo, who sees him in the forge every day, hardly recognises this well-groomed and soberly elegant young man. Marianna is in her room, waiting for a hairdresser from Sassari to come.

Mercede makes a cup of hot milk the way Gavino likes it and, beside it, another cup full of pieces of *pane carasau* to dip into the milk. Then just as she is putting the cups on the table it occurs to her to say, "One day you will thank your father and me for everything we've done for you."

Michele Angelo looks at his wife, critical but trying not to show it, since he feels this is not the best thing to say to someone who is forcing himself to accept a situation he clearly disapproves of. Mercede meets Michele Angelo's glare with the haughty self-righteousness of a woman who always defends the logic of what she says and thinks.

Gavino meanwhile crumbles a snow of breadcrumbs onto the skin that has formed on the surface of his milk; he feels nothing and does not want to feel anything. So he does not speak. Though there are certainly things he could say . . .

"There are biscuits for your milk too, if you want them," Mercede says drily.

"It's fine as it is," he answers, trying hard not to seem abrupt. He has made a promise and wants to keep it. In an hour or two the house will be full of people. And he will need a good deal of self-control.

"But what have we done to you? Eh? What have we done to you? You can't think it's been easy for us? Do you think you're the only one who has suffered? Eh?" Mercede bursts out, as if anxious to take advantage of this unique opportunity to speak to her son, now that he is the prisoner of the promise he has made.

"Leave him alone." Michele Angelo tries to intervene.

But she silences him as never before by raising her voice. "No!" she shouts. "What can he be thinking? What indeed?" she goes on, looking at her husband, but, in fact, asking this empty, sterile and weak question of her son.

Marianna comes into the kitchen, still dishevelled, in a dressing-gown. "What's going on?" she asks.

Mercede looks at her. It is as if she has fainted and been brought back to consciousness by a slap.

Gavino buries his spoon in his milk.

Michele Angelo speaks in a parody of a calm voice. "Nothing, nothing's going on. You're getting married; that's all that's happening, isn't it?"

Which was how that Sunday in November began. It could have been worse, because everyone expected heavy rain from the thick clouds just above the summit of Monte Orthobène. The rain held off, thanks to the arrival of a light but capricious wind, which saved the ceremony but certainly not the festoons in the courtyard, which were half blown down before the ceremony even started.

In any case Michele Angelo was spared from adding to the general answer he had given his daughter, because the hairdresser from Sassari arrived immediately afterwards. Despite the fact that she was an outsider and a city woman, she was not much different from her counterparts from Nuoro, just that in Nuoro no-one would normally have spent money on something they could have done for free on their own.

All the same, this business of the hairdresser fetched all the way from Capo di Sopra became the main topic of discussion of the whole Serra-Pintus-Chironi wedding. And the very fact that people were talking about it disturbed Michele Angelo, because he was very conscious of the rule that to survive we must always float on the very surface of the water.

Never be under the water and never above it, just float on it . . . In between, to avoid both envy and pity. Above, on high, is the livid green beast that gulps without digesting. Below, under the surface, is a merry buffoon dressed in mourning, who flatters with one hand while he stabs with the other.

This was certainly nothing to do with "fatalism". More to the point would be "realism", an intimate knowledge of one's own genetics. There are no odds there, only evens. When people say "You are me", they mean "I am you": what you have and what you show are exactly subtracted by you from me. That makes us equal: this is the surface of the water; anything else is an offence, a failure to meet an obligation. If we are not equal, it follows that from time to time I must be either superior or inferior, to be envied or pitied; if I am not equal with you, you will be forced to rise to my level or sink without trace.

It is like walking on red-hot embers; we must walk ever so lightly so as not to burn ourselves, so as not to make a noise or draw attention to ourselves.

It is not given to us to understand whether that city hairdresser signified rising above the surface or sinking beneath it. But she undoubtedly provided a subject for conversation and therefore a distraction from the serenity of the autumn leaves swirled about by the wind and the ferment of public opinion.

In fact, what people were saying was, "Let's see what sort of work this hairdresser from Sassari is capable of. Then we'll find out how they're planning to use their money. You know what happens when people have too much money? They throw it about. And this shows disrespect for God, for those who don't have enough to eat."

Then they pointed out that the groom came from a family with a name but no money, whereas all the bride's family had was money.

So the match was well balanced and it could be argued that all this posing as townsfolk on the part of the Chironi family was merely an attempt to prove themselves worthy of the surname, or rather the surnames, they were buying themselves through this marriage.

Michele Angelo knew this perfectly well, and he had made certain basics quite clear to those that mattered years before in the vineyard. And this was the only reason he felt uneasy.

When the relatives of the bridal couple come into the courtyard for the second time, they find it full of wedding guests. The friends of Biagio Serra-Pintus divide the little crowd like a blackshirt guard of honour; looking as if they have just disembarked at Terranova after the March on Rome (which they describe as having been a high point of enthusiasm and a key moment in the History of Italy). In fact, none of them has been to Rome, or has marched anywhere except perhaps in his own courtyard at home, but the virile plain-speaking of these young men dressed in mourning that is not mourning does have a certain effect.

A few veterans of the battlefields of the Carso dismiss them as like lovers helping themselves to the most alluring features of other men's wives while rejecting the women's less attractive aspects. These soldiers without trenches, these marchers with no road to march on, are an open book. Though none of them are able to explain what they really mean when they talk about the National Fascist Party. We are in the furthest reaches of the Empire; what happens in Sardinia, in Barbagia, is so completely unimportant that there is no point in wasting time talking about it. So all explanation is snuffed out by their triumphalist tone even if no-one knows what that signifies. Perhaps a martial attitude, black shirts, male choruses and aggressively masculine demonstrations have the same effect on the local peasants as pearls and mirrors do on native Africans. It is also whispered in corners of the courtyard that if there are Sardinians in the National Fascist Party, this can only be because someone has made it worth their while . . .

Never mind that Biagio Serra-Pintus does not even know how to pronounce the word "politics"; he will be given a prestigious position – as soon as he is in a position to pay for it.

See him in the midst of his powerful-jawed If etymologically challenged comrades of the avant-garde: he too has a black shirt on under his double-breasted grey jacket.

Gavino stays on the sidelines despite his official position as next-of-kin. He has already entirely understood all this theatrical protruding of chests and rigid straightening of backs. He is making the most of this chaotic phase of the ritual, when the families have to square off over sweetmeats and liqueurs before deciding the order of the procession to the church, where they will divide. Mercede, simple and beautiful as the mother of the bride must be, keeps an eye on Gavino from a distance, this son who is both a pain and a delight.

Finally the bride appears, elegant and stunningly beautiful. Her hair coils like a twisted mass of shining snakes round her head. She is like Artemis ready for the hunt. A simple veil held in place by two pins hides her face down to the chin. Her white dress, delicately tinged with gold, hangs straight on her small body without accentuating her silhouette, like a home-made stage costume from Olympus. On closer inspection, however, it is obvious that the dress is covered with a constellation of pearls. And over it, this November bride will wear a mantle with a collar of bleached astrakhan.

The women draw in their breath and, as if by reflex, adjust anything out of place on their own traditional or bourgeois dresses.

With the procession falling into line and everyone ready to head to the church, Gavino waits for the last guest to leave before he moves.

The expected rain arrives the next day, by which time the married couple have already been on the steamer to Livorno for several hours, on their way to their honeymoon in Florence and Venice.

The emptiness that takes over a house after a ceremony, any kind of ceremony, brings a combination of relief and sadness. Mercede, Michele Angelo and Gavino sit in silence in the kitchen eating scraps. No-one has done any cooking, nor will they for the next three days, and many of the leftovers have been given to the parish for the poor.

The wedding and their new relatives have brought benefits to the Chironi family, because it seems Rome has major projects for this outpost; and land near their home is already being urgently expropriated for the construction of large public buildings. Yes, dear friends, the place is looking forward to gaining official status as a city. And, the rooting out of brigandage everywhere has finally removed what was until now an obstacle to progress. For the Chironi master blacksmiths, and from now on for the Serra-Pintus too, there will be no shortage of work.

Via Majore has been renamed corso Garibaldi. Like the bed of a dried-up river, it is a chain that links two apparently diverse entities. The road that used to unite Nur to Nuoro, now, higher up, on the first part of the ridge, has begun to be divided into plots and building sites. The great mule-track winding directly from the prison almost as far as Séuna will become a new artery named after Attilio Deffenu, a young hero dear to the gods. Along this line, as a flood of directives from the new regime about roads and politics makes abundantly clear, the nerve-centres of the Fascist city are set to develop in the form of public buildings and residential apartment blocks. Meanwhile at Ponte di Ferro, where the new city meets the old, a massive Palace of Labour has been erected. In what is now a city in reality no less than in name, complete with Prefettura and provincial headquarters, there will be a need for labourers, but for railings and balconies as well.

It is a time for architecture, of a kind that knows that to keep up with the latest trends you must have style. Like Marianna's wedding dress which at first sight did not seem much, but was completely in tune with continental fashion. In the same way, springing up like a mushroom where a vineyard used to be, there is now an Office of Finances – in a place where "office" and "finances" are both utterly alien words. This makes it essential to upgrade the second-rate via La Marmora, which until then had been the entrance to the city on the Ogliastra side. As it is a continuation of the corso, and parallel to the ultramodern via Deffenu, it has to lead to the new narrow-gauge railway station. The diesel-powered railcar arrives, like a horse-drawn coach, at the Macomer junction. An occasional real train also passes. It moves more slowly than time itself which, conversely, is now rushing by.

After four years of marriage, in the Fifth Year of the Fascist Era, a new Mercede is born to Biagio and Marianna, though everyone calls her Dina to distinguish her from her grandmother.

The Serra-Pintus-Chironi family lives in the new district in a villa with a garden fit for a mafia boss. Gavino has never set foot in the house, not a fact to distress Biagio, to whom his brother-in-law is like a clause in small print at the end of the marriage contract: one of those obscure factors that have to be accepted with Christian resignation. Biagio's comrades have been ordered not to touch him, because in any case the fool, the Chironi family draft dodger, can at worst only harm himself. When signals relating to his brother-in-law reach Biagio – flyposting, talk of defeatism, some unauthorised public gathering – he raises his eyes to the sky and slides the document into the bottom drawer of his desk. Occasionally, faced with an awkward situation, he will speak to his wife at home and ask her to have a word with her unfortunate brother, who is only safe from trouble thanks to the respect Biagio commands among his comrades.

The fact is that Biagio hopes to be transferred as soon as possible to Cagliari as a member of the prefect's personal staff. Once there it would be a very different matter, far from this hole that no-one apart from Mussolini himself wants to turn into a city.

Marianna seldom returns to her parents' home because she is too busy and because her new status as a lady forces her, whether she likes it or not, to make certain sacrifices. If Mercede wants to see her little granddaughter, she must start at dawn as if going to early Mass and enter the house via the kitchen.

Now that History is dealing the cards anew, it has begun to occur to the Serra-Pintus family that it is just possible that accepting this hasty alliance with the Chironi – thoroughly decent simple people, no question – may indeed have rescued them economically, but it has contaminated their blood. Marianna, the rich and modest wife, has become someone to keep a close eye on. Especially now that Biagio is in the good graces of the federal government, and that the possibility of a prestigious transfer to Cagliari is growing ever more likely. Bosses can never be less than bosses even when there is not much to be boss over, because they are brought up to believe, generation after generation, that everything is owed to them. Biagio, as far as it goes, is undoubtedly fond of his wife, but has not the character to stand up to his mother, who remains in charge despite everything, and even if the money at her disposal is not her own. So Mercede, who knows her place, only calls on her daughter and granddaughter at times when she will not be noticed. And occasionally, in the early afternoon and if the weather is good, Marianna almost surreptitiously takes the little girl to see her grandparents at San Pietro.

Knowing his daughter is a hostage does not help Michele Angelo sleep soundly. So one day, washed and cleaned, he decides to call on his son-in-law at his office at the Fascist headquarters. He plans to

179

point out that being ashamed of one's relatives is not a good idea at all.

Biagio receives him affectionately, with an expression on his face as if to say, You're absolutely right, but he stops short of admitting any such thing. He does, of course, understand, but Michele Angelo for his part must also understand that Biagio has an important job and a name to keep up.

Michele Angelo, invited repeatedly to take a seat, obstinately remains standing: "Our ancestor came to this part of the world in the retinue of the Archbishop of Galtellí... At a time when you had not even been thought of, we the Quiròn, Kirone and Chironi family, were already here."

Biagio has put on weight in the last few years, evidence that, even with all the new fitness propaganda, he has not been taking as much care of his body as he could. Michele Angelo, standing there with his whitening hair, looks like a Church elder having just pronounced an anathema. He informs Biagio that the Serra-Pintus family are just recent arrivals and so have nothing to make a fuss about, and that the only reason for their double-barrelled name is because if you say just Serra or Pintus no-one has any idea who you are talking about, whereas in Nuoro if you say Chironi everyone knows you mean Michele Angelo Chironi, master blacksmith.

An extremely long silence follows. Biagio is conscious of a mixture of surprise and fear. His red face turns white; he seems about to roar with laughter, but it is just nerves. "We each have our sacraments," he says, "and I believe you also understand things that you claim not to understand. Even if your family were here first things have since changed, and I didn't make up the rules."

They take leave of one another for the last time. Michele Angelo and Biagio will never meet again.

That night Gavino is dragged home by two men who dump him at the entrance to the courtyard, more dead than alive.

As he leaves Gavino's room, Doctor Romagna recovers his composure. To do his job properly he has rolled his shirtsleeves above his elbows, but as he closes the door behind him he pulls them down again to cover his hairy forearms.

Michele Angelo stands before him in silence, because he knows that when his friend the doctor speaks, his words matter. In fact he says, "The boy's been badly beaten up. What's he been playing at?"

Michele Angelo shakes his head.

"I suppose he has been mixing with bad company . . ." the doctor says. "Whoever beat him up knew what they were doing. These are times when we have to close our ears and wait till people walk past." Michele Angelo nods in agreement. "But he's a tough lad, this boy of yours. In fact, Chirò, you have relatives who count for something . . ."

"Influential connections," Michele Angelo specifies. And this says everything.

"But at least you know where you can turn, lots of unfortunate people can't even do that."

There is a short but pregnant silence.

"Doctor, what have they done to him?"

The doctor finishes adjusting his shirt before answering. "Let's sit down a minute," he says. "Have you got a strong drink?"

No, he certainly hadn't expected anything like that. How can you even imagine such things? Nothing of the kind had entered his head, because Michele Angelo could not even conceive of a Universe where such things as the doctor was describing could happen. And while the doctor is saying "tied up, beaten and abused", Mercede walks round and round the kitchen table like a madwoman in an asylum, unable to keep still, driven insane by understanding yet at the same time not understanding. She is on the edge of a precipice of foreboding and has no idea how to face it. The doctor's words carry heavier and more terrible implications than she would be able at present to grasp, even if she were brave enough to stand on the edge of the cliff. Gavino himself is no help. He does not speak.

Michele Angelo indicates she should settle down because if she goes on walking round and round he cannot properly take in what the doctor is trying to say. But there is little to take in. It is a very ugly story, his son's injuries and lacerations leave no room for doubt. Dr Romagna is saying that he has watched the Chironi children grow over the years and thank God there has never previously been much need for his professional skills because they have always been so healthy, but now he does not feel up to telling the whole truth, at least not in plain words.

Mercede, who is in no sense a fool, has been forced to see things she would much rather not have had to see: Gavino's blood-soaked trousers and linen, which she has always washed with soda and ironed with a charcoal-heated iron. Now she looks at her husband and asks him to stop asking whether they have heard the worst yet, because in any case the unimaginable has happened, like a fear hovering outside the home for years and which one fine morning has come to knock on the door.

Now it seems that the moment has come when she must make a decision: either to accept once and for all that she is in the wrong, or to start on a careful analysis of the signs over time. Because if the facts, the little tiny indications, fit together, all this unexpected disorder, this unforeseen shock, will fall into place. But once you start arranging signs in order there is no going back.

Gavino, in his room, has the strained expression of a dying man, but is not about to die. He has lost a lot of blood. He is dreaming of a time when he was unconscious of his own body, almost as though it were a sort of secondary appendix. A time when he believed his happiness depended on how much of the surrounding world he could manage to watch. It was in those days, like a message floating in a bottle on an ocean, that the realisation reached him that he was attracted to other men. But see how subtle and cunning the stratagems of thought can be: as a child Gavino understood something he was not yet living, but as an adult he is now living something he does not understand. Personal salvation depends exclusively on never letting the two coincide. When one shouts out, the other keeps silent.

So, abuse it is. That word that scares Mercede so much.

Gavino remembers the first time well, but he later told himself firmly that one should not wish for pardon for having followed one's nature.

That first time was a miraculous morning with a sky of enamel just crossed by the fragrance of the north wind, the *tramontana*. And he, the other man, was a perfect adult, both attainable and unattainable. The man had since died in the war, had never come home, had become food for worms. At the time, though, he had the most beautiful smile it was possible for a man to have. And a combined scent of rain and tobacco, of work at the sheepfold, and of an attentive mother who knew how to wash shirts.

That first time he had not even taken his clothes off nor expected Gavino to do so; they embraced like two interdependent bodies. It was then that Gavino had learned that the adult body is solid where the adolescent body is soft. And that no matter how much what goes before might seem infinite, what comes afterwards is hurried; that no matter how much the before might seem well-directed and precise, the afterwards is always oblique and full of hints. A fullness containing an emptiness.

So, at sixteen, Gavino had learned only too well where his flesh would take him: in height and in depth, in euphoria and in depression, in plentifulness and in frugality.

———

In her headlong flight Mercede understands that if she does not stop, in every sense, despair will gain the upper hand in her, especially now that the signs, ignored for so many years, are accumulating in her head. The times he came home late and had not gone to school, and those older boys he spent his time with, and . . .

A few steps away from her, Michele Angelo too is beginning to understand something that, battering away like the skull of a ram, is beginning to break through the extremely solid defences of his wilful blindness.

"It's an illness, Chirò," the doctor persists in explaining as if to make the concept more palatable to that brain so eager to reject it. "Gavino has ended up in the hands of some pederast, Chirò, heaven knows how long it has been going on." Dr Romagna lowers his voice a little to articulate the individual sounds of the word "pederast", as if to rescue it from the list of words that sound more terrifying than their meaning.

"But he isn't a child, doctor . . ." is all Michele Angelo manages to mumble.

But in any case, he is not about to give in; he cannot even visualise that terrible word, with its derivation from ancient Greek and its vaguely amorous significance. But now that it has been spoken, it must be accepted.

The light in the room has grown weak, like when a candle burns down and you only become aware of darkness at the moment when the wick finally goes out, and little by little the colours fade. This diffused pallor corresponds exactly to the state of bloodless stupor that is making Michele Angelo tremble. The man beside him in the room is one with whom he has spent hours, even days of his life. A man into whose eyes he has peered deeply. He has seen him sweat, do backbreaking work. He has watched him grow up, his face change, his jaw grow dark. And now? Now he knows, without a shadow of doubt, that what he had thought an open book was in fact an armour-plated strongbox. The pain of having been deceived is tempered only by the knowledge that Gavino's secret was not one it would have given him any pleasure to share. And in fact, now, as the doctor explains, while at the same time trying to skate over the details, he is not in the least curious to know, even if he realises he must show some interest not to challenge what the doctor would expect of a father.

For her part, Mercede has discovered her own solution: that the being she brought into the world must be faultless. Let them not claim he had it coming to him. He was assaulted by criminals who deliberately set out to hurt him: that is what happened. For her, Gavino is a Christian martyr, a defenceless soul, a lily. Though even now that she has understood the way things are, she does not dare enter the room where he is lying in a sedated sleep.

He has lost a lot of blood and runs the risk of internal haemorrhage, but has survived. That's the fact of the matter; you cannot tell a mother more than that.

"Be careful what you tell your wife, Chirò," the doctor sums up before going. "Speaking as your brother, I advise you to err on the vague side; these things are better not explained to mothers . . . Apart from that, he will recover. But don't let him make sudden movements. Keep him in bed, and I'll keep a check on him . . ."

"Yes, doctor . . ." Michele Angelo says, not fully in control of his words. "Please . . ." he begins, but stops.

The doctor feigns indignation. "Don't even mention it, Chirò," he says, thumping his own chest. "Say no more and I'll do the same."

Michele Angelo, crushed, bows his head.

They tell Marianna that Gavino has been unwell. And that while she is still breast-feeding she should not even come to see him because sick people by causing pain and anxiety can make a mother's milk bitter. So she stays away, in obedient suffering, and almost feels as if she is back in the days of the trousseau when, relegated to a sort of limbo of embroidery with the cloistered nuns, she had even thought she might never emerge from it again.

But eventually she did emerge and now has to concentrate on her child, who must always come first. Even Gavino obviously now comes second.

Though hardly conscious of the fact, Marianna knows her family has entered the terrible period when debts must be paid back.

Marianna repeats to herself the words of the mother prioress, to the effect that we are all workers on the land, and must give back to our Lord and Master some of what we have been allowed to cultivate and reap. And that He is good but also relentless, generous in giving but also unrelenting in exacting repayment. Like a tax-collector. It is easy for us to understand our own suffering when we remember that others have done wrong to us, but do we ever think how God must suffer when He is placed in the terrible position of being implacable with his children?

All she knew of Gavino was what her husband told her as a warning: "Things have now reached a point where, you must understand, we should keep a certain distance . . . We have a reputation to protect, we are of a certain rank, and we have a daughter."

Michele Angelo and Mercede told Marianna hardly more than that, just that Gavino was slowly getting better.

The rumour in Nuoro was that he had been taught a lesson for political reasons, and in any case everyone knew that he had never in any sense embraced the ideals of Mussolini. But spreading this rumour was the only act of affection Biagio Serra-Pintus carried out for his wife, and perhaps not even that . . . In any case, and with their transfer to Cagliari imminent, Marianna preferred to assume this was the case, and in the evening at dinner she pretended to be cross with him for not having kept his promise to protect her brother from the gangs. For his part, Biagio pretended to accept this fiction, the kind of compromise necessary if any marriage is to last.

The sky is dripping thick blood from violet clouds. A terrible alloy of Nothing and Everything . . . Like our consciousness that roams among things too explicitly stated until the result is nothing but silence. All the things we would like to hear people say to us but no-one ever does say.

In the silence of the rooms there are gods hampered by their vestments. He is a tired old man, like a father forced to punish his children. His very thin body is held together by a fevered set of bones, his shoulders bowed beneath the weight of the papal tiara. All round, angels display the symbols of supreme martyrdom.

A subdued pain that cannot be described.

Memory is an extremely thin and unspoken thread. Each mute memory is a figure from the Apocalypse. Which dazzles and screams.

Section deleted.

But this dazzling image of an Apocalypse is in itself a contradiction, it is narcissism on the part of its inventor and of its interpreters, St John the Divine who wrote it down and all the artists who have since portrayed it. Each in his own image. John absorbing words in a perpetual fever, the artists setting down sign after sign with the minute exactitude of nightmare. John certainly cannot have imagined wondrous robes or the virtuosity of the chisel. But a painter can only interpret the Apocalypse in terms of himself. How can you describe the silence of neglected memory? With silence or with signs? The painters responded

191

by depicting angelic butchers showing off the perfection of their vest-
ments, while their victims mimed a terror never expressed in words. The
saints responded with silence when asked to recant. Some with theatrical
amazement, others with the machine-like wisdom of persuasion.

Section deleted.

Yet in John's text, I imagine the Apocalypse shot through with Levant-
ine warmth, stained with desert sand and smelling of sweat. I imagine
it like a line of reconstituted bodies in a hangar or on the forecourt of
a station . . . I see angels exhausted from killing, streaming with per-
spiration and fighting for breath. I imagine them struck dumb and
dressed in uniform, incapable of ever speaking again. And I can also
hear the terrible lamentations of mutilated souls.

Section deleted.

But not here. What we have here is a struggle between straight lines
and curves. The direct route of Good against the massive contortions of
Evil. The signs are the soul of a painter almost tempted by order, by an
urge to conquer the calm of the icon. Yet in that foaming north-east sky
a vibrant storm is raging, with white wings flashing and candelabra
flames blazing. Then silences, terrible silences, often dressed in horrify-
ing revelations.

The numbers are seven, twelve, three and four. The infinite cabbala
of returns. How many tribes are there, how many horsemen? Twelve,
which is three times four. Four: war, famine, death and pestilence. And
how many candelabra? Seven, which is three plus four. And the precise
number of the sealed? One hundred and forty-four thousand: twelve
thousand times twelve. Then seven trumpets and seven seals, the seven
heads of the monster. And seven stars in the open palm of God's hand,
white with the terrible whiteness of the Just.

Gavino, wrapped in his shroud, is pretending to sleep. Aware of noises and muted smells.

Opening his eyes is as exhausting as trying to sit up. And, in fact, he fails, at least at the first attempt. The pain in his legs and back is terrible. But he tries again and again.

A permanent penumbra has overtaken the room with its half-closed shutters, so it is difficult to tell whether the light outside is from a sliver of moon or some other source. It could be a quiet afternoon, or the dense silence of the last sleep before dawn. Perhaps it simply does not exist at all, so that Gavino's attempt to sit up is nothing more than a dreaming about himself in the deep heart of the night. Whether in drug-induced sleep or half awake, he gropes his way towards consciousness of himself as if raising his arms to feel his way blindfolded down a corridor. He does not want to remember what has happened to him. Yet, unable to do anything about it, he does remember. He remembers everything.

He remembers the gaze of the unknown young man leaning on the bar in the tavern like a rope thrown to a drowning man, and how welcoming the smile was that opened behind that gaze. And how his heart began beating fit to explode. All this he remembers. And the thoughts that flashed through his mind at that precise moment, when he asked himself what others would have felt if they had been able to understand the amorous communication between those two bodies and the looks and gestures of that precise instant, as the two stood before the landlord who was busy filling a line of glasses to the brim with wine. The unknown man gave off a good aura, a secretive but subtle smile full of zest, and brown eyes like hard stones. He did not drop his eyes until Gavino lowered his first.

Yet that instant lasted a whole geological era, passing from ice age to cosmic spring when warm breath fertilised cells and melted glaciers, and the water flowing into the ocean beds carried a broth of teeming life as species fought to survive over others. It lasted no longer than the single instant God needed to separate dark from light and the beasts of the sky from the beasts of land and water. In the same way that look and that hint divided life and death in the fraction of a second for Gavino. Just as had happened to Luigi Ippolito when, between one state of unconsciousness and another, buried in his madness, he had succeeded in grasping the instant of lucidity that led him to kill himself. It was just the same, though the other way round, when exchanging glances with this unknown man. Gavino grasped an instant of madness after so many years of prudent make-believe. He had never before put more faith in his body than in his head. He left that musty tavern knowing he had exposed himself more than he should, and he was afraid. As he crossed the threshold, just as he had hoped and prayed, he heard the unknown man walking behind him, gliding along as if hardly touching the ground. So instead of going home he headed through the fragrant night to the limit of the built-up area, where the countryside opens up and the dry grass crackles with every step.

Luigi Ippolito's dead body is heavy enough to weigh down the corner of the mattress. When Gavino sees him he waves his hand.

I thought I was dreaming, he murmurs. But here you are.

I'm here, the other confirms. Did I ever tell you how I came to decide what had to be decided?

He waits for an answer. Gavino hesitates, then shakes his head.

That afternoon we had just cleared out a bakery when a young-ster in uniform fired from the platoon at a child covered with flour. I was responsible for that platoon. And all those people who had raided the bakery were ghosts. They would have died anyway, so risking their own lives to defend their loot made sense. We took up positions outside the bakery and they came out in silence, pale and white with flour like dusty corpses. We ordered them to drop what they had stolen and put their hands up in the air, but no-one moved or spoke. The children in front were clutching loaves of bread like favourite toys. Behind them were women driven mad by hunger, homeless in the dead city we claimed we had liberated. And behind them in the river were the swollen corpses of soldiers who had died in the mountains and who had been swallowed into gorges, sucked into the currents and snared by the teeth of glaciers, regardless of what uniform they were wearing. The air was heavy with the stench of decay, all humanity a sewer open to the sky. And my head began to realise I had come all the way to this place at the end of the world to tear bread from the arms of these children. "Stop, stand still, all of you!" I shouted. But who was I addressing, since no-one was moving? It seemed they had used the last of their strength to break open the flimsy bakery door and hurl themselves on the piles of freshly baked bread. The fragrance of fresh bread from inside the shop was competing with the stench of death. A war against war. And it was there, during this wait so long in the telling but barely lasting the moment of a glance, that it all happened: a child opened his mouth to shout and stones and insults rained down from the windows of the houses. A caporale, himself almost a boy, fired. The bullet passed through the bread and entered the flesh of a child, a ghost . . .

Luigi Ippolito is weeping without tears and Gavino reaches out his hand to touch him; bitter grief welling over from his own pain. You and me, you and me, he says. But his brother shakes his head, and explains to him that that quick glance, possibly misunderstood, possibly deceptive, the one that lost him, was perhaps the obstacle that made him realise that the invincible hero he thought he was had been defeated, and nothing can be judged until you have been defeated.

He talks about himself:

When the autumn weather is hazy the body can flow from a soul of glass. And it is certainly possible to see the flame that originates in water, like watching a death in flight by drowning.

Oh, during the solemn winters, bodies have little meaning, no more than thoughts which have been stubbornly thought through and lands left behind when ships set sail . . . It is possible not to know why . . .

All that's left, dear brother, my own flesh, dear soul, blood of my blood, is the torment; but it is an unconscious torment since it seems impossible for one to be deracinated, pulled up by the roots like a weed, carried off in flight as if weightless, an uncertain entity against the heavy weight of certainty . . . Certainty does exist, oh yes, the certainty that all this can happen . . .

Then there are the words, like geographical names one does not know how to pronounce, and springtimes of the year we know we shall never see again, but that our earliest ancestors described to their children who described them to those who came after: enormous flowers picked in distant lands and pressed between the pages of a book, great fertile flowers of thought, unlike the small pansies and wallflowers that are starved of light here, and unlike the ones Mamma grows in the courtyard or the ones that seed themselves in our cemetery.

At this point Gavino tries to speak.

No, listen to me: out there, beyond the horizon, drunk on light: lemons explode, prickly pears ripen, oleanders are clothed in finery; and with these, grown during those ecstatic summers, we sustain our smiles, welcoming them like a formula reserved, with the choreography of their origins, for the children of our children.

Gavino leans forward, but Luigi Ippolito lifts a finger to stop him again.

Listen: after we left we greeted the sea, the hills and the summits of unknown mountains. And the distant horizon of the plain.

Then we stepped into the Theatre of War, the field of battle, which was nonetheless more peaceful than what we had carried inside ourselves. Poor, forlorn, seeing ourselves as prisoners of Destiny . . . and as sad as if that was what we really were.

We recited the seasons like beads on a rosary: Ave Maria *and* Our Father *and* Gloria *and* Peace. *Peace on earth. Listen: peace on earth! Now softly I say goodbye.*

For as long as the season of love lasts . . .

*

Gavino studies his dead brother and notices there is not a scratch on him. His body is unmarked, so pale that it seems to generate a light of its own. While he was speaking he had been moving his bony hands, a lock of hair falling gently over his brow each time he bent his head. Now Luigi Ippolito has finished, and Gavino feels the silence between them is growing unbearable. His brother looks round the room as if searching for something unfamiliar. But nothing has changed. The same smell, even the same light. Gavino clears his throat.

How does the story end? he asks.

Luigi Ippolito takes his time. It ends with Quiròn in danger . . .

Well, the Inquisitor's faithful assistants are not very happy that such humiliation has been inflicted on Diego de Gamiz, and they plan further revenge. But Don Giovanni de Quiròn is not concerned with that. He is in the midst of a war and doesn't even know it, doesn't even want to know. His destiny is in all respects linked to the Royal Treasury. He has taken an oath, kissed the floor of the apse of San Tomè and entrusted himself to the Infallible Lord. Now they advise him to go into hiding, and that it is best not to provoke the Holy Office too far. They tell him that Don Angelo Jagaracho, at his own request, is already leaving for the Indies. In this particular war even doing one's duty, even honouring one's own word as one would honour a banner or standard, is considered an act of insolence. You have won, they tell him, the King has received satisfaction, the Holy Office will not stand by and watch. You see, dear brother, it always ends like this. I understood something in this war when it became clear to me that no matter what happened no-one would win. You panic, you try to understand the incomprehensible. And I believe this is what happened to Don Giovanni de Quiròn. Because he too asked himself how his life could possibly be in danger now that he had done his duty. I don't know if those were his exact thoughts, but I can state definitely that they were mine: We've won, they told me. But if we had won, how was it possible that I felt defeated? When they transferred me to the firing squads these questions became overwhelming no matter what anyone might say. Because, quite simply, there were no possible answers. I desperately needed to find a reason, I was begging for one. When it came to my third execution I knew that the truth I upheld could not stand it any longer. Just as with Quiròn when he understood that to run away and hide, as everyone advised him to do, would mean going against his own nature. So he did the opposite: he made a great show of himself and paraded around. One night he realised he was being followed, but carried on his way without turning round. The chief treasury official sent for him the following morning and explained that *force majeure* compelled him to recommend an immediate transfer. You do understand, don't you? You know how things are . . . Sometimes opposing powers pretend to be enemies and indulge in a bit of play-acting, but in the end they always come to an agreement.

When Capitano Sermonti came to find me he pretended I looked alright, but it was clear to me that something in my appearance must have disturbed him. He just said, "Tenente." Nothing more.

Then he sat down, and after a pause told me that for my own good I must be admitted to hospital for a while. So I told him that in just the same way, my ancestor Don Giovanni de Quiròn had been advised to return to Spain, but had begged instead for a job in the remote interior of Sardinia, which was inhabited by savages and where they would call him Kirone . . . and where he might face even greater dangers than the ones they were trying to save him from. I added that I realised he was offering me an escape and that this was not something I could accept. I asked to be sent to the front line, into danger, like Quiròn.

The capitano shook his head, a signal for two men dressed in white to enter the room. I backed away: "May everyone present be witness to the fact that I have stated my decision not to accompany the envoys of the Viceroy and that I refuse to leave this Hall unless forced to do so." Having stated that I began taking off my clothes.

"What are you doing, tenente? Our orders are to transfer you; and as far as your health is concerned, there will be doctors to pronounce on that!"

The nurses hesitated, understandably enough. After all, I was naked and must have suddenly seemed untouchable. "I refuse to come with you," I said.

"That's how the story ends, brother. The rest was just a matter of finding the right moment."

Mercede, eavesdropping at the half-open door, hears Gavino praying in his delirium, and lifts her eyes to heaven.

Michele Angelo works on but still has an ugly sense of foreboding. No-one could ever accuse him of being in a good mood. He cannot believe that this son so nearly murdered could be the same child that he fathered.

He is squaring up an iron bar to be inserted with twenty-four others like it to form a banister. From his point of view, the fact that he has not beaten all these bars in an identical way does not affect the fact that eventually, lined up and fixed into the stairs, they will all look the same: all that is needed is the skill to make different objects seem identical. In the same way he is confident that he has worked out a solution for his suffering son. He is not sure what he feels, but discipline is something he has some experience of. As soon as the boy is back on his feet, I'll take charge, he tells himself. And he begins to plan what to say: "What's past is past" will do as a start.

"What's past is past. You made a mistake. Alright. Now let's start again, and remember, my son, the only incurable illness is death. At present everything must seem confused to you, but that's not how it is at all. Believe me. Believe the words of your father, who loves you."

He imagines it might be a good idea to hug the boy while he says this. And just as he knows that iron bars can be bent to make a railing, he believes he will be able to overcome Gavino's stubborn silence in the same way. He will manage.

Mercede still has her ear to the door. Gavino is talking in his sleep; she could clearly hear earlier that he was praying. Now he is talking to someone in a language she cannot understand, but he has done this ever since he was a child. Mercede feels she can say now that his life has been a *Via Crucis*, a Way of the Cross. She watches life fading from objects in the pale afternoon light, as it neutralises colours and blurs contours.

Yet she has no idea of the great number of happy moments that have been lived in that house, or of how much despair her family has been spared during this terrible period.

And how much laughter there has certainly been. It is possible that laughter is less interesting in the telling than weeping, because we tend to be more moved by passion lurking in misfortune, but there has been a lot of laughter, there can be no doubt of that. It would be a discourtesy to God to say that happiness has never entered the master blacksmith's home.

Like the time Luigi Ippolito and Gavino decided to show Mercede the sea. How that came about cannot yet be told, because there are no words for it, no words at all.

Now Mercede is moved to the point of tears. She escapes to the kitchen with her eyes shining and her lips moving of their own accord and collapses into a chair.

Because, you see, she has only just admitted as she thanks heaven, that her life has not lacked happiness, together with all the pain, yet she weeps. That is always the way it goes.

So she jumps to her feet and pulls herself together as if someone is watching her, but there is no-one there. She decides her son must eat something. She pours some vegetable soup into a bowl, grabs a spoon and hurries to his room.

The liquid diet Gavino has been living on has caused his body to wither away. He cannot have any solid food until his stitches have healed. So they have been feeding him on meat broth, honey and hot water, semolina and vegetable soup. For several days now he has been able to sit up, but it is not his physical condition that worries them; he is remarkably strong. But the expression on his face frightens them.

Inside himself, he has come to a decision. Worse than dying.

"I was thinking about the time you two took me to the sea," Mercede says as she feeds him. He barely moves his lips to admit he remembers. "I was so terrified," she goes on. "So terrified. Who could have imagined anything so big, and such a smell . . . Eh?" Gavino looks at her with what seems to be tenderness. "Do you remember how I didn't even want to come? But your brother arranged for Pani to take us down to Orosei in his coach. Do you remember?"

Do you remember? It was all a constant repeating. Do you remember?

"I'm leaving. As soon as I'm back on my feet, I'm leaving," Gavino announces. The first thing he has said for weeks, perhaps that is why it comes as such a shock to Mercede.

"What about us?" is all she says. Gavino seems to have nothing more to add. She stops dead, spoon in mid-air.

*

That very night Mercede dreamed it was snowing. Big round flakes. Her children were all still little: Pietro, Paolo, the stillborn Giovanni Maria and Franceschina, Luigi Ippolito, Marianna and Gavino. All together, like the litter of a wild boar.

In dreams she can predict things she is unable to see directly. A characteristic of dreaming is to be able to look down on things from high places, such as the top of a bell tower, or the head of a hawk. Thus her dream in every sense replaced her usual limited vision with another, more precise vision. For example, it made it possible for her to watch each individual snowflake joining the billions and billions of other snowflakes and deceive herself into believing that she was not counting them, whereas in fact she was, because in a shower of snow every single flake matters. And at the same time she was able to watch her children, including those who had never been born, playing in front of a lighted fire as if that was how they had always been, but this time she was able to get her own back and get into the house. There, lit up and warmed by the flames, the children were laughing, boys and girls, living and dead, chasing each other without coming to any harm. Now, for example, she was able to see each snowflake, the children, and beyond the mountain good weather coming towards them, because the snow-storm was nothing more than winter resisting the approach of warm weather.

And she dreamed the flames of the fire were of a colour that did not exist in nature or at least that she did not know. Exactly like her first sight of the sea when, though prepared for blue, she had not been aware that such a blue as that could exist. This was the wonder that she dreamed. Her response to the imminent disappearance of yet another child. Just when, overtaken by misfortune, he had been restored to her loving care.

"What about us?" Mercede says, spoon in mid-air.

"Don't say anything to Babbo," Gavino begs, but without insisting, as if he expects nothing from her, not even confirmation that she has heard him. "It's you I'm telling."

"My child," she sighs. "My child. What choice do we have except to give birth to you and love you?" She moves her shoulders and suddenly seems to have become a little girl herself.

Gavino clenches his jaw and eyebrows in a huge effort not to weep. By a miracle he achieves it, but stays on the edge of tears. "He was beautiful," he says, knowing that if he does not say it now he never will. "And I told myself: He is too beautiful for me. I looked at him and he looked at me, then I went out and heard him behind me." Mercede, who has understood now, lowers her head and puts down the spoon. She starts to stand up, but he holds her back and raises his voice: "We walked in the dark . . ."

"No," she implores him, "no," trying once more to get to her feet.

As Gavino holds her down, her plate, soup and spoon fall to the floor. "Let's see how much you can both love me now," he hisses. His arms are surprisingly strong. "It was me who sought him out; and when he started hitting me, and when his friends came up and told me what I was, and I fell to the ground, I felt no pain, only relief, and I said to them: Kill me."

"Kill me."

But they said, "Killing's too good for you."

Exactly four years have passed since the day Gavino left. Four years during which Dina has grown bigger, Mercede and Michele Angelo have aged, and Marianna has been living the life of a lady in Cagliari.

The forge has been enlarged after months of construction work. Michele Angelo employs three young men from the area. Sons of the forge like the Cyclopes of Vulcan. He takes life a little more easily now, knowing how to make his apprentices work. Gavino's place has not been filled: no-one dares go near his anvil. It has been a time of building and inaugurations. The new Fascist province of Nuoro is like a malleable substance ready for the layout of new buildings, including the main Post Office behind the Royal Institute of Teachers. It dominates the crossroads between the former via Majore and the brand-new via Deffenu where scaffolding has just been removed from the dazzling new Palace of Civil Engineering complete with balconies.

Work has been done to develop the area in front of the Salotti fountain just below the summit of Monte Orthobène into a recreation spot for the summer. Here, barefoot like pilgrims, local urchins climb the rocks roped together in small groups. All in the name of a new belief in fitness: healthy food, fresh air, the elimination of rickets, and sunbathing. Beyond the ocean Mr Kellogg has just invented Rice Krispies. Youth leaders, bilingual in Italian and Sardinian, egg the smaller children on to climb to the summit. In the central grassy area two teams of small boys, whose slender chests indicate a need for tonics, compete in a tug-of-war. In the background are girls who have been excluded for biological reasons from tests of strength, along with older boys whose only experience of healthy exercise and the agonies of performance has been *strumpa*, the traditional Sardinian form of wrestling, whether with humans or animals. In the middle stands a curly-haired young trainer with his hands on his hips.

It is an age of dispensaries and fortifying tonics, of public health, daily personal hygiene, universal education and school canteens. Many young boys and a handful of young girls will sit down at a long shared table to eat healthy food – mineral salts against cretinism, citric acid against scurvy, football and sun against rickets.

One is struck by a precocious and immediate general acceptance of anything modern, without the least sign of resistance. In addition to the bricks-and-mortar buildings that function as dormitories, there is also an outdoor dormitory in the form of a large tent in the Anglo-Saxon boy-scout style. Stripped and shorn, the needy little beneficiaries are ready to be classified by height, weight, condition of teeth and chest measurement. For many of these children, in a few years, another very similar examination will decide whether they are ready to fight in yet another war. Others will find themselves compelled to contribute by their mere existence to the compilation of statistics on the physiognomy of criminals. A few will survive their destiny as cannon or prison fodder. But for the moment, Italianised but still cautious, the urchins are allowing themselves to be catalogued. They have been admitted into History through a process that goes beyond a simple chronicling of the past. In this peripheral region of the state, these children are also breathing in a myth of themselves that is being constructed without any substantial basis. Out of their element, they are the bewildered sons and grandsons of heroes whose names are carved on ugly memorials in every village square. Children who have already become rhetoric.

As for Gavino, they know he left by sea for Livorno intending to go on from there to Toulon, and that he planned to make his way via England to Australia. It is impossible to imagine anywhere more distant for him to go, even if some have confused Australia with Argentina. Neither Mercede nor Michele Angelo, questioned on the subject, know what to say; to them, Australia and Argentina sound much the same. The simple fact is Gavino left as he had vowed, and as he promised to himself has never got in touch.

Gavino has already been gone a year before Mercede realises that he has taken all Luigi Ippolito's letters with him from their hiding place, as if unwilling to travel alone without the company of his brother.

Marianna occasionally makes the journey from Cagliari with her daughter to visit her parents. She is in every respect a lady, complete with gloves and hat. Dina is becoming as beautiful as the day; it almost seems as if there must have been something good even in that ungrateful son-in-law Biagio Serra-Pintus, who has recently been raised to the rank of commendatore and, it is said, will soon be appointed podestà, mayor of Ozieri.

What people say of the Chironi family is that these former foundlings can now at last enjoy the fruits of their silent labour. Admittedly they have been unfortunate in their children, and would certainly have sacrificed their status to have been able to keep them all, but this has been decided by a higher power and nothing comes free in this world. Nevertheless, now that they are getting on in years and own their own house and land plus a thriving business that employs others, and have a son in Australia or wherever and a well-married daughter – a marriage with foresight, so to speak – they are at least ensured the security of a respectable old age. And they also have a grandchild. A girl, rather than the boy the Serra-Pintus family would have preferred, but Marianna Chironi and Biagio Serra-Pintus are both still young.

Popular rumour can play as many variations on the same theme as a well-tuned instrument. After Gavino's departure and before Marianna's fateful journey to Ozieri, the word was that Mercede and Michele Angelo were living like two hawks on a crag: beautiful, silent and inaccessible. People noticed that Michele Angelo no longer liked to go out himself to negotiate contracts or take measurements for work, but would often send one or other of his apprentices. In fact, the Chironi were seldom seen outside their home at all. So that everyone saw it as a major event when a little later Mercede went to Orgósolo to attend a High Mass for the soul of the martyr Antonia Mesina, killed the year before. They interpreted this journey in honour of the murdered girl as a tribute to her own martyred sons. And how could it be otherwise?

*

The story was that Antonia Mesina, sixteen years old and living in Orgósolo, had left the village to look for firewood and had been seen by a young man from the area, though people were quick to disown him there. This youth, Ignazio Giovanni Catgiu, was destined from his baptism to be a channel for suffering. Others before him had been born in darkness rather than facing the light, so that like Judas Iscariot, or Alessandro Serenelli who murdered Maria Goretti,* Catgiu was also born to prove that without someone to shoulder the weight of evil, good cannot possibly result. Countries need History and martyrs, even places where History never passes and martyrdom is so common as scarcely to be worthy of notice.

Even so, when she went out to look for firewood that morning in May, the month of Maria, Antonia Mesina knew quite well that divine providence had special plans for her. So when she saw a dark young man following her on the country lane she was immediately tempted to turn back but, at the same time, equally certain that she must go forward. In fact, she pressed on. As had happened with the blessed martyr Maria Goretti, and also certainly with the Chironi brothers, Pietro and Paolo, on their way to the vineyard.

That was the story they told in the bus on the winding road from the valley to Orgósolo, but Mercede was only thinking of her own murdered sons whom she had never been able to see after their deaths because, as they whispered in her presence: "Holy Jesus, Mother of God, think of the poor, poor creatures, stuffed into their

* Maria Goretti (1890–1902) is a virgin-martyr of the Roman Catholic Church and one of its youngest canonised saints.

coffin in pieces."

It was there and then that Mercede came to understand how that August day thirty-five years ago had been the moment that had overturned her whole existence. She felt sorry for herself and condemned herself as the worst possible mother, because she had passively allowed herself be eaten up by grief and had offered herself as a martyr as though she had never had any choice in the matter.

She now completely understood this, and faced with the flower-decked image of the little Antonia Mesina who had been stoned to death, she even managed to tell herself that she had never wanted to love any other of her children as much as the first, for fear of being defenceless on any further occasions of martyrdom.

Thus, in front of the grave containing the body of this little virgin which was said to have remained unbelievably perfumed, Mercede felt she had grown so old as almost to find herself back at the point of departure.

On the day of this beginning, on which she also became aware of the end, she remembered this rediscovered evil and all the pain she had succeeded in ignoring.

The little Antonia had been as beautiful as a statue and as small as a child, but strong. So much so that she managed to escape from Catgiu's grasp not once but twice, running towards the road that led to the village . . . But the boy, surprised and frightened by her unexpected resistance, and persuaded that the fleeing child represented his own death and, above all, his failure as the devil's left hand, grabbed a rock and flung it violently from a distance, striking the young girl on the neck.

The impact stunned her, but there was no blood because her hair prevented any laceration of her skin. She fell to the ground, and through misted eyes saw Catgiu reach her. He was on her in a couple of leaps, but still she refused to give in and had almost succeeded in getting up again, when the boy punched her in the throat. The maddened chirping of amorous insects mingled with Ignazio Giovanni's panting and Antonia's puppy-like whimpering.

Turning her back on him, closing and drawing up her legs, Antonia clenches herself in a tight knot while, his lungs beating against his ribs, he struggles to turn her round. She seems paralysed and withdrawn into herself like a tortoise. But Ignazio Giovanni is determined to turn her round, just that and nothing more. Realising he cannot go back, he decides he must go forward, but forward where? Antonia has stopped moaning, conscious that the boy lying on top of her is strong and excitable. With her mouth full of earth and realising he is as frightened as she is, she begs him to let her go, but he does not even hear, determined to penetrate deeper into himself like someone who knows he has fallen down a well and is simply waiting for the relief of reaching the bottom. With a final effort he overpowers her and manages to force her round. Yet even now that he is looking into her eyes he has no idea what to do. She crosses her arms over her chest and shuts her mouth tightly, quietly murmuring: Get off me . . . Get off me. Ignazio Giovanni shakes his head; he could easily explain why it is pointless to keep asking him to get off her, but he doesn't, afraid that if he opens his mouth he will see and hear himself trying to rape this pleading child. In the end a blow to the temple with a stone loosens her ligaments:

her arms fall open and her legs go into an uncontrollable spasm. But though now utterly defenceless, to the eyes of her executioner she suddenly seems no longer accessible. Her eyes are staring at him. So he strikes her one, two, three times more to force her to close them. He goes on striking her even when he realises she is dead. Yet even now her eyes still watch him. Trembling, he gets to his feet; he is stained with blood and tries to clean himself, then looks around and finds just what he is looking for: a heavy flat rock. He lifts it with difficulty, staggers over to her and drops it on that face, on that stare. Antonia's soul leaves her little body, dazzling that afternoon of terror. Someone from the village will swear they saw the orb of the sun explode for an instant. When Ignazio Giovanni gets his breath back he realises what he has done. Like Adam ashamed of his nakedness or Cain being interrogated by God, he tries to hide the young girl's martyred body. He lifts the rock from that face which is no longer a face and drags the body as far as a large, thick bush.

This detail of the bush distresses Mercede most of all. Her sons were cut to pieces and hidden under a great tangle of brambles in the hope that a wild boar would dispose of their little bodies.

The whole story embitters her, as does the thought that during the thirty-five years that have passed from then until her encounter with this new holy martyr, nothing had seemingly happened. There had been no murderers found, no bodies . . . Nothing at all.

They say that thanks to intercession by the Bishop of Cabras, Antonia Mesina will be beatified like the Blessed Maria Goretti, whose hagiography she knew by heart.

In silence, Mercede asks for peace. And to receive all the pain that was her due, but that she never felt when they told her Pietro and Paolo were now sitting on the best seats in Paradise. Except you could never get Paolo to keep still anywhere. Pietro maybe, but Paolo never.

She does not even know how much the peace she is begging for may cost her. But returning from this Mass for the soul of the young girl from Orgósolo she feels better, as if she is finally ready to live with a truth she had always obstinately resisted.

At home she prepares *filindeu*, an extremely fine pasta dish that must be made with a combination of calm and tenacity, warming the pasta with her hands until it is sufficiently elastic to stretch when pulled. Every part of the mixture is like a dense interwoven warp and weft until it takes on the appearance of canvas.

Entering the kitchen that evening Michele Angelo notices the smell of lamb broth and fresh cheese still simmering on the heat.

But by this time Mercede is already ill.

It was not easy to diagnose Mercede's illness. Doctor Romagna, after he had managed to examine her, tried to help Michele Angelo understand the incomprehensible by suggesting that it was like two different people living in one body. Or like a dam, did he know what a dam was? Well, a dam can crack slowly, starting with almost invisible chinks that slowly grow bigger until finally the whole structure gives way.

But would any woman have been able to cope after what happened to Biagio and the child?

Though none of this, the doctor added, would have happened if people only made promises they were able to keep . . . And, of course, this madness might only be a passing phase. Passing phase, my foot! he burst out; a glass too many always loosened the doctor's tongue. So much for the socialists, who said Mussolini wouldn't last a year and yet . . . Then they said people couldn't be so stupid as to believe in that puppet . . . and yet.

And yet only yesterday the Duce had come to Nuoro and everyone had thronged the streets and squares. All except Mercede, who had looked forward to the day with trepidation, but when the time came had stayed in bed, and then, still in her night clothes, had gone into the courtyard to water the plants. This despite the fact that the week before two boys from the local Militia had brought a pass from Commendatore Serra-Pintus, reserving a place for his Respected Parents-in-Law on the platform with the Authorities for the speech to be delivered by His Excellency the Prime Minister, Benito Mussolini.

Exactly half an hour after Biagio Serra-Pintus had signed this pass for his parents-in-law, he had got into a car with Marianna and little Dina and set out for Ozieri, to take up his new position as mayor.

Go back a year before the pilgrimage to Orgósolo.

September was so cold everyone said it was general proof of a new ice age and people asked each other: If this is September, what will December be like?

Well, two carabinieri and a lawyer appeared at the Chironi home and requested a personal interview with the head of the family.

"I'm sure you heard of the murder of the young Antonia Mesina last May in the countryside near Orgósolo," the lawyer began. Michele Angelo gave a non-committal nod. "Excellent," the lawyer said, "excellent."

Michele Angelo looked at him and waited. He was a very thin man of about thirty with an inexplicably sorrowful expression and he wore a Fascist badge.

"Excellent," he repeated after a pause. "So you know that Catgiu Ignazio Giovanni, son of the late Bartolomeo, was arrested *in flagrante* and confessed his guilt?" Michele Angelo nodded again. And waited. "Good, excellent, excellent," the lawyer went on, apparently unwilling to come to the point. "This Catgiu has made a full detailed statement, in the course of which he has referred to events that happened a long time ago and which, although they have no bearing on the case in question, nonetheless involve a particularly savage double murder that has never been solved."

"Well?" Michele Angelo asked, hoping against hope he had not understood.

The man did not reply at once; being a lawyer and thus used to pausing for effect, he wanted to find out how much Michele Angelo could guess of what he was about to say. "The murder of your sons, Signor Chironi."

Michele Angelo nodded, thankful at least that this male-dominated regime had blessedly excluded Mercede from the interview. "In what way could this . . . ?"

". . . Catgiu."

"Catgiu. How could he have had anything to do with . . . with my sons?" Michele Angelo stammered. "I don't understand. At that time he wasn't even born."

"Indeed." The lawyer set out to explain. "Hoping for clemency on the part of the Court, Catgiu alleged he had heard certain things said while in prison awaiting trial, one of which referred to the unsolved case in question. It would seem, though we have no direct evidence of this, that another prisoner talked to Catgiu about a pair of twins murdered by two vagabonds, one of whom, the only one still alive, was being held in the same prison on a charge of killing his wife. And this man would seem to answer to the description of Carroni Giovanni Antonio, son of the late Michele, who at the time of those earlier murders was seventeen years of age."

217

"The case . . ." Michele Angelo repeated. "Two vagabonds . . ."

"Exactly," the lawyer confirmed. "We can now state with confidence that after more than thirty years that case has been solved."

"Solved . . ."

"Do you understand?"

"Yes, yes . . ."

"When the accusation has been made official you will receive a summons to appear in court in the capacity of injured party. Please convey my respects to your son-in-law the commendatore."

Silence.

Michele Angelo needed to broach the subject with his wife with the greatest possible calm. To help him, he summoned Marianna from Cagliari. She arrived, like a film star or a lady from an illustrated magazine. She seemed out of place in such humble surroundings, but partly for this very reason was careful to play her part.

Parents feel they are getting old and must stand aside when their children suddenly become self-confident like ducklings whose down is changing to feathers. Or so Mercede assumed when she heard a note of reproach in Marianna's voice. "Don't even dream of it, Mà," she exclaimed when Mercede said she wanted to go to the prison to talk with Carroni. "Oh, Bà, you tell her, please."

"What do you expect me to say?" Michele Angelo shrugged. "When she gets an idea into her head . . ."

"Tell her she can't go!"

"You're right," Mercede interposed unexpectedly. "Going or not going won't change anything; perhaps it won't change anything, or, just possibly, it will. Do you know, my dear, the first time I saw the sea I was already grown up? Your brothers decided it was time for me to see it. You won't remember that . . ."

"But I do remember." Marianna's voice was suddenly gentle.

"I was always afraid of the sea before I saw it. There." Silence. "That's all."

"You're mad, you're completely mad, both of you! How can you ever have thought of such a thing, oh dear, poor me . . . You do exactly what you like with your mother, just what you like!"

Yet when she got out of the bus supported by her sons she felt happier than ever before.

"Notice the smell, Mà," Luigi Ippolito said.

How utterly beautiful that son had been! Like an angel!

It had only been late spring, but it was already hot; Orosei smelled of fish, stagnant water and citrus fruit. And the sea could be felt before it could be seen, with its regal murmur and a smell so strong you could faint.

When malaria had forced their ancestor Quiròn to flee he had missed that wonderful fragrance of bushes, soil, berries and animal hair, kept moist and scented by a constant light rain.

You're mad, both of you!

When she placed her bare foot on the sand, she had not realised that the open space would be something that her unprepared gaze would find hard to sustain. It seemed too much. So much greater than anything she could have imagined.

Far off a sailing-ship passed, the first ship Mercede had seen in her life. She sat down abruptly on the sand. A few cows were grazing near the waterline.

The boys tried to get her to touch the water, but she refused as if the idea embarrassed her. So Gavino took off his shirt and rolled his trousers over his knees, then went down to the water's edge and collected a little water in the joined palms of his hands and took it to her.

She put her hands together in response and he, as golden and hairy as John the Baptist, poured the water into her palms.

Luigi Ippolito was throwing stones into the water.

"It must be warm!" Gavino shouted to his brother.

The other shook his head, because at that time of year, it was only May, the water could not be warm. But Gavino insisted, taking off his trousers and standing there in his underpants.

"Get dressed!" Mercede shouted. "Shame on you, someone could see you!"

Gavino laughed as only he could laugh. Luigi Ippolito struggled to keep a serious expression on his face, then, on an impulse, began undressing too.

Mercede pretended to be angry. Yet in her heart she was thinking, in fact she was certain, that days like that never end. She began to weep tearlessly.

Gavino was swimming like a fish; he had always loved the sea. Luigi Ippolito, with his shining broad white shoulders and narrow thighs, walked slowly towards his brother without daring to dive.

"Jump in! Jump in!" Gavino was shouting . . .

That's all. What more could there be to explain? Nothing. In fact, two days after Marianna arrived from Cagliari, Mercede was given permission to interview Carroni Giovanni Antonio, son of the late Michele. Another sea to be viewed if she were to overcome her fear of it.

In front of her was a trembling old man. Fifty-one years old, but he looked a hundred. A life of privation, and being in prison . . .

However hard Mercede tried, his face brought back no memories. She could not visualise it in any of her earlier lives, when she had been a mother. She really had no idea where he had come from. There she was, face to face with the man who had turned her existence upside down like a plough turning over a clod of earth, yet the only thing that came into her mind was to try to remember if she had ever seen him as a boy, barefoot, dirty, perhaps hanging about his home or the forge; but she could recall nothing.

"What did they say?" she asked the man. He struggled to speak and shook his head; he was like a rough sketch for an unfinished body. "What did they say?" she repeated as she would have with the stubborn Gavino, who once he had decided to clam up and say nothing would not respond even when threatened with blows. The man began scratching his face; he really did not know what to say.

"Answer!" the warder ordered him, striking him on the neck.

The man sighed. "Nothing," he said, emphasising the word with a movement of his head.

"Did they cry?" she insisted, conscious that her adored sons were now really dying.

"No," the man answered, not looking at her.

*

That night Mercede could not sleep. Nor the next night . . . Instead of sleeping she began walking round the house, sometimes busying herself in the kitchen, or sitting to pray in front of the fireplace. It seemed as if a phase of her life was over and there was nothing left to follow. A girl martyred at sixteen had taken away her sons who had died thirty-four years before, and had probably taken them with her to the perfect place where the souls dearest to God must be. But the girl had also removed them from the inflexibility of Mercede's mind, leaving very little for her to cling to.

No-one knows the use of grief except arrogant cowards who have tried to run away from it.

With her eyes open, Mercede dreamed of the sea, and the sailing-ship she had seen in the distance.

Listen!

For an instant the ship seemed like a volcano in the midst of the ocean, spitting out flesh, iron and wood . . .

We sprang from the silence, landing in the crash of the huge prow as it first rose, then, defeated, let itself be engulfed by the maelstrom.

Listen!

Cries are heard from the lifeboats, shipwrecked people illuminated by diesel oil wave their arms, like the sirens waving to Ulysses.

All round more and more bodies are floating , .

Listen: poor floundering bodies, catapulted from uncertainty to uncertainty, staring into bottomless depths with wide-open eyes. We too called out with broken voices, slimy as foetuses begging for new life, and a few of us were hauled on board, pulled up by the hair with mouths flung open and throats on fire, necks chafed by our lifejackets, eyes staring with terror, hands rigid with cramps . . .

Listen: in the lifeboat we were afraid to die dry. Chests torn apart as we panted for oxygen; legs trembling with fatigue; tense arms searching for space.

Even being saved didn't make us feel safe.

Jump! Jump! Throw yourself in!

No . . .

Come on! Come on! Jump!

I can't jump, I'm scared!

You must, jump, jump!

No, I'm scared, I'm scared!

Now seen from the lifeboat the ship's snout seems immense. We rowed for all we were worth to escape the undertow . . .

In the end the bows disappeared under the water and, like when a stone is thrown into a pond, we were struck by a big circular wave like molten lead that seemed to spread slowly but hit us treacherously, a wicked backwash . . .

You're safe, they said . . . we'll reach land . . . you're safe.

But what then . . . on land?

Listen: *goodbye, we'll meet again,* goodbye, we'll meet again, goodbye, goodbye . . .

It was not until Mercede went out into the courtyard barefoot in her nightdress that Michele Angelo really began to worry about her. Until then he had tried not to understand, even if things were clearly going from bad to worse. Normally she would not even leave the bedroom unless fully dressed. She had always been punctilious in her rituals, but now for some time she had been forgetting things.

Then one morning she got out of bed and barefoot and in her nightdress went out into the courtyard to water the plants. The neighbour who saw her from the balcony of the house opposite was astonished, because in all the years she had known Mercede Lai, the master blacksmith's wife, she had never seen her with a hair out of place, let alone barefoot like a pilgrim and in her nightdress with her hair loose!

When the neighbour calls down to her she does not even reply, murmuring some film song she heard in Cagliari on her daughter's gramophone. Her daughter in Cagliari lives like a lady and even has a telephone . . . Well, seeing Mercede out there like that the neighbour calls her husband. By now it has become clear that there are major problems, so much so that father and daughter have decided to employ a maid to help with the housekeeping. In fact, the maid is the first person to come out of the house; she had been tidying the larder and had not noticed anything. Then, attracted by the voices in the courtyard, she goes out and sees her employer in the condition we have described.

By the time Michele Angelo arrives, Mercede is sitting on her stool in front of the fire with her arms folded. Before he has time to speak, she suddenly seems to become aware of the situation of her own accord. Put out, she responds aggressively to every question: no, she doesn't want to get dressed! She's at home in her own house and will do as she pleases! She's not hungry or thirsty or anything, let them just leave her alone! What do they want? And why is Michele Angelo Chironi at home and not at the forge? In short, she's a fury.

Hearing these events described, Doctor Romagna gives his opinion that it sounds like a case of somnambulism, since she is behaving as if fully awake while in fact asleep. Even her bad temper makes sense, because there's nothing worse than waking a sleepwalker. He can well imagine the neighbour and the maid shouting and pushing Mercede: but what can such ignorant and clucking hens be expected to know about somnambulism? The doctor sums up: if it happens again, be careful to treat her gently and make no noise or quick movements. And give her a few drops of this – he scribbles something illegible on a piece of paper. Get them to prepare it for you at the pharmacy . . . Something to calm her down because she has suffered too much; what can you expect after what happened to her little granddaughter? . . .

Because meanwhile – and in terrible circumstances – nine-year-old Dina is dead, and Biagio with her. It happened after Mercede was allowed into the prison to interview Carroni Giovanni Antonio, son of the late Michele, but before the two young fez-wearing officials brought the Chironi their pass to the dignitaries' stand for the Duce's visit to Nuoro.

During the funeral Mass for the commendatore and his child, the bishop, Monsignor Cogoni, mentioned the massacre of the innocents, presumably referring to the extraordinary number of children from the Chironi household who had died, but also to God's design that could not have foreseen the spilling of so much blood in the home of the master blacksmith.

But we must return to Biagio Serra-Pintus, who having signed the pass for his in-laws, got into the car with Marianna and little Dina bound for Ozieri, where he had just been nominated podestà.

The drive from Cagliari should take about six hours, road conditions permitting. But it will take longer because they have planned two stops: at Oristano (to avoid the terrible road via Tortolí); and at Nuoro, where they will spend the night and call on their relatives. Some of their luggage has already arrived at their destination by military transport put at the service of the local federal secretariat. The podestà's residence has just been redecorated and fitted with all modern comforts.

Reports in the local papers describe the journey in great detail: route, kilometres per hour, even the colour of the dress of the signora commendatoressa, and the white bow in the hair of the innocent little passenger. The national papers treat the news like Nobile's expedition to the Pole. But no newspaper headline reveals that what had been passed off as a road accident was in fact an attempted robbery that ended badly. Nevertheless, despite the attempt at an official cover-up, rumours spread rapidly. So much so that Doctor Romagna was able to affirm that you must only make promises you can keep and not sacrifice the truth to lies. Biagio Serra-Pintus, newly elected podestà of Ozieri, had been killed together with his little daughter and his driver while resisting an attempted robbery; but according to the regime no such thing had happened, because to admit that such a thing had happened would have meant admitting that banditry had not been eradicated in the area, or worse still, that a truce agreed with local criminals had collapsed. Years earlier the bandit Samuele Stochino had died in mysterious circumstances and now here was the merry-go-round starting up all over again. But this time, the doctor went on, it was not so easy to sweep the dust under the carpet.

The result was that, having spoken once too often, the doctor was locked up in jail for two days to coincide with the Duce's visit to Nuoro.

In the Chironi home, whatever the official version of the incident, the real news was that the official story, however plausible, did not ring true.

Michele Angelo's instinct was to spread his arms and curse heaven. And so he did: of course Job had had his boils and the trusting Jeremiah his lamentations, but what Michele Angelo felt like now was Lucifer, ready to fall and be lost for ever as an affirmation of his right to curse his own ill fate for eternity.

So alone in the courtyard he thumped his knees and shook his fist at the sky: Curse you!

*

It was a little before this – who knows? – that Marianna found herself deep in the countryside at night with only one shoe, her dress torn and her breathing convulsed by terror. She had come across a sheep pen in the middle of nowhere. If you had asked her where she was she would not have been able to say, just that from one moment to the next she had found herself no longer in the car with her child but outside in a sweet-smelling clump of bushes.

She was not a countrywoman, and had no experience of country life beyond olive groves, and the vineyard at Lollove before it was abandoned to thorns. But this place, as her heart thumped madly in the pitch darkness of an overcast night, proved to be a space of immense fragrance, as indecent as the scent of a naked belly. When she became aware that there were animals shut up inside the sheep pen, she briefly felt an irrational surge of happiness. Then she started screaming and some of the sheep bleated with her, until a little old man with a huge greatcoat over his shoulders emerged from a primitive shelter that looked as if it had grown out of the rock, and asked, "What is it?"

Marianna did not answer, simply because she was out of breath. The old man studied her with the eyes of a bat since to him darkness was like broad daylight, and he realised that she was a lady, a woman from the city.

In the village a fat maresciallo from the carabinieri gave her something to eat and drink and started asking questions.

Once she realised she could still speak, she said she really had no idea, but that on leaving Oristano, after a meal to which the local bishop had invited them, she had dozed off on the back seat of the car, then suddenly, with no idea how she came to be alone, had found herself deep in the countryside.

Thus, little by little, and with growing amazement, the maresciallo realised that the woman sitting before him shivering violently with a shawl round her shoulders was none other than Commendatoressa Marianna Serra-Pintus. And he suspected, no, he was certain, that something terrible must have happened. So he hurried to wake the radio telegraphist and told him to contact Nuoro, and also to get the local medical officer out of his bed to assist the commendatoressa in the most appropriate way possible.

The maresciallo was used to dealing with the local criminal fraternity, but when it came to ladies from the city, especially ladies with high-up connections, he had no idea what to do. So he called in not only the local doctor, but also a midwife and the parish priest.

Marianna was moved to somewhere more comfortable. As they waited for instructions from Nuoro, the maresciallo, assisted by the local authorities, ventured a few more questions.

"What exactly can you remember?"

"Very little. First I was asleep, then I wasn't. We were travelling..."

"Try to remember how long you were travelling for."

Marianna shook her head.

"Who was with you in the car, exactly?"

"I was dreaming of doing things I don't know how to do..."

This answer made the maresciallo look at the doctor who nodded as if to say: The signora has lost her mind.

A suspicion reinforced by the woman's utterly impassive expression.

They made immediate contact with Fascist headquarters in Cagliari, whose reaction was: What, didn't they know? Hadn't they read the orders of the day? Commendatore Serra-Pintus was travelling with his family to Ozieri to take up his new appointment as podestà.

The maresciallo closed his eyes, and deep inside – himself a father used to inspiring fear – tried to select an oath worthy of the situation. Then he turned again to the signora commendatoressa and tactfully asked, "Were your husband and your daughter travelling with you?"

He spoke as if the question were a purely formal one, in a tone of voice chosen to make any possible answer easy. His psychology was as subtle as it was unconscious. For the first time Marianna clearly understood what she was being asked. In fact, with an almost imperceptible movement of her face, she seemed to be repeating to herself every word the police officer had said.

This was how she came to remember the child. And that the child was her daughter and that she had been sleeping on the rear seat with her head against her mother's legs. Marianna gave a lurch forward. Her face twisted like a sheet of paper. And her mouth fell open, though no sound came out of it.

When she woke in hospital her father was standing beside her bed.

There was an accident, he said, a terrible accident, the car had run off the road, didn't she remember?

No, she didn't remember, except that she had found herself goodness knows where in the dark with only one shoe, her clothes torn and her legs scratched . . .

The police report stated: "A traffic accident, resulting in three deaths: the commendatore Serra-Pintus, the female child Serra-Pintus-Chironi Mercede, and the driver Senette Giuseppangelo. Sole survivor: Serra-Pintus Marianna née Chironi, admitted to the New Medical Clinic at Nuoro in a confused state."

However, the people of the area told a different story. That there had been no ordinary accident, but that the car had tried to avoid a barricade of rocks and tree trunks deliberately placed on the road, meaning that criminals had been waiting for the car and its passengers; and that the obstruction had not stopped the car so much as forced the driver to make an impulsive attempt to reverse; and that as he struggled to execute this manoeuvre the car had fallen into a ditch beside the road; and that the people in the car, though possibly stunned, had all been alive at the moment this happened; and that they had then been approached by men on horseback who had ordered them to get out of the car because they wanted to seize the podestà; that the driver had responded by firing his revolver at the attackers; that they had replied with a volley of shots at the car which had killed the driver and the child who was asleep on the back seat and had no time to realise what was happening; that Serra-Pintus had then told one of the attackers that he recognised him; that this man had come up to him as he tried to escape and killed him with a rifle shot to the face without even getting off his horse; and that finally the commendatoressa, unconscious inside the car, had been thought dead and thus escaped the massacre.

The first account, the official story, was ever so simple; but the second, the unofficial one, was simpler still. The first version was approved, the second ruthlessly suppressed. The first agreed with the policy of national pacification, the second was defeatist.

So there it was.

All that was left for the Duce in the city square, after he had proclaimed his steely determination to win for the umpteenth time ("We're Victorious And We Shall Always Win"), was to touch upon the tragedy that had struck the fertile capital of the Barbagia region with the loss of Commendatore Serra-Pintus, a Fascist of the first rank, and his little daughter, a sapling cut down – in the wisdom of the Omniscient – long before her time, demanding the condolences of all Fascist Italy, not least those of the Duce himself.

But Mercede was not there to hear him, nor to be moved by these gracious words from His Excellency the Prime Minister.

The fact was that her neighbour, looking out that morning from her balcony, had seen her watering her plants barefoot in her night-dress and with her hair loose.

An immediate connection is made: her daughter's life has been in serious danger, her granddaughter is dead, and her powerful son-in-law too. Mercede gives up. She has no need to know the details or that there are conflicting accounts of what happened. Mercede, quite simply, gives up.

They take Mercede back inside since she seems to have recovered. Do you want proof that she really has become a sleepwalker? they ask Michele Angelo. He can't think of any answer to that, though he realises he has to do the right thing. He is without illusions and does not forgive. By now, with full lucidity, he has understood the way things are going. It seems to have been obvious from the first. He knows only too well that when a job starts badly you can of course struggle on, doing a bit more hammering or a bit more heating, but when it's not right it's not right. If limits have been set, you have to take them into account. And in his case the limit, the error in manufacture, the curse, was surviving people dear to him.

Suddenly that mournful memory that had seemed to belong to the past shook him again: it is night-time and cold, and he hears a very long lament, almost like a sustained howl.

When she dies, he thought . . . Then he pushed the thought away. When she dies . . . And the lament became terrible.

Darkness and cold followed by the lament.

When she dies, I shall survive. This was clear to him and he repeated it to himself. Even if I tried to kill myself I would survive. He knew that well. He was ready. At what point had this become clear? When he stopped worrying about the fact that everyone else died, but he survived. He had already understood that when he looked down from the top of the ladder, in the church, to where Mercede was sitting.

Apart from this stupid detail things had not gone badly, but that did not mean much: he knew only too well that all you had to do was to open yourself for an instant to misery to negate whole years of happiness.

This is what he understands now, faced with the incredulous look on the face of his wife who still cannot believe that she went out into the courtyard "half naked".

It was alarming, but also, in the opinion of everyone who called in to see her, an isolated event, caused by the shock of her adored granddaughter's death. The fact was, Mercede seemed to get better rapidly, while Marianna struggled.

Physically Marianna was fine, but seemed permanently tired, as if afflicted by some painless but chronic form of inertia.

Her reaction seemed less disturbing than Mercede's, because something in the blacksmith's wife had not returned to normal, something that caused unease. Admittedly she no longer went about half dressed, but she seemed to react in an unnatural way to everything, like someone who knows she is out of harmony, but feigns indifference. She never mentioned her little dead grand-daughter, but went to church with exaggerated regularity. She had always been a practising believer, but for some time now her attendance had been excessive: Mass morning and evening every day without exception.

Marianna had had to adjust to being alone again. Without the matter ever being discussed, she had returned to her family home and the room she had slept in as a girl, enabling her father to go to work without worrying that his wife, even with the daily help present, would ever be left unsupervised. Marianna's response to the tragedy had been a practical one, as if the most important thing was to meet misfortune on equal terms.

She was thirty-five now and a rich widow, but with no idea what to do with her money.

She and her father had developed a silent understanding, so that when Mercede announced she was going to Orgósolo for the Mass to commemorate the first anniversary of the death of poor Antonia Mesina, Michele Angelo caught his daughter's eye before nodding his assent.

Returning from the ceremony Mercede seems relaxed and

calm just as in the old days, when one could see a sort of seraphic wholeness in her expression.

Yes, she is calm. She sets to work the minute she enters the kitchen, waiting only to take off her shawl, knot the corners of a handkerchief on her head and wash her hands. Then she quickly pours bran onto the marble table top, and making a little hollow in the mound, adds water and salt and begins kneading.

It takes a long time for the dough to become elastic enough to weave. Mercede sings while she works on the strands, murmuring the ritual formulas:

> Never attract attention,
> never fear the abyss,
> give without seeking advantage,
> be sincere when you speak,
> never be unjust,
> be committed in what you do,
> be docile in adversity, but never docile towards adversity.

Leaving the pasta time to dry she puts the lamb on the fire to stew; so it can boil slowly with the spices. Fresh cheese will have to be added at the last minute before putting in the pasta.

When he comes into the kitchen that evening Michele Angelo smells the fragrance of lamb broth and fresh cheese simmering on the heat.

It is ready for the pasta to be added.

But Mercede is not there.

Thinking she must have gone to church again Michele Angelo

asks Marianna, but she has been busy all day emptying the other house, and says she hadn't even noticed that Mercede was back from Orgósolo; it was the maid's day off.

When darkness fell they reported Mercede missing.

After three days they realised there was no point in searching any longer because she did not want to be found. Her final gift to her husband was to have no grave, calling in question his firm belief that everyone else would die before him, since no-one could ever be quite sure that Mercede was dead.

The consequence is that early one morning Michele Angelo goes to the forge and informs his workers that from now on they must only complete work they have already started and accept no new orders, because by autumn the whole business will be shut down.

When he comes home again Marianna is fussing round the kitchen like a busy housewife, but there is no-one else there. She hears her father come in and moves her head in greeting without turning round, just as Mercede would have done.

"I've closed it all down, I've had enough," he announces. Marianna carries on with what she is doing without paying any attention. "Don't you believe me?" he continues.

Marianna dries her hands: "What?"

"I have a right to rest too . . . Haven't I worked enough in my life?"

"Enough, yes, you have," his daughter agrees. But she notices he is slowly growing paler. "What's the matter?" she asks, beginning to worry.

Michele Angelo shakes his head, thinking: Here we go. He had always assumed death would strike him obliquely and not in such an arrogant and cowardly way. Not like this: closing his business, sending everyone home, bolting the door, sitting down in the kitchen where his widowed daughter is working. He feels his head grow light as if it is about to take off and fly from his shoulders, he feels his sight growing dim and his whole body being dragged into a slippery descent, as if incapable of resistance. He feels the pulse in his temples beating louder and louder, louder and louder . . .

Marianna runs to him with a glass of water, then grabs his head as if to force him to drink.

Through the cotton wool blocking his hearing, Michele Angelo is aware she is saying something, but he doesn't know what.

"Don't frighten me, don't frighten me, drink!" she is saying. "What's the matter?"

But how can he answer such a question? I'm dying, daughter, that's all. I'm dying. Which would be fine apart from the fact that I expected a more gradual, more respectful death. But already at this mere thought he seems to come back to himself and here is his head which had so suddenly taken flight returning to fix itself again exactly where it ought to be and his hearing is again strong and clear and his sight as sharp as the sight of an old man can be.

The fact is, this advance notice of death has departed just as it came. As if it were nothing more than a rehearsal, a joke in poor taste.

Marianna notices her father is better, but this does not stop her worrying.

"I'm fine, I'm fine," he says, shaking her off.

She takes a step back like a painter looking for an overall view of her work and sees the colour is back in his cheeks. "But you must let the doctor look at you," she says, recovering her composure.

"Doctor my foot," her father says, trying not to seem too brusque as he realises his daughter may have been frightened. "Look, I'm fine, really, I don't know what it was, but anyway it's gone now." He tries to reassure her.

But she insists. "We need Dr Romagna to tell us what happened to you. What if it happens again?"

"You are your mother's daughter!" he bursts out, in the tone of someone administering a reproach while knowing he is in fact making a compliment.

"Of course," she agrees. "But we'll get the doctor all the same." She unties her apron, grabs her coat from its hook and goes out.

Only Marianna knows how she manages to cover the distance to the doctor's house. Her urgency is not so much to know exactly what has happened to her father, as to adjust to this umpteenth declaration of war. She is heading towards a point that is not as secure as it seems. Or, rather, she has an address, an objective, an appearance of sense. She is moving towards a definite place, there can be no doubt of that. So she pushes everything else from her mind and hurries towards the white gate of the modern house where Doctor Romagna lives. A short, direct, simple journey, were it not that Marianna now feels she is walking in a strange place. Everything seems transformed by urgency, like the time when, stunned, dishevelled and with a shoe missing, she found herself in the middle of the countryside in the dark. And even before that, when the car was running on the road towards Nuoro.

That memory was lying in wait for her, ready to strike like an assassin. Marianna thought she heard the tyres screech on the badly asphalted road. She remembers there was a wide curve. But not immediately, first there was a long straight section. Biagio, sitting by the driver, was addressing her without looking round. Talking about Gavino, saying it was for the best, very much for the best that he'd gone, that no-one would ever have tried to stop him when he decided to leave Italy. Biagio was speaking with the confidence of someone who knows what he is talking about, because he wanted to make it clear that these were times when any attempt at opposition must invite resistance. Little Dina was asleep, and Marianna had settled the child across the back seat with her head against her left thigh. She remembers what she was thinking while her husband was speaking: leaving Italy, she was thinking, meant travelling far enough to frustrate any attempt at adjustment. This was what was passing through her mind, and she felt sadly impotent. Then she thought of the cold, brusque tone of her husband, the commendatore who had just been made podestà. These things matter, she had thought, the nuances are important. So, careful to make sure Dina was still sleeping peacefully, she said Gavino had done exactly what he wanted. Biagio had clearly insinuated that this brother of hers, this champion, had not only compromised himself politically, and he had emphasised the "not only" as if to say: As a gentleman I will say no more and you may think what you like, but best not to press me to say anything else. A smile had twitched the corner of the driver's mouth. Marianna couldn't see it, but she had felt it.

Gavino will do as he likes, it's his life, she had insisted. He's a grown man.

Biagio shook his head. This has always been the problem with your family, he remarked with insincere regret.

The problem? What problem? she asked.

Living without rules. Without rules you can have no sense of duty and without a sense of duty there can be no spirit of sacrifice.

Yes, yes, Marianna had said. That's true, and of course it's your sense of duty that has got you to where you are now.

That seemed the right answer, the perfect response of a devoted wife. Biagio pretended to take it that way, though still brooding on the possibility that his vixen of a wife had somehow made a fool of him.

It was while he was thinking this that the car entered a blind curve on a slight rise. Perhaps it was the burst on the accelerator necessary to tackle it that made the manoeuvre seem rather abrupt. The tyres screeched on a surface that seemed little better than gravel. Dina gave a start, but continued to sleep; Marianna had to brace herself so as not to lean on her daughter. After the curve the road straightened again, still climbing slightly, bordered by two lines of large plane trees. Levelling again, it veered to the right. It was after this curve that they came on the barricade. The driver saw it, and with the greatest respect, swore. When Biagio realised what had happened he turned to his wife. A look combining terror and pity that said many things that had been hidden for years.

It was a barricade of branches and stones, nothing that could have got there without deliberate intent.

The driver instantly reversed, causing a horrible sound like steel scraping on stone . . . the car shot back as if sucked by an enormous magnet. This unnatural movement woke Dina. The little girl tried to sit up, but Biagio reached out an arm to force her down again. Marianna, looking at her husband, had time to reflect on how a man's face can change when he is brought face to face with his primary instincts. The Biagio she knew seemed to have vanished, swallowed up in the need to protect his child. Marianna naively did not realise this was a sign that should have alarmed her; instead she had a warm feeling and convinced herself that she had made no mistake; she could even have loved that man who had turned to protect his daughter. But an instant later the driver, after his brief retreat, lost control of the car as he tried to negotiate the curve. A brief fall followed before the car became stuck in a ditch with its nose pointing upwards.

From the edge of the road the men on horseback towered over the people inside the vehicle. There were four of them, masked and armed with rifles. They ordered the occupants out of the car in a sharp voice, as if commanding a herd of animals to change direction.

Keep down! Biagio told his wife and daughter without turning or moving his mouth. The driver, paralysed, awaited orders.

We are getting out, what do you want from us? the podestà shouted to the masked horsemen.

They answered that what they wanted would not interest the

242

commendatore, but everyone must get out of the car unarmed.

Dina began crying with her face buried in her mother's breast.

It's nothing, Marianna reassured her, but without the conviction a mother should have in such circumstances, so that the child understood at once that they were lost, and that she must grow up instantly if she wanted a chance of surviving.

Meanwhile the men on horseback were shouting in loud voices.

What have we done to you?

Out! Hurry up!

We have no money!

Come on, out!

Just before getting out Biagio looked at his wife in a way he had never looked at her before, a sign that deep down in the confusion of life, terrible events can be significant. His look revealed a dimension to their union he had never previously shown. Gratitude, possibly. As if, stripped of his shell, Biagio had offered himself naked to his wife for the first time. To her he had become unexpectedly beautiful. And he must have felt the same of her because in that tiny moment there was just time to hint at a reciprocal smile, the only one they had ever shared.

Outside the car, Biagio recovered his usual manner, insensitive rather than courageous, emboldened by the insignia he was wearing. The passengers in the rear of the car, buried in the ditch, remained hidden to the horsemen.

Like a man at a livestock market, Biagio began bargaining: hinting a little, complying a little, but also threatening a little.

The apparent leader of the bandits listened with a mixture of surprise and admiration; he was a worldly countryman, who could recognise a man with balls when he met one, and it cannot be denied that he even slightly admired this man he was about to kill.

The driver, who had also got out of the car, was standing to one side without taking part in the negotiations. Though it was hardly a case of negotiations: the men on horseback were dictating conditions and those on foot had to do what they were told. All they knew was that they would be killed or, if they were lucky, be taken into the bush and held for a ransom.

In the car, Dina was beginning to get agitated, and despite Marianna's best efforts to hold her still, the child became startled at each snort from the horses.

One of men heard the noises inside the car.

Who's there? Come on out! he ordered.

A woman and a small girl, Biagio explained. Are you even chasing women and children now?

These are hard times, the mounted leader said with unmistakable scorn.

Come out, another horseman shouted. *Ajò*, what are we waiting for?

Marianna had no idea what to do. Days seemed to have passed since the car crashed into the ditch though it was hardly any time at all. She waited for a signal from her husband but none came.

A woman and a small girl, Biagio repeated. Crooks, he hissed.

The man on horseback took this as a compliment. Just a question of point of view, he said. We certainly see you lot as crooks. Isn't that why we're in this position now?

At the very moment when Marianna decided to start struggling to get out of the back door of the car, one of the four men began to get off his horse.

It was then that the driver pulled out a pistol that shone in the darkness, and fired. A dense flame like a small incandescent spray came from the mouth of the gun. The man getting off the horse dropped to the ground dead, with his foot still in the stirrup, and as he fell his rifle went off. It was as if the guns were having a conversation of their own; the revolver had asked a question and the rifle had replied. Marianna and Dina heard the body of the driver fall heavily against the side of the vehicle. Then they heard bullets scorch the sheet-metal. A few bright tracks pierced the darkness of the passenger seat. Dina gave a sort of sob that only Marianna heard. She called to the child, who did not respond. Meanwhile, outside, Biagio was shouting. Two more men dismounted to find out what had happened inside the car. They saw the child dead, and the woman as if annihilated, almost euphoric in her ridiculous attempt at dignity despite the circumstances. Biagio turned and caught sight of his wife so briefly he had no time to understand whether she was alive or not. But he realised with a wrench that something terrible had happened when the spray of bullets had riddled the side of the car. Without thinking he said the first thing that came into his head.

I know you, you criminal! To hell with you and your family! May you and all your evil race be reduced to scavenging from the dustbins of the poor! I curse you, Vindice Deiana!

Hearing his name, the leader pulled the reins of his horse in such a way as to make his animal rear up.

Eja, he said. Yes that's me. And fired.

The hail of lead hit Biagio full in the face, forcing his eyes upwards like a punch to the chin. He saw that ultra-cursed sky that always dazzles those with no time to think of beauty, that very beauty they have themselves neglected. So he just had time to take in the terrible brightness of that firmament still astonishingly suspended over everyone, even over that tormented corner of the world.

Silence.

All three bandits got down from their horses. Like cave explorers, they shone a torch into the car. They saw Marianna, motionless, and Dina. Silence.

When Marianna realised they were looking at her, she begged them: Kill me.

Even killing you would be too much trouble, they said.

And mounted their horses again.

In the darkness that followed, Marianna realised that in some way everything was returning to its origin. There in the countryside, stained with blood and beginning to feel the cold, with one shoe on and one shoe off, she was driven to survive by the very consciousness of her lack of feeling. Because inside that motionless darkness everything apart from her own existence seemed to have had some meaning: the look on Biagio's face, the rapid trajectory of Dina's life. There seemed to be an explanation for almost everything. Only she, Marianna Chironi, seemed without significance. Which was why there had seemed no point in yielding to her first instinct, which had been to end her own life. What can you take from someone who has nothing? Too easy, she told herself; too easy, Marianna Chironi: before you give up anything it would be better if you possessed something. But the very clear idea flashed through her mind that she had absolutely nothing.

In Cagliari she had been a householder without a real house of her own, an outsider in a hostile environment. She had certainly altered herself, questioned herself as she tried to adjust to circumstances, but she had still remained nothing. At Nuoro she played the lady and probably was one, but as if playing a part in a play. Perhaps this was the message of what had happened to her: learning that inside every design is another design, and inside that yet another, and another, and so on . . .

It was then she had seen a light in the pitch darkness.

When she realised there were animals inside the sheep pen, she had briefly felt an irrational surge of happiness. Then she had started screaming and some of the sheep bleated with her, until a little old man with a huge greatcoat round his shoulders emerged from a primitive structure that looked as if it had grown out of the rock, and asked, "What is it?"

"What is it?" Doctor Romagna's housekeeper asks. She is a brisk woman who can't stand the doctor being disturbed at mealtimes. And if anyone knocks on the door at such times she looks out of the window into the lane and lets her displeasure be known.

"Excuse me, this is urgent," Marianna calls up without raising her voice.

"At this hour?" the housekeeper answers. "The doctor is eating." Doctor Romagna appears behind his housekeeper, with his napkin tucked in his collar. "Let her in, Gesuina," he says without making his words a command. "Come up, Marianna, come up."

But once inside the house Marianna is tongue-tied and does not even know how to describe what has happened. Michele Angelo has undoubtedly had a turn, but she has no idea what it was. The doctor continues eating while asking questions to help him understand, but Marianna cannot think what to say. The housekeeper gives the glare she inevitably turns on all untimely callers who imagine the doctor must be a magician who can even understand those who do not speak.

"Have you put him to bed?" the doctor asks, finally.

"No, why? Babbo in bed? No, no . . . he's better now, in fact he says he's fine, but, doctor, I want to be able to feel calm and not worry."

"Of course," the housekeeper grumbles. "Feel calm at the expense of others."

"I'll come as soon as I can," Doctor Romagna assures her, giving his housekeeper a sour look. She holds her employer's gaze, far from intimidated.

"She rules here," the doctor remarks.

From the doctor's brief visit it appears that the problem was a sudden dip in blood pressure, and that there is no immediate threat to Michele Angelo's life.

Doctor Romagna is firm with him: "You're as strong as an ox; why not go back to work? Keeping busy will do you good."

But Michele Angelo is categorical. "No. I have no reason to go back to the forge."

"You're wrong," Marianna interrupts. "Just think of all the decent young men you could save from the street by giving them the chance to work for you . . ."

"Just words!" Michele Angelo exclaims, turning to the doctor.

"No, she's quite right, Chirò. That's the only medicine I can prescribe you."

Michele Angelo was a man who never seemed to listen, but eventually did. Early one morning Marianna found him in the kitchen dressed in his best clothes and freshly shaved, which made him almost look young again.

"I've been thinking," he said. She waited for him to go on. "These are ugly times with so many unfortunate people who have lost everything. I want to give something back . . . Is there still an orphanage at Cúglieri?"

Marianna spread her arms. "Why go all the way to Cúglieri? There are orphans here too. But have your breakfast first."

"Alright."

But the search for an orphan was fruitless. Michele Angelo was looking for a face he could not find and Marianna realised that it was impossible to get him to come to a decision.

They very soon gave up the search.

Exactly five years after Mercede disappeared, news reached them of Gavino.

Every Wednesday morning, after seeing to her father and getting him to go out for a walk, Marianna opened up all the rooms and pulled back the bedclothes, including those no longer in use. This ritual caused the maid to pull a face and say to herself: You see? When gentlefolk have no work they invent it for themselves.

For Marianna, putting clean sheets on the beds was a complicated ritual that began with opening doors and windows, then continued with throwing back the bedclothes to air the beds, and finished with changing the sheets, even those that had not been slept in. That particular Wednesday was no different from any other except that a previously unused pillowcase was found in a trunk. The maid viewed it with a critical eye, since the linen in the Chironi household had always been perfect, and more than once she had thought to ask her employer to lend her a towel so she could copy the embroidery. But the pattern on this particular pillowcase made no sense: was it a fish perhaps, or just a bunch of grapes gone wrong?

The maid approached Marianna while she was remaking the beds in the brothers' room with fresh, stretched sheets which had never been used before. She drew her attention to this pillowcase with its unbelievably poor embroidery. "What shall I do with this?" she said. "Shall I put it back?" Marianna told her not to, and it occurred to her that if that forgotten pillowcase had resurfaced from the bottom of a trunk, there must undoubtedly be a reason for it. "Put it on my bed," Marianna said, making a quick decision. The maid had another look at the strange embroidery trying to be a bunch of grapes while looking like a fish, said nothing and went to her employer's room.

That night Marianna dreamed about the Battle of the Tritons . . .

"What's disturbing your sleep, Marià?" Michele Angelo asked, disturbing her in turn.

"A huge battle at sea," she murmured, eyes still closed, "making the water boil like a shoal of fish being pulled to the surface, *oh what pitiless blows* . . . They were men, they were fish . . . gouging out eyes, crushing flesh, pushing each other aside to delay the moment of being suffocated in the air . . . Then the sheep massed in the sheep-fold all started moaning in unison . . ."

"What sheep?" her father asked. "What are you talking about?"

But he was wasting his time; Marianna was deeply asleep again.

"The night of the devil," said Michele Angelo, returning to his own room and going back to sleep himself.

Next morning the sky was the colour of iron with sounds like a hammer striking an anvil, followed by a promise of wind, then a distant bleating . . .

And indeed, next morning the telegram came for Marianna.

Now Michele Angelo had stopped working, all that was left for him was to listen to the silence round him. He was certainly resigned to growing old; he had never asked for anything and did not expect anything.

The closed forge seemed a sad place full of ghosts, and sometimes he seemed to hear noises from the position where Gavino used to work. But it was only a playful mouse taking advantage of the cat's absence. I should reduce the whole place to rubble, Michele Angelo would tell himself, trying to work out how much time he might still have to waste. And that was his vendetta against himself, to give up on whatever had always gone well in his life: That's how you learn, he would say to whoever had condemned him to this unequal burden. What could possibly still afflict the Quiròn family? Nothing. Marianna was beyond childbearing age and he, he told himself, was too old to be a father again. Though like the patriarch Abraham, if he had received the call and been sent a young concubine, he would certainly not have refused the challenge. His good health was part of the curse, in fact the main symptom of the menace of his survival. He was seventy years old now, but if he had wanted to he could still have worked as hard as when he was a young boy.

The closed forge reminded him that this time it was he who had made the decision. Certainly his days had become long and silent. Beyond the courtyard another war was raging, but even this did not seem to matter.

Marianna still liked buying women's magazines, full of film stars and patterns for clothes.

Occasionally, during the long autumn evenings, she would read aloud and comment that, seen from the magazines, the world seemed a harmless place, but that to judge from the marketplace, where people came to blows over bread or a piece of meat, the world seemed much more sunk in suffering.

They lacked nothing, and could buy anything they needed from local shepherds or the many travelling salesmen who offered goods on the black market.

When the Second World War officially broke out, it skimmed over the Chironi home like an illness against which they had been well vaccinated. Though, of course, young men were once more being driven away to see a world turned upside down, leaving parts of their bodies and even their lives in hitherto unheard-of places.

Then, after the first air raids on Cagliari, evacuees began to arrive.

In late June the people of Cagliari were shaken by the roar of engines as French planes unleashed a storm of bombs on the port.

But this was news that, in the total silence of an outpost like Barbagia, could only be discussed in a whisper. The radio told only one story: we were winning, the enemy was in retreat and, soaked in the blood of heroes, the soil of our country was revealing the unshakeable resolve of the manly Italian soldier.

But the evacuees said it was a terrible war. They told stories of explosions transforming night into day and driving poor people underground to hide like mice. And they said that overseas it was even worse, because the war was breaking out wherever money and affluence could be found . . .

"Luckily we're too poor here for the war to reach us, though not rich enough to avoid mass recruitment," Michele Angelo remarked. And Marianna told him to be quiet because these were times when enemies were everywhere. Times when the slightest thing could see you ending up in front of a firing squad at Prato Sardo.

They were passengers in a ship buffeted by huge waves.

Every story the evacuees tell begins with the sky, like a tumultuous overture of purple clouds . . .

In August they report that in some places people are living naked like savages. It's hot in the Campidano district. But not here, not where you are.

No indeed. With us August is like rough local wine, strong and sour, full of promise but no longer satisfying.

It is also the time of year when in the Chironi household the dead are mourned and the palette of endless winter is prepared.

It is the month when the sea seems to recommend abandoning the pastures nearest the beaches and stockpiling firewood. It is time to rebuild the sheep pens.

Even in August the prospect of winter can send a shiver up your spine.

The stories the evacuees tell refer to the sky, because the sea is directed from the sky, when the cold wind's breath begins to seethe.

But the thunder they heard was coming from the ground, not from darts hurled down by gods. It was the thunder of anti-aircraft howitzers, of underwater torpedoes, of tonnes of shipping being swallowed up by the sea.

From the Castello district of Cagliari, itself no larger than a small ship, you could see flashes from the guns of warships out at sea and the astonishing sight of flames floating on the water.

From there too one could hear at night the laments of the ship-wrecked, as their already heavy bodies gulped down more and more water.

A year-long war between sky and sea, on every possible horizon.

For a long time they prayed and searched for unripe fruit in the countryside, but then were forced to give up.

And start walking.

They reported that that tempest of humanity, that rattling and crackling on the horizon, also brought gifts from the sea: crates of food, floating fish, suitcases with valuables in them . . . sailors' caps and even, occasionally, roses.

But nothing reached Nuoro except black flying devils with crosses on them that ripped the fabric of the sky.

And stories.

The house in via Deffenu, formerly home to the Serra-Pintus-Chironi family, now half empty but still comfortable, was put at the disposal of tormented souls who had been forced to flee from the flames of the Cagliari district. They had succeeded in reaching Barbagia, which, as a bastion of Nothingness, was considered a safe refuge.

Constant new arrivals kept the fire going. That particular History was like a tiny flame with too many cold hands pressing round it. It was the story of a story, because the sad fate of Cagliari, a place many people in Nuoro had never even set eyes on, was nothing more than a pale reflection of what was happening elsewhere.

Whatever the case, the latest news was that a huge bomb with half a tonne of high explosive had been dropped on the capital, and on hitting the ground it had pulverised everything within the radius of a kilometre. And – a particularly gruesome detail – it had wrecked the cemetery, blowing open graves and sending skeletons and fragments of corpses flying in all directions.

Terrible things you could lose sleep over, were it not for the fact that Marianna had something else working away at her mind: a telegram had arrived the day before.

She had been a woman of the world, the wife of a commendatore, so she knew things others did not. She knew, for instance, that with a telegram the information reaches you at a different pace than the ordinary postal service. Even so, she did not open it at once.

That evening in the kitchen, with her father watching her, she started ironing. She heated the iron on the fire and checked the embers inside it, then cleaned it with a rag to make sure there were no fragments of charcoal left on the outside.

Michele Angelo watched her in silence; his daughter knew how to use the iron's incandescent tip on the most delicate lace without tearing it, and when necessary she knew how to apply exactly the right pressure and the lightest possible touch.

"What's the matter?" he asked suddenly.

Marianna shrugged and went on with what she was doing. "Nothing."

"Nothing?"

"Just one thing."

Michele Angelo waited patiently for her to go on; they had all the time in the world: all eternity lay before them.

She took her time, then said: "Something happened last month. I had almost forgotten about it," she lied, pausing again. But Michele Angelo was determined to wait, so he waited, watching her. "Yes, I saw an article in a magazine, but I didn't tell you."

It was almost the end of August. They had entered the period they associated with sleeplessness.

"Yes," he said, and no more. As if he could only expect the very worst from the last days of that singularly cursed month.

"Last month it must have been, no, what am I saying, it must have been *Ferragosto*." She corrected herself. "Less than a month . . . There was a news item about a ship sinking, a large ship."

"Yes," Michele Angelo said again, to give her time to change her mind and not say whatever it was she had been about to say.

"There were pictures of people missing in the shipwreck and I thought I recognised . . ."

"Recognised who?" Michele Angelo demanded so aggressively that Marianna took a step backwards. "What do you mean? Why not leave everything as it is?"

"Nothing, nothing," Marianna parried his question. "I'm really stupid, I don't know why I'm telling you this. The article upset me and I let myself be carried away. I had a strange dream . . ."

Suddenly Michele Angelo remembered the night when he had had to get up and go to his daughter who was crying out in her sleep about fish and drowning. "Recognised who?" he repeated when he had pulled himself together.

Marianna put fresh embers in the iron. "Gavino," she said.

"I knew it," Michele Angelo murmured.

According to the magazine article, when Italy declared war, they started rounding up Italian nationals in England to deport them, calling them a fifth column, because they assumed every Italian must be a Fascist.

The main picture in the magazine showed a large ship in Liverpool, the transatlantic liner *Victoria*, one of those ships on which the rich travel the world and where bankers gamble away fortunes and fashionable ladies start adulterous love-affairs with enterprising valets. Ships big enough to hold the entire population of the San Pietro quarter of Nuoro and a good many more besides. According to the article, this wonderful liner had changed its function in time of war and become a means for removing Italians and Germans no longer welcome on British soil.

Well, the story was that, loaded with "prisoners" from this supposed fifth column, the ship had been torpedoed by a German U-boat off Ireland while on its way to Australia.

What this could have to do with Gavino was not clear even to Marianna, though like most women she responded emotionally to things she did not yet understand.

Which was why she had not been able to sleep that night, and she explained it to herself by the fact that the mere name "Australia" evoked her absent brother. It had been said in some quarters that, through Josto Corbu, Gavino had let it be known that he had found work in England as an assistant in a shop selling Italian cloth. Perhaps it was because Marianna had put all these details together that she was so upset, though she didn't show it. But she knew.

In fact Gavino had come to find her that night. He had put on a little weight and was strangely relaxed in an extremely elegant grey suit.

One should know where one is born and, later, where one dies.

One should know why one is born and, later, why one dies.

So for the first I would say Nuoro, and for the last a nameless though precise place off the north-west coast of Ireland.

65° 30′ N   10° 38′ W. That's where.

"Why" is a game of cards: one is born from love if one is born well, but to die well one must die of terror, and in fact die an instant before death . . .

In the first-class saloon of the *Victoria* some of us rushed for the exits immediately after the explosion . . . To be able to survive in the world one must be capable of perceiving the dangers of life; everyone told me I was a reliable man who knew how to work iron and who understood cloth better than most . . .

Someone who constructs things, a creator with the patience of an artisan, can also recognise destruction: the ship's timbers began to groan, but not with the caterwauling of a choppy sea; but the clear crash of a fragmented hull.

When the impact came, when the missile rammed into the ship, it seemed almost as if we had scraped against a submerged rock . . . From where we were we hardly heard the explosion as more than a reverberation. Like the shattering of crystal accurately struck at its weakest point, or the splitting of pack-ice struck by an axe.

Do you know what pack-ice is, little sister? You'd be surprised what you can learn when you go round the world.

It was as if the ship had suddenly lost substance, and I thought of the mystery of molecules that can join together to make solid matter, creating good or bad mortar according to how they are mixed, like an alloy, and I thought of that unique moment when the touchstone must be inserted.

In fact it was a slight blow; the ship coughed like a whale in a fairy tale. Inside that floating palace, the eighth wonder of the modern world, we all looked at one another and clearly heard the protestation of the parquet floor, then the protestation of steel girders as bolts shot out of their sockets.

Then shouting, and the alarm signal, and everything went dark, followed by the sound of something like the footsteps of an army marching on the bridge above.

Then a mad rush began and some swore, but not me: I didn't run, and I didn't swear.

The only thing I thought about was the last second before a collapsing building falls and the sound it makes before it falls: I know instinct wants me to resist, but I'm falling . . .

I'm falling.

So many tears that night for that soul telling its grief.

My little girl is dead, Gaví.

I know, I saw it . . . You told me without knowing it, my darling.

I wanted to write to you. Mamma has gone too.

Yes, yes.

But you, where are you?

Someone who had been to sea was saying it: unless you identify reference points you won't get far . . .

But look, that was speaking in order to say the opposite, like when you say: Do you want to see that it's raining? Like when you look up into the sky, trying to read its riddles. Because it seems the very sky itself is not convinced; while the earth, in contrast, allows itself to be trodden and tolerates hesitant footsteps.

I tell you: it's like having a new bed; first you feel it with your hands, then you sit on it, and finally, you lie down.

The earth takes your weight, the sky doesn't. The London sky was a mischief-maker and treacherous. I used to look up and say to my love: Look up! *Gaze at it!*

He would look up and shake his head the way you often do. You would have liked my love, darling sister, dear heart.

Like you, he would ask, What is it? And I would say, It's as if it is alive; when the earth is soft the sky is hard.

Then I would tell him that I had left the loving care of a blue sky to find refuge under the cold care of a leaden sky . . . I had left a hard stubborn earth to run aground on a soft flirtatious earth. It was like buying shoes the wrong size because you've been too lazy to try them on and then pretending they don't pinch your feet.

When they came for me my love wept.

I'm a British subject, I said. He confirmed it. The youngest of the soldiers looked at me and shrugged, with the thoughtful look of someone who hopes to understand what he is doing.

As I left in handcuffs, I looked up at the upturned sea billowing above our heads.

Then I thought perhaps I should take off those shoes that were too tight for me and go back to swearing at the sky the way people did in Barbagia before I left.

Confused by the noise of embarkation, I never even noticed the colour of the ship . . . and those who did understand such things, people perhaps from Livorno or strays from Mediterranean ports, they said that that those bare grey sides with no identification marks were not a good sign.

We won't be going far, they said. To me, aware the ship and the sky were the same colour, all this was natural. I had come to that land, been accepted with reservations, and found there a love hidden from the world; and then been expelled because of external hostility . . . In the first-class cabins someone was singing Mozart's "In diesen heil'gen Hallen" . . . And someone else, in the first-class saloon, was accompanying on an accordion. "Within our sacred Temple".

The ship passed the Isle of Man.

Are you him? Is it you?

When Marianna woke it was still three hours to dawn. She got up, closed the curtains and lit the lamp. Then, sitting on her bed, she opened the telegram:

SIGNAL RECEIVED STOP SORRY COMMUNICATE OFFICIAL
RECOGNITION BODY RECOVERED ISLAND OF COLONSAY

STOP CONCERNING CHIRONI GAVINO CLASS 1896 STOP
DEEPEST SYMPATHY

*

They found me on the morning of August 16 after I had been drifting for forty-five days . . .

What can this mean? You are all authorised to ask: a washed-up
body, turned to sponge by salt water; but what story can it ever tell?

Well: I never survived the battle . . . When we realised the
ship was sinking we fought each other to get to the lifeboats – *oh
merciless blows* like maddened mice, crushed together in the liner's
first-class saloon we attempted a desperate rush like a school
of beached sperm-whales, fighting each other with hard blows,
trampling everything in our way . . .

Inverting the dream it could be said that in our desperation
we were like fish brought to the surface in fishermen's nets. The
fact was we struggled in vain to force open the locked doors and
escape from the pens intended to divide us into groups.

Don't listen to anyone who tells you we waited impotent and
resigned.

Certainly a few muttered the rosary, *Ora pro nobis*.

And a few undoubtedly surrendered without joining the crazed
horde, but most of us, who had become enemies in our first meta-
morphosis, then became ferocious beasts . . .

———

The following morning Marianna gave her father his milk and she
told him the man she had taken for Gavino in the out-of-focus

photograph in the magazine account of the Italians missing on the *Victoria* had not in fact been him at all. Then she told her father to go out because she did not want him hanging round the house all morning. Michele Angelo protested, saying he no longer knew his way about, everything was changing so fast and even the wine in the taverns was no good. But Marianna refused to listen to any arguments, because she had things to do and she had to go out herself without explaining too much to her father.

Ten minutes after he had left the house complaining, Marianna put on her little commendatoressa hat and best overcoat.

The official at the Prefettura told her her brother's body had been washed up on an island off the Scottish coast and that a local family had given it a compassionate burial. Marianna asked for the family's address.

Back home, smoothing out a new sheet of paper she had just bought, she wrote in Italian as follows:

Dear Friends,

Your compassion has given meaning to our grief: the seasonal harsh weather we have heard about makes it impossible for us to be with our dear one at present. Thank you, thank you so much for your compassion in burying him . . . I hope the cheque we have enclosed will not cause offence; it is a very small thing, but please lay a wreath of flowers for us on the grave of our beloved relative.
Signed: Marianna Serra-Pintus-Chironi

She blew on the ink to dry it, then folded the paper and slipped it into an envelope, on which she copied out the very complicated address given to her by the official at the Prefettura.

That concludes the brief history of this family. Folded and sealed inside the envelope on its way to Scotland.

Marianna hardly dares sigh because eternity is about to knock on the door.

Third Canto – Purgatory
(1943)

Scire

I shall be waiting for you. Standing on the threshold.

And with fierce determination panting at my side. But this circumstance, this waiting for you, piles damage on damage. A progressive agony, for everything I could have told you but never did tell you. For every time I believed in your smile which was as open as an open drawer. For every time I replaced the fragility of your thoughts with complexity. Here, I am waiting for you. Standing here. Calm as a painter infatuated with the feverish minutiae of a brushstroke, the sinuous weave of a basket, or the white plumage of a reflection. This is the work of a housewife who has plumped up ice as if softening a pillow for a fakir. And has beaten sheets and carpets exposed to the midday sun, white as a burst of laughter. I am waiting for you, no doubt about that. I intend to give meaning to that bubbling of the pot, to that crystalline froth, to that turbulent vapour. It is my intention to yield myself to that chaos, but not without a fight. Standing on the threshold as if spying on that excited bride as she counts the repeated clinking of glass during her wedding toast, when every hand is a raised glass, and every happiness seems possible. Before entering the uncertain picture of the morrow, before letting herself be swept away, ambushed by a morning kiss. Before every hope has once and for all been violated by life. Nor can one know how many and what kind of thoughts this violation may lead to, since regret, loneliness, happiness, and love – and love – are just splashes of light and

shade in a nature too intensely alive to be self-sustaining, and already
dead on the canvas. All that is here is merely an absurd surrender in the
face of a half-formed destiny with no name, and which even if it ever
had one, could still not be named. The mystery of reflection, the contrast
between what can be said and what cannot be said . . .

Then came the day when Michele Angelo found the face he had been waiting for. A man he immediately recognised. Thirty years old at the most, but with the eyes of a man with greater experience of the world. A refugee and undoubtedly in very poor shape, but no more so than the times they were living in.

The year of famine in Nuoro was just one more crisis in a chronic litany. Those who had never known plenty had no fear of famine. Yet the closeness of the countryside turned them all into animals and the presence of livestock turned them all into cattle rustlers. And into foxes haunting hen-houses and even into freshwater fishermen.

One morning, when Michele Angelo was alone at home while Marianna was out shopping, he heard a knock on the kitchen door. The old man was on his feet as if he knew someone was about to arrive. Through the window he saw a young man in a shabby jacket, with large trousers stretched at the knees and a shirt that had once been white. But nothing stays white in times of such hardship. So he opened the door to this young man in his dirty shirt.

"It was open," the man said, pointing at the courtyard gate as if in apology.

Michele Angelo stood aside to let him in. From his accent he realised the stranger was not local, but had perhaps brought news of Gavino. This was what Michele Angelo hoped, but dared not ask. Yet the man seemed to have no news to give. He said nothing; not from embarrassment, but as if simply waiting for the frenetic and mute dialogue between them to end.

Even the old blacksmith felt they had been talking, because the stranger's silence was beautiful, full of glances and pauses; something that seemed familiar to Michele Angelo, he did not know why, as if his own blood was breathing.

Marianna came in just as the man was about to introduce himself.

What she saw immediately stopped her breath. She pressed her fist against her mouth so as not to cry out, then looked at her father as if to say: How can you not have realised?

"You left the courtyard gate open," was all Michele Angelo said to her.

Marianna, astonished, moved closer to the man. "Who are you? What do you want?" she asked, but as if looking for confirmation rather than asking a question.

Her father gave her the sort of look people give little girls when they are rude. "I was thinking I might open the forge again," he said. The stranger stared blankly at him, but Michele Angelo's words were meant not for him, but for Marianna. And she had not heard, or if she had, she only registered what he said on the surface of her mind.

"I got this address from the Prefettura through the port authorities," the stranger finally said, as though anxious to explain that he was not there by accident.

At the sound of his voice, Marianna shuddered and stared.

Michele Angelo adjusted himself to her reaction.

"He's similar in everything and nothing," she said to her father as if the visitor was not even there.

She had helped her father to understand something he had not been able to grasp rationally: at times the stranger seemed unexpectedly familiar. A particular gesture, a way of moving his shoulders or drawing a breath when about to speak, or a turn of his head. She saw it clearly and it had a name; Michele Angelo saw it too but he could put no name to it.

They spent a long time staring at each other. At one point the unknown man put his hand in his pocket and pulled out an envelope that seemed to have something bulky in it.

Michele Angelo lifted his hand to stop him.

"Do have something to eat," he said, using the polite form in the way one addressed people from the mainland. Then he nodded to Marianna who went to the larder.

The stranger and the old man continued to stare at each other, but they said nothing until Marianna came back to the table with some *pane carasau* and mature cheese, as well as some broad beans and a stump of dry sausage.

"It's bread," the old man explained to the visitor, pointing at the crisp pieces. The young man nodded with the trace of a smile. Ignoring the rest of the food, he picked up the sausage and bit into it. Michele Angelo nodded to encourage him. "Is it long since you last ate?" he said.

The man swallowed. "I can't remember," he answered, grasping the bread and cheese.

273

Michele Angelo looked at Marianna. "Bring some wine," he said gently, as if tactfully suggesting something she should have thought of in the first place.

Marianna woke from the spell. Now she saw the man eating he seemed to match the light filling the room perfectly, with his dirty hair falling over his brow, his bony hands, black neglected nails and slender but strong wrists, the kind of slenderness and strength sometimes inherited in old families.

He fitted exactly, as if he had just returned to a place he once occupied.

Yet they understood he had come from Friuli and that something he had not yet said had brought him to their home, to the kitchen where he was sitting.

They were hunter and prey, the old man and the mysterious stranger. But now the prey was looking at the hunter as though he knew him well.

Stories often explain things that cannot otherwise be told. Lying in wait, you have to anticipate their movements, then pounce.

The old man searches in his pocket, then looks at his daughter. Marianna knows what he is looking for. Then smiles when Michele Angelo places the keys to the forge on the table.

Michele Angelo would have told the stranger everything he was able to tell. Now that he had him in front of him he knew this very well, and he also knew why he had been willing to wait so long. He understood this because he had known how to absorb the terrible blows with which the Blacksmith of Life had maimed his own existence. One glance at this stranger and absolutely everything had acquired form and meaning.

It was like the first time Gavino had come to work in the forge. Things were still possible back then. He thought he had accumulated enough funds to to get by. It had still been a time of certainties . . . a time when plants and animals still reproduced in spring and summer and rested in autumn and winter. When there were never fewer than five people round the table for meals and they could claim they had paid for the index finger that the statue of the Redeemer raised in blessing. Certainly Gavino caused problems, but at that time those problems were like the vulnerability of a chick's skin when it loses its down, or the moment when a snake looks for a narrow space between two rocks to shed its old skin. In the transparency and ostentatious pride of those new times, it was possible to assume solutions would always be found.

Indeed, when Gavino first came to work in the forge, he seemed like a strong self-confident person who, with that confidence, would know how to look after himself.

But even then Michele Angelo had told him what he was able to tell.

Above all we must know how to see, to touch things with a look, even to understand what is to come before it happens. For this reason, son, the blacksmith sees in the dark. When he places the iron bar in the blaze of the fire he observes the colour the metal becomes: red, orange, yellow . . . white. But there is only one single moment, just one, when the metal is ready for working, as orange passes into yellow, like dawn shading into broad day. This is why a blacksmith can see in the dark, to be able to spot that fleeting moment with precision, that absolute instant.

But we must give things their names: this work is called forging, my son.

Forging is when you are the one giving form. You are the one who has to battle with the matter, which grows increasingly docile the more conscious it becomes of the hand of its master. If you are trying to tame a difficult horse, or teach a dog to obey you . . . it is always a question of earning the animal's respect. In the same way the metal would like to resist you, because when you place it on the cold flat anvil it is like waking it from sleep. But it must learn that you are in charge, and that you are a just master full of authority. The metal knows who it has to deal with from the very first blow, understands the hand modelling it, and sometimes perhaps ventures an opinion of its own.

Gavino nods. A time when wonder at the world could still leap from his eyes, and every possibility was still open to him.

The iron will understand you and sense the steadiness of your wrist, the strength with which you grasp the hammer, and the confidence with which you deal the blow. You will find that the art is to modify without losing control.

From the first blow I shall be able to sense the music your heart makes when the pact has been signed.

But forging is a combination of many things.

There's traction, for example, which means pulling, lengthening the bar to exhaust it, make it thinner, sharpen it. Like your gaze, my son, the sharp look you turn on worldly things. It contains wisdom, knowing when to stop, the skill of gaining the upper hand without crushing. A chisel can only tame wood or stone when it has been previously sharpened and challenged, but not defeated. Even you know what a word or look too many can mean.

Gavino nods again.

And this is where the bending comes in; this is an act of love, because you have to seduce the metal, you have to convince it, son, that if it submits to you it will achieve perfection for itself. Because bending doesn't always involve surrender, but can mean change. You may swear now that you will never bend, but I tell you, you will have to, because if you yourself cannot bend, you will never be able to bend an incandescent bar.

You will be sad. You will feel the weight of the Universe on your shoulders as though you were the only person carrying it. You will feel crushed by responsibility, yet the wisdom that will help you to learn how to turn this evil to good will enable you to declare yourself a man. In the forge we call it "compression", which means causing pain to the metal to condense it, like threatening it in order to reduce it to the correct degree of compactness. And it involves learning to submit in order to grow stronger, accepting questions without fearing the answers, and conceiving victory even through defeat.

You will feel on your own when one blow more or one blow less transforms movement into an extension of yourself. Yet it is only through this loneliness that you will be able to experience the power of feeling, perceiving and anticipating in your own body. You will feel the pressure of images traced in pencil on carbon paper, and for which you will always be accountable. Another name for compression is, in fact, "tracing" or "transfer". Which is to say that, like metal, your body is nothing more than the expression of a concept permanently established. For ever. You take after me in your colouring, and also after your brother and mother. You have her character, as your brother has mine. For ever. You have broad shoulders and Luigi Ippolito is slim. You have my solidity and emit my light; your brother has your mother's density and depth.

I am afraid when I see my own restlessness in you . . . Then I grow calm by telling myself that you mirror me in everything, from the width of your feet to the thickness of your hair, but not in character – or when you tell me you would react to my questions with Mercede's answers.

Next comes "stamping", which means leaving a mark, a depression or hole. Oh, you will feel tremendous wounds, arrows that will pierce your flesh. You will expose your heart to all and sundry by pulling apart the sides of your chest, as if to say: Here I am. You will make every mistake it is possible to make and a few more besides. Every one of these mistakes will leave its mark. That is when, my son, you will have to remember that these are not wounds so much as trophies and decorations. Proof of your strength. An incision telling you you have survived another day in the prison that is the world, and then another, and yet another. It is just the same with metal: every defect can be turned into an ornament if the blacksmith has a sure hand and a sense of harmony. He can ask the lock of a cell to look sober and the lock of a jewel-case to look flirtatious, but in each case he will have to strike the right point and make the incision accurately in the relevant place. Like a tribal sign. A ritual scar.

And you will have to wait a long time before you can understand the secretive paths through which the overall design can be glimpsed, because your mind will reason in fragments and betray you three times over like St Peter and then three times more. Your mind will deny you if you have not been able to grasp the whole because you were too busy concentrating on the parts.

And finally we come to what we call "combination", like the jewel that is your sister Marianna, who is a stranger to everything yet at the same time accepts everything, perfect in her harmonious perfection, earned through humble hard work. She is as dependable as dough in the hands of an expert housewife, who senses its warmth and elasticity and knows when it's ready.

Forging, therefore, is the art of uniting traction, flexibility, compression and stamping. It all depends on knowing when to stop and when to go forward. Like your sister who thinks before she speaks and has neither your insecurity nor your brother's over-confidence. She observes before passing judgement and does not have your indecision or your brother's blind impetuousness.

You must learn all this, my son, but I can't promise you that even knowing it thoroughly will bring you happiness.

Hunter and prey, the old man and the unknown stranger. Hound and game. But now the prey is looking at the hunter as if he knows him well. They are sitting face to face, each lost in the other's gaze, only the table between them. Motionless: the hound and the sheep, the deer and the mouth of the rifle . . .

Yet, notwithstanding the levelled weapon, the prey does not run away, but moves towards the hunter and, as in fairy tales, is the first to speak.

His soft mellow voice is full of foreign sounds. But though he sings an unfamiliar tune, the way his lips move is dictated by genetics.

And Marianna stares at his lips, bewitched by how perfectly they reflect their ancestry.

The man has a story to tell, but for the moment all he will say is that he took the ferry from Livorno to Terranova. The old man realises the stranger is not as old as he seems, a tall slender young man with light skin and a piercing gaze. He says he towered over the poor people that surrounded him on the journey: families with hardly any luggage, soldiers without shoes or identifying insignia, groups of children led by nuns or Red Cross workers. He knows well that anyone landing in Sardinia that day has fled a terrible inferno; a terrifying final regurgitation of the war that is effectively recreating the Apocalypse on earth.

So this solitary refugee from a devastated land tells them he promised his mother that if she died he would go to find his father's family. And she for her part promised him that where he went he would not suffer hunger and cold . . .

He tells them he went straight from the ship to ask the port authorities how to get to Nuoro, where the surviving members of his father's family still lived.

He shows Michele Angelo his documents, just as he did to the duty officer at the port offices: "Chironi Vincenzo, son of Chironi Luigi Ippolito and Sut Erminia, born Cordenons 15 February, 1916, paternity officially documented by notary's certificate signed 6 May, 1916 at Plesnicar Notary Office, Gorizia."

So then everything was clear. Gold and purple, precious as the most precious secret possible. Then. Because there's always a *then* waiting concealed in the precarious obstinacy of the hour. In the brilliance of the gold. In the liquid density of the period before birth. When we are not yet present, still only conditional. Adapted to every period, we experience the complete cycle of a trial existence, and every single instant of centuries. Because by then we are already something beyond the absolute authority of possibility. And the secret cycle of our precarious condition is still whirling. Just when everything seems immobile, stable within a complex stability, just at that moment, when equilibrium seems immortal, when it seems stasis has got the upper hand; that is when the woodworm of uncertainty insinuates itself, the subtle anxiety of duration, the anguish of time. In the precariousness of head-on symmetry there is an untold story. Yes, indeed. Unreality pervades the specificity of completed sense. An area of truth that has no words in which to express itself. In the manner of a great still life fixed in time, glued to the canvas, no longer subject to change. It is only in expectation that we can reconcile ourselves with that iconic immovability. Waiting for the chalice to fall, for the glass, finally, to shatter . . .

And the end is no end.

This is an invented story, but nonetheless true. As soon as possible I shall start it again from the beginning.

M.F.

MARCELLO FOIS was born in Sardinia in 1960 and is one of a gifted group of writers called "Group 13", who explore the cultural roots of their various regions. He writes for the theatre, television and cinema, and is the author several novels, including *The Advocate* (2003) and *Memory of the Abyss* (2012).

SILVESTER MAZZARELLA is a translator of Swedish and Italian Literature, including stories by Tove Jansson and novels by Davide Longo and Michela Murgia. He lives in Canterbury.

Marcello Fois

MEMORY OF THE ABYSS

Translated from the Italian by Patrick Creagh

As a colonial soldier in Northern Africa, recruited from one subject land to subdue another, sixteen-year-old Samuele Stocchino learns to kill before he has learned to love. It is a skill he hones to perfection on the pitiless battlefields of the Carso Front in the Great War.

Returning to Sardinia a hero to a pauper's welcome, he finds his family swindled and his sweetheart stolen away by the richest clan in the region. From one first crime of passion a bitter feud is born. Stocchino terrorises his wealthy neighbours and anyone who dares to till their land until, with Italy now firmly under Mussolini's boot, his elimination becomes *Il Duce*'s priority. As he goes on eluding capture, the seeds of myth are sown and the enduring legend of Samuele Stocchino is forged.

MACLEHOSE PRESS

www.maclehosepress.com

Subscribe to our quarterly newsletter